dear plant daddy

shenee howard

chapter one

PlantDaddy54: Question! What do you think is the sexiest type of plant?

PlantDaddy13: Oh, this is a great question. There's so much to think about when making this decision.

PlantDaddy54: Absolutely. I think you gotta consider texture, size, and colors in your decision. Is it just about looking at a plant and being like wow that's sexy or is it like being attractive like a bee orchid that masquerades as a sexy bee to other bees?

PlantDaddy13: Is it about seeing a plant that looks like . . . something else?

PlantDaddy54: Right, like how the Nepenthes looks like . . . . well it seems like . . .

PlantDaddy13: A dick! A member? As I'm saying this, I'm wondering if I should still be calling a dick a dick. I'm sorry that was immature, but that's what it looks like! The ones out of Cambodia are huge. Did you know that they're going extinct because people keep plucking them?

PlantDaddy54: For novelty? Is it like a party trick? Is that a Nepenthes in your pocket or are you just glad to see me?

PlantDaddy13: . . . . .

PlantDaddy54: I know, that was bad. I'm gonna go now.

PlantDaddy13: Honestly, we are on the same level. I'm not gonna judge you.

PlantDaddy54: Does it bother you that we are two strangers making plant dick jokes?

PlantDaddy13: Well . . . we could switch to clit jokes?

PlantDaddy54: I like you a lot.

———

"Are you guys having sex?" Allison's high-pitched voice is louder than I would like. But it serves its purpose, and I snap my head up towards her as I realize then that I've abandoned whatever I was doing and have just been standing in the middle of my plant store, staring at my phone.

I look around to make sure nobody else heard my best friend, but the store is predictably empty. It's the end of the day, so the rush is over. All that remains are little piles of dirt from knocked-over plants after tornados of kids had swept through the room during the after-school rush and displaced plants from professional hobbyists who'd moved things around while trying to pick and choose between different varieties of hoyas.

"This is a business establishment!" I hiss, pocketing my phone. I decide this is a good time to take care of those little piles of dirt, so I grab my broom from nearby and start sweeping. It won't take long. Plant Therapy isn't big—around the size of a small one-bedroom New York apartment. And it's cozy. I'd tried to channel the feel of Anthropologie more than Home Depot, to give customers a preview of how a plant will feel in their home. It's a nightmare to have so many plants alongside cozy couches and antique furniture and art, but the result is worth it. I love coming to work every day, and I think my customers appreciate the space too.

"You didn't answer my question," she points out.

She must know it's a silly question. How can you have sex with someone you've never met? I don't even know his name. If I had to tell someone about him, I'd have to call him "54." A number. That's all I have of this guy—at least I think it's a guy?—who I talk to all the time, someone whom I've been messaging for months. And that's for the best. He could be anyone. He could be a scammer. (He's probably a scammer. I have a crush on a scammer like one of those rich women on those Netflix shows. When he cons me out of my life savings and unused audiobook credits, everyone is going to say I deserved it because who starts a texting relationship with someone they met on Reddit?)

Of course, I have wondered what 54 is like offline. What he looks like, what he'd feel like. It's been a very long time since I've looked forward to talking to someone this much. But then I remember the Netflix women and snap out of it. Hopefully, he'll ask me for money soon and put me out of my misery.

"We've never met," I remind Allison, suppressing the urge to take my phone back out of my pocket and check my Reddit inbox to see if he's written back.

"You're smiling at your phone like he's asking you what you're wearing."

I laugh a little thinking about the conversation 54 and I are having about sexy plants. It's not really like he's asking me what I'm wearing, but it might as well be.

I roll my eyes and give her a look. "Don't you have a store to run?"

The answer is yes. Allison owns one of those aesthetic boutiques that show up in every neighborhood and somehow manage to stay open even though there are never any customers. Phoenix is more or less a carbon copy of her perfect closet. Lots of neutral colors and flowy dresses. Earth mother but rich. And it suits her. Allison is beautiful in the way everyone likes. Racially ambiguous and slender with perfect curly hair and bright green eyes. She kind of looks like those models of what everyone will look like in a hundred years when all races blend. We're pretty much opposites in that way. I'm unambiguously black and thick, complete with full lips, a fleshy stomach, wider hips, and bigger boobs that bother my back sometimes. My hair can only barely retain a curl pattern after a full day of work, so I tend to go for more protective styles or a slicked back ponytail, like today's style.

In any case, if I didn't know Allison personally, I'd think her store is a front for drugs, targeting the wealthy yoga moms of Long Beach. Nobody is ever there, but she never seems to be that bothered by that.

Once I finish with one of the dirt piles, I'm momentarily distracted by the Cebu blue in the corner that needs a little water, and my mind drifts to 54 again.

PlantDaddy54: We don't talk enough about the Cebu blue.
PlantDaddy13: What would we say? It's a very thirsty but low-maintenance plant.
PlantDaddy54: It's romantic. It doesn't want much but it needs you.

"You're doing it again!" Allison shouts. I'm still being watched. Dammit. "You're smiling. Are you thinking about him?"

"Stop looking at me!"

"I mean, what do you guys do with all that pent-up sexual frustration . . . ? Do you hook up? Are you sending photos or sexting?"

I can't blush—my darker skin doesn't allow it—but my skin does feel hot all of a sudden.

"No! We aren't having sex." Her mouth opens, and before she can be annoying, I add, "We aren't having digital sex, either. We just talk."

She stares at me as if she feels sorry for me, and her reaction tells me something I guess I didn't really know—Allison probably sexts a lot. Maybe that's how she and John, her boyfriend of three years, keep things interesting. He recently moved to Riverside for a job, and since Long Beach is about as far as you can get from Riverside, it's almost like they're in a long-distance relationship.

"You have to admit there is something post-coital about the way you smile at your phone."

"He's just funny, that's all. It's a smile like I'm laughing. Like haha, that's funny and then you smile." I reach for a smile, but I can't make it work. And I know it doesn't work because she gives me that look again, kind of like pity. I decide to change the subject. "Did you know that there's a plant in Cambodia that looks like a dick and is endangered?"

"Did 69 tell you that?"

I roll my eyes. "54."

"Still calling each other Plant Daddy? That's kind of kinky too."

When it was time to pick my username for the LA Reddit plant forum r/plantssocal, I chose PlantDaddy as a joke because it was funny. There were a few other people who had the same idea, but 54 and I were both the most active. The two of us kept getting confused with each other for months, and I finally introduced myself to him.

PlantDaddy13: You stole my username!

PlantDaddy54: I'm for sure more of a plant daddy, so I'm pretty sure you stole it from me.

PlantDaddy13: What are your qualifications?

PlantDaddy54: I feel connected with Plant Daddy culture.

PlantDaddy13: Is that like some type of porn category?

PlantDaddy54: I wish.

PlantDaddy13: HAHA. Do you?

PlantDaddy54: Not really, was just trying to be clever. Are you an actual daddy?

PlantDaddy13: Of course I am!

PlantDaddy54: Because in your profile you say your pronouns are she/thatbitch

PlantDaddy13: Are you saying a bitch can't be a Plant Daddy?

PlantDaddy54: No, you're right. I'm sorry.

There is something old-school about us writing back and forth, so we haven't pushed for anything more. I don't really know how he feels, but for me, I just don't want to ruin a good thing. I don't do much online dating anymore, but when I have, the messages back and forth were always the best part. They always felt the safest. And since the Reddit board technically has a rule against sharing your identity on the board, I enjoy just being anonymous to someone. I like not having the pressure of being me.

"No names, that's the point." I'm feeling defensive, and I don't know why. If it was anyone else, I'd have just as many questions and be even more suspicious. It feels like a scam. Maybe it is a scam. Perhaps this is how scams work. You get seduced by cute, nerdy facts about dick plants, and while you're giggling at his comments about philodendrons, he's draining money from your bank account.

My thought is interrupted by the ding of the door and the signature shuffling of Miss Anette, one of my regular customers. Great timing. Save me, Miss Anette.

Wildcat, my Belgian Malinois, jumps up from her sleeping spot to greet our visitor. She's goofy, all tail wags, and licks Miss Anette's walking stick. Wildcat was meant to be a police dog, but she developed a degenerative eye disease that made her unqualified to serve. I adopted her after my first year of living here when I realized I was probably going to stay put in Long Beach for a while, and she's been my constant companion since. She was raised in the plant store and acts as its guardian and greeter.

"Tessa, be a dear and find me something nice for the living room." Miss Anette sits in the antique chair near the door to rest. Wildcat settles at her feet.

Miss Anette is at least eighty-five. Plant Therapy is just another stop on her weekly route down the strip. I love that I can always rely on her to do the same thing every time I see her. It's soothing. First, she stops at Allison's shop next door and complains about the prices, and then she moves on to my neighbor Bill's to buy something obscure and antique. Finally, she trudges through my shop, looks at every plant, and acts like she's finally ready to make a purchase. She doesn't ever actually buy a plant because she thinks she'll kill it. I understand not wanting to flirt with death, which is a huge part of growing plants, although it's really the only risk I find myself fine with taking.

She notices Allison. "Your prices are too high, Allison. Thirty-five dollars for a scarf?"

"I sell investment pieces, Miss Anette. Beauty is worth the investment."

Miss Anette scoffs, and as they continue their conversation, I pocket my phone—is it weird that I'm so aware of it against my thigh, even through the heavy denim of my overalls? probably—and take the opportunity to grab the few options I have ready for Miss Anette this week. Maybe this will be the week I'll finally entice her to take one home.

I bring her a particularly hearty sansevieria. Strong and bright green and yellow. It looks old, almost Jurassic, which also seems to give it a sort of indestructible energy. Perfect for her. I hold it out for her.

"Snake plant. You can't kill it. It thrives off neglect." I hand it to her, and she holds it, considering. She won't buy it, but it never stops me from trying. There's nothing that makes me happier than helping someone find the perfect plant.

"So you smile like that, and you aren't getting laid," Allison pipes up from behind me.

I pretend to ignore her, grabbing my watering can and crossing the room to my live wall. It's a display of rare and common plants, all lush and textured, covering the wall under a spotlight. The top layer has a row of pothos and then a row of philodendrons and a row of dracaenas, all flowing down. The live wall is what the store is known for, and it's a headache to take care of, but I love it.

Allison follows me as I climb up the ladder to water the top layer. "I'm just saying."

"You *are* smiling in a particular way," Miss Anette interjects. She's old, but I guess her hearing hasn't started to go.

I raise an eyebrow at Miss Anette and gripe to Allison behind me. "Did you just come here to talk about my digital sex life?"

When she doesn't respond immediately, I stop what I'm doing and look at her.

"Actually . . ." She drags the word out, and I freeze. This is her bad news voice. It sounds a lot like—

The condom just broke.

Another store has closed.

I didn't mean to puke in the rare monstera pot.

"Yeah?" I prod, feeling a tad nauseated.

"Have you talked to Elliot?"

Elliot is our landlord. He's relatively new, just took over in the last five years or so. Before that, the building was managed by his father, who owned all the buildings on the block for over thirty years, which is almost as long as my store has been here. Well, technically it's not my store. It belongs to Norma, who is living her best life at a retirement home. But I'm the co-owner. I've worked at the shop since the day Norma took me in almost eight years ago now. Elliot's father was nicer, and by nicer I mean he was less . . . hands-on. He was fine just collecting our checks and living his life. But that's definitely not Elliot. Elliot has been spending too much time reading passive income forums to figure out how to make more of a profit.

Allison grimaces as I shake my head. "He's raising the rent. Another $500."

The plant store does okay, but another $500 is a pretty big hike, especially considering how dead our part of the street is now. Plant Therapy exists on a block on 4th Street that is slightly away from the action. Not many businesses have survived here over the years, and it's gotten even worse as things have moved closer to downtown. You'd think that would make things cheaper, but it's actually had the opposite effect. This is going to be our second rent increase in only a few years.

"Isn't there some type of law against this type of thing?" I ask while climbing back up the ladder to reach the next level.

"I don't know. Maybe. But it's something to think about."

"What do you mean?"

"I just mean . . ." Her voice grows serious, and I look down at her from my watering spot. She's pretending to be distracted by a fern, but Allison doesn't care about plants, despite my best efforts. She just entertains me. "The neighborhood keeps changing, and this area is still so empty. With the prices going up . . ."

"Yeah, but this is our home. This store has been here for like forty years. Whatever is happening with the price hike, we'll deal with it, right? We'll figure it out."

Allison looks like she wants to say something else, and so I wait. But before she can continue, the door bursts open like we're all starring in one of those sitcoms where a rotating cast of characters file in to applause and a laugh track.

"Have you heard?"

This time it's Bill, who owns Bill's Antiques, the store next to mine. Bill is the type of "cool" that most white men aspire to. He's eighty-two but looks like he's in his sixties. He also has a cool car and plays in a Clash cover band that is pretty good. Everyone thinks he's cool, especially Wildcat, who jumps up and scurries to his side, nuzzling his pocket until he produces a treat from the stash he keeps there just for her. Bill gives Miss Anette a quick nod.

"I already told her about the rent hike," Allison says.

"Rent hike. Hmph! Another one. Why? I tell you what, capitalism is such a burden on our system. It's like Bernie Sanders once said . . ." Bill starts ranting. This is one of his decidedly old-man traits—he goes off on wild tangents. Wildcat, who also does not want to hear Bill's daily socialist rant, paws at his jeans in a bid to get his attention and get another treat.

"Bill, what were you going to tell us?" I press lightly, but my voice feels a little tight as my anxiety builds.

"Right. Well . . . There's something else." He gives me a look that feels a bit like pity. I hate pity. How is this my second pitying look of the day?

Bill pauses for dramatic effect.

"Bill!" all of us, even Miss Anette, exclaim.

He takes a deep breath, and subconsciously, I take one too.

"There's a new plant store coming to town," he says, looking at all of us expectantly.

I exhale the breath I was holding. This is hardly a big deal. Plant stores have become more popular over the years, and now there are a few in downtown and North Long Beach. Not an issue.

"Oh god, you scared me." I relax my raised shoulders, flexing my neck, which is already so tight from all the watering and moving things around. "Lots of plant stores. No big deal."

"This one is on our street," Bill explains, his voice soft. "The old community center."

"Wait, where?" Allison asks, and I'm struggling to picture it, too. The community center is huge, taking up a whole block. There's no way a plant store could take up that big a space. It would practically be a plant IKEA. Right?

"Wait, I gotta see this." Allison makes her way out the door. "Come on, Tessa."

"What about the store?!" I protest, my arms wide. Besides Miss Anette, who is now taking her daily nap on the cozy couch I have in the corner for her, the store is empty. Wildcat and Allison both give me a knowing look.

"Fine," I sigh. "Wildcat needs a walk anyways."

I am curious what a plant superstore looks like, and I'm also secretly hoping Bill's news is just some type of rumor. If it is, this is more proof that I need to stop thinking about Plant Daddy and stay focused on what really matters, which is making sure the store is up and running. That takes up pretty much all of my time as it is.

Wildcat jumps up from her spot by Miss Anette's feet and grabs her chain to show she's ready to go.

————

Our part of 4th Street feels like a before and after or like crossing from the "bad" to the "good" side of the railroad tracks, but there aren't any tracks. Our quiet, somewhat dead part of the street is the "before." That used to be true of the whole strip, until last year, when a local chef won a TV cooking competition making Cambodian food. He decided to use his winnings to open a hybrid coworking café/high-end restaurant in the abandoned laundromat on the corner a few blocks away. Soon enough, more businesses started to pop up around it. A mystery bookstore called Sleuth. A vegan ice cream place called Save Cows. There's also A Little Witchy, another store a little farther down that sells crystals and provides spells.

You'd think the new energy would benefit us, just a few blocks over. But the revitalization of 4th Street started a little too far away. While we do get quite a few people who wander from the new Argentinian restaurant to our block, it's rare. And it's a bit of a walk. To get to the new plant shop, Bill, Allison, and I have to pass a bunch of houses, freestanding apartment buildings, and abandoned buildings.

What used to be the community center is sandwiched between a vintage boutique and our neighborhood movie theater. From the front, it doesn't look that big, but the building stretches back pretty far. Bill and I attended a few community meetings over the years and had expected that the location might eventually be turned into a grocery store or a gym. A plant store was the last thing that had been on anyone's mind.

As we make our way up the street, I can spot the fresh white façade among the more weather-worn buildings. As I get closer, I can see the beginnings of a mural—thick black lines shaped as banana leaves and birds of paradise. We stop directly across the street and get a look at a giant sign with the words "Botanical Brothers" written in Hipster Script.

"Name seems kind of cliché," Allison says.

I barely have time to register her comment because I'm too focused on all the trendy neon lights, the thumping music, and the huge displays. This feels more like a club than a plant store. The only signs of plant life are the dozens of brown bags on the ground, the telltale sign of a fresh delivery. I can also smell the distinct scent of dirt and leaves. It would be oddly comforting if it wasn't coming from such an overwhelming source.

Bill and Allison are both looking at me.

"You okay?" Allison asks.

I can't say anything right away because, honestly, I feel a little nauseated. I'm not even sure what this place is yet—can a plant store really be this . . . flashy?—but Botanical Brothers already feels like a vortex of energy, like it's going to suck in everything around it, including me.

After another minute, I force a nod. "Yeah. Yeah, of course." I know my optimism sounds fake, but it's too late to back out now. "It's fine." As I'm talking, I start to believe it more. "So there's a huge plant store just a few blocks from my much smaller store! That's okay! There are lots of plant stores. People need options."

"Right," Bill and Allison say in unison.

"Sometimes I want a different kind of coffee, so I go to a different coffee shop!"

"Exactly!" Bill nods a bit too enthusiastically.

"So there's nothing to worry about."

"Nothing at all!" Bill affirms.

Allison is noticeably quiet.

"Allison what do you think?" She'll tell me the truth, I know, because she always tells me the truth.

"Ummm . . ." Allison begins, but whatever she is about to say gets drowned out by a squeal from across the street.

"EEEEEEEEKKKKKKKKKK!!!!!!!!!!!!!!"

"Jesus Christ." I jump at the sound, my heart beating fast. I look over at the small group of adolescent girls huddling around the door to the new store, taking selfies with the sign.

"Is it a celebrity plant store or something? Something with Snoop Dogg?" Allison says, plugging her ears. Somehow, the girls' screaming is getting louder.

"I don't think Snoop Dogg is into plants." I'm trying to think who the Guy Ferri of plants would be, but I'm coming up blank.

Another shriek pierces my ears. Is there a *Rhaphidophora tetrasperma albo* in there or something? What could possibly be THAT exciting?

I don't know the answer, but I can't ignore the goosebumps forming on the back of my neck, always my signal that something big and disruptive is coming.

chapter two

PlantDaddy13: I was looking at this gorgeous hoya and it made me think of you instantly. Is that weird? There was something about it that felt so you and I was overwhelmed by that feeling. Maybe that's weird, because I don't know you, but I feel like I do, and I felt guilty not saying anything about it.
PlantDaddy54: Not weird at all. Plants make me think of you all the time.

———

Is it weird to be jealous of your dog? Because when Wildcat runs at the beach, I can't help but feel envious. The dog beach is less than a mile west of the shop and is a three-mile stretch of dog paradise—one of the few places my seventy-five-pound dog gets to really run like she wants, and so she does. As soon as we cross the parking lot and step onto the sand, you can feel it, how free she is. Wildcat takes a beat when her feet hit the sand and then sprints towards the water. I slip off my shoes and follow her across the sand, but she's already a barely visible brown blur in the distance.

Wildcat likes to make a wide circle when she runs, and sometimes she goes so far it almost feels like she's running away. She inevitably loops back around to me, tongue flying, so I can throw her a ball or stick or something else she finds on the ground.

It's midday, so the beach is mostly empty beyond a smattering of other people with dogs a little too wild to come to the beach at peak time. We all seem to have a silent agreement among us, to let each of our dogs have the space they need to truly RUN.

"Tessa! I can barely hear you," my mom complains over the phone.

We talk to each other most days, whether I want to or not. I like talking to her when I'm in the middle of doing something. Her words don't land as hard when I'm in motion. My mom is one of those people who worries. Even a tiny shift in the tone of my voice can trigger a freakout. It's been eight years since I left home, and she still requires proof of life daily. Of course, if it was up to her, I would never have even left home.

"Are you sure you're okay?" Mom yells over the sound of the wind. "It's so loud there."

"Yes, I'm okay." At least I'm trying to be okay. Botanical Brothers lingers in my mind, but I know that if I tell my mom what's really going on, she'll have me on the first flight home. That's always her response to everything challenging.

I've reached the part of the beach where the warm, dry sand turns cool and damp. It feels good beneath my feet, like it always does, and I focus my attention on the bracing shock of the water passing over my toes as I walk along the shore. The water is freezing because the Pacific Ocean is always cold.

"You know you can always come home." There it is. Predictable. It's meant to be comforting, but sometimes it feels more like a threat. I know she means well, which is why I don't fight her on it. But I also don't tell her that moving back home is the last thing I want to do.

"I know."

Wildcat brings me a ball I don't recognize because she's also a thief. The ball looks well loved (that is to say, thoroughly chewed), so I pick it up carefully, a little grossed out because it's covered in drool. I'm just preparing to launch it back down the beach when a blur whizzes past me. The blur is small and gray and fast, and it makes three tight circles around me and Wildcat before taking off. Wildcat chases after it, galloping at full speed, and I take off running too. Wildcat isn't dangerous, which feels obnoxious to even think, because don't all dog owners say that? But I can just imagine the viral outrage if someone were to post a video online, Wildcat sprinting at full speed down the beach, chasing the "poor little dog" who's running for its life. *Dangerous dog totally out of control! Owner has no idea what she's doing!*

But she's just goofy and big, and this speedy terrier is small. I'm screaming and whistling for Wildcat, and she tries to stop and heel, but the little blur is toying with her. She gives me an apologetic look before taking off again.

"Shit, shit, shit!" I scream, continuing after her while huffing and puffing. Running in the sand is hard, and the heaviness weighs on me with each step.

"Tessa?" Right, Mom's still on the phone. "Are you okay? Should I call the local police?" She sounds frantic too, so I force myself to relax.

"No, it's okay, it's okay. It's just Wildcat. She's—"

"That dog of yours," Mom says with a sigh.

She loves Wildcat the way you love a weird cousin—they're there, and they're family, but you don't fully approve. I take a deep breath and give myself a moment to watch Wildcat with the little gray dog. They're playing.

"Don't worry," the sexiest voice I've ever heard says. The hairs on the back of my neck stand up, but not in a bad way. More like in shock that I'm reacting so strongly to a random voice. A random really, really sexy voice. "Alfred can take care of himself," the voice continues.

I slowly turn towards the sexiest voice I've ever heard, and I come face-to-face with whom I can only describe as Sexy Man^{TM}. He's slightly taller than me, but we're still standing eye to eye, which is pretty impressive because I'm five foot eleven. His black hair is under a baseball cap—a typical hot-man move—and beneath the brim, I see his bright white hot-man smile. Sexy Man^{TM} has the nerve to have a dimple on his left cheek. His golden skin seems to glow, and for a moment, I wonder if he is a merman from the sea. Then I realize I've been staring too long, and I shake myself out of it.

"Mom, I'll call you back," I say into my phone. I quickly hang up before she has the chance to start throwing questions at me. I'm sure she's delighted to hear the voice of a man. Her big dream is for me to be married and move into a house across the street from her where she can babysit my babies I don't have. But I don't need another distraction right now. Sexy Man^{TM} is enough of a distraction as it is.

I cross my arms over my chest and then uncross them again, unsure of what to do with my body. He's not saying anything, either. He's just . . . looking at me. I don't know remember the last time anyone looked at me like this—so direct and focused. When you live somewhere for a long time, you tend to fade into the background. People know you're there, but they don't see you. Not like this.

"Oh, um, is that your dog?" I somehow choke out.

He nods and gives a loud, high-pitched, clear whistle without breaking eye contact. My whole body reacts. Is that some kind of pussy whistle? Both Wildcat and the small blur, who has now been identified as Alfred, stop in their tracks. Alfred spins around and bounds towards us, and Wildcat follows. Alfred runs straight up to me, wagging his tail and greeting me. He's as cute as his owner is hot. His gray face and big, open eyes remind me of a seal pup. I bend down to pet him, and he wiggles around aggressively before settling and rolling onto his back so I can rub his belly.

Taking Alfred's lead, Wildcat struts up to Sexy Man^{TM}, flops down on her back, and spreads her legs for a stomach pat. Can't say I blame her.

"And who is this?" His voice is what I imagine butter on toast would sound like if it had a voice. That doesn't really make sense, but this reaction I'm having also doesn't really make sense. I feel like maybe I should drink more water. This could be a dehydration issue.

"This is Wildcat."

"Wildcat!" His smile grows even wider, and at the sound of her name, Wildcat jumps up to give him a kiss. I start to apologize, but Sexy Merman™—yep, that's what I'm going to call him, Sexy Merman™—loves it, playing around with Wildcat with a confident ease while I meet Alfred's squirmy energy with more affection. We're both quiet for a moment, meeting each other's dogs before we meet each other. I take a moment to peek up at him. His legs are wet, which supports my merman theory. Alfred gives my hands a few more licks before he wiggles out of my grasp and takes off again. Wildcat does the same, leaving me alone with Sexy Merman™.

"Your dog is very cute," I say, fully meaning it. Alfred's fluffy gray face and whiskers make him look like an old man and a baby both at once, his eyes big and bright. I can't say I'd really expect a guy like this to have a dog like that.

"And your dog is—is the word majestic? She's a gorgeous dog." I linger on the way he says "gorgeous." It buries itself beneath my skin. You don't hear people use that word very often. "Beautiful" is a good word, gets tossed around a lot, but there's something about "gorgeous." It feels deeper, truer. "She's one of those police dogs, right?"

"Noooo. She's retired. Well, she's a police dog academy dropout. She didn't qualify because she has this eye disease. Now she's just my way-too-big lapdog. How about your dog?" I'm finding my footing now. I can be normal. He's just a dude. I talk to men all the time.

He walks closer to me, and I have to fight the urge to take a step back. I'm struggling a little here. His eyebrow raises just a little, like he knows what I'm thinking, and I blurt out, "I don't think I've ever seen a dog run that fast before."

Sexy Merman™ grins. "Maybe he's running away from me."

Are his eyes fucking sparkling right now? I consider walking into the sea. *Come on, Tessa. Stay in.* "Now why would he want to do that?"

That makes him a little shy. His gaze drops to his feet, though he's still smiling that gorgeous smile, and it feels like a little victory.

When it comes to dating, or men in general, I've never been that good at it. Suffering through small talk over drinks always feels so hard, and my store has always been my first priority anyways. At one point, I was all about casual hookups with friends of friends or random men I'd meet when I'd join Allison on one of her big adventures as the main character. She'd always have some kind of Garden State-esque grand sexy adventure with a poet or artist or something, and I'd take home a less-exciting friend with a bit of a fat fetish that I'd ignore for the sake of trying to get off. But it'd never really work that well, and I'd always leave feeling unfulfilled.

It's one of my favorite things about Plant Daddy. Things just flow so easily with him—no awkward small talk, and I don't have to worry about how I look or what he thinks of how I look or anything like that.

I wonder if Sexy Merman™ ever has to worry about making good conversation. Probably not. People likely just fill the silence to keep him around.

"Lots of reasons. We've only been together for a little while. He was my grandmother's dog, and I took him when she died." His smile fades a little as he watches Alfred run away from the incoming tide. "I don't know how my ninety-three-year-old grandma handled all of his energy."

Of course, he's an angel. A perfect sexy angel merman from the sea.

"Well, I appreciate Alfred's service. Wildcat is likely going to sleep for the rest of the day because of him."

"Anytime." He looks at me when he says it. He's so confident, and I fight to maintain his unwavering eye contact. "What's your name?" he asks.

My name. It's been a while since anyone asked for that, too.

"Oh, I'm Tessa." I extend my right hand for a shake, a habit I picked up from my father, who believes in a strong handshake, says it sets the tone. When he takes my hand, I feel a thrill run up my forearm. His hand is surprisingly soft, and his grip is firm. The tone is horny.

"I'm Leo," he says. "It's nice to meet you."

We keep shaking hands until it starts to feel silly, and I giggle a little and pull away. His hands are so soft, and I wonder if his lips are too. Then I start to feel a little guilty, thinking about Plant Daddy. Am I betraying him somehow? It sorta feels like it.

Our moment is interrupted by our dogs, who make another exhausted circle around us before falling in a heap at our feet, both of them panting hard, pink tongues lolling out the sides of their mouths.

"Mission accomplished," Leo says, reaching into his backpack to get a squeezable water bottle and one of those little collapsible dog bowls. Both Wildcat and Alfred drag themselves back to their feet and lap peacefully from the bowl, taking turns like well-behaved siblings. It's cute.

I wish I could stay with him a little longer. I have questions, and he has one of those faces I just want to tell everything to. *What do you think I should do about the new store? Should I stop talking to 54? Do you think I'm being scammed?* But my break is almost over, and I need to open the store back up.

"We should probably get going, I need to get back to work. Maybe we'll see you around again?"

"I hope so." It's like he's threatening me with that dimple again when he says it. He's so scary. What do you want from me, hot man?

There's an awkward silence for a moment, and I give a weird wave before turning and walking away. Maybe I should have said something?

I try my best not to look back, but I can't help it. I feel a little self-conscious knowing that he's seeing me from behind. It's something I've always been a little insecure about. When I glance back, he's still looking at me. He gives me another wave, and I wave back.

Wildcat makes a slow circle around me as we continue down the beach. She's totally exhausted, which makes sense. I reach down and give her a pat and then glance back toward Leo again. He's finally started walking away, and I get a good look at him from behind. Strong shoulders and a great back. Nice butt. Of course.

My phone rings too loudly for the quiet beach, and he turns towards the noise, giving me a shy nod when he catches me staring. I turn back around.

"Hey, Mom! Sorry!"

"You okay? You sound nervous."

"Yep, I'm fine."

chapter three

PlantDaddy13: Are you married? I realize it might be a little late to ask but I'm just curious. This thing we have going feels kind of in between flirting and friendship. Flirship? Friending? What do you prefer? I just want to make sure I'm being more friendly than flirty if you are in fact married. I shouldn't keep sending you pictures of plants that look like body parts because we think it's funny. I don't want your partner to be going through your phone and see a photo of a very erotic orchid and get mad and confused because technically it's just a flower but it's also a really sexy flower.

PlantDaddy54: Do you consider sharing photos of fly orchids and rhodochitons cheating? I guess if I found those on someone's phone I would also be confused. It's silly but also I totally get thinking "wait, what?" I'm not married or in a relationship. I'm single. I agree that there is a bit of a flirship here and I look forward to it every day. I really like talking to you. I guess we'll just warn each other if we need to transition from flirship to friendship?

PlantDaddy13: Okay, sounds good. I'm single too, by the way. Very single.

PlantDaddy13: I didn't have to say that last part.

———

"This Leo guy sounds really hot."

After work, I find myself at Allison's apartment. She lives downtown in one of the few high rises in the city, and her home has views of the ocean during the day and the city at night. When I go to her house, I feel like I'm in another world, even though she lives just down the street.

Allison is aggressively baking, and she has been since I arrived. I'll admit that scares me a bit. She doesn't bake unless she's worried about something. When I try to push her on it, however, she directs the attention back to my Leo encounter.

"And he's real!" she says, whisking whatever white stuff is in the bowl in front of her so fast I wouldn't be shocked if she takes flight.

I roll my eyes. Plant Daddy is real too.

"And I know what you're going to say," Allison inserts. "Plant Daddy is real, and you guys are just friends, and blah blah blah. Oh wait, is this a love triangle?"

I would be more annoyed, but it's nice to see her smile, even for a bit. I wish she would tell me what's bothering her.

Her aggressive whisking turns the white concoction foamy. She stops immediately and holds the stiffened substance up to the light, scrutinizing it carefully. "Did you ask for his number?"

Allison can ask this question with confidence because she's the kind of hot everyone likes. She can always get any man she wants because every race of man wants her. I don't say all that to Allison, though. I just say, "No."

She points her whisk at me, and I wince, expecting whatever that white foam is to come flying right off the end of the whisk and in my direction. Thankfully it stays put.

"You are young, beautiful, and successful," she says. "And you haven't been on a date in like two years." She sets the whisk down and sifts flour into the bowl with even more aggression.

My last date, two years ago, apparently, was with an accountant Allison knows. He seemed normal at first, maybe a bit boring. He was a foodie, so we talked *a lot* about food. It took me a little too long, but eventually I realized he was getting turned on by watching me eat. The last date I'd been on before that was with the son of one of Bill's bandmates. He's actually totally cool, but he keeps inviting me to his orgies, and I'm running out of polite ways to turn him down. I'd just rather not date. It's distracting, and people are messy.

That's the whole appeal of PlantDaddy54. It's the best of both worlds. We flirt and talk, and I don't have to worry about the weirdness of dating or wonder if he likes thicker Black girls because it doesn't matter. We just talk, and there's no pressure for me to be anything or anyone else.

"I know you really like 55 and you two have this connection, but when are you guys planning on, you know, actually meeting?"

I don't even think to correct her number usage, and I don't feel the need to respond. Allison already knows the answer anyways. Plant Daddy and I have never talked about meeting face-to-face. It might be because I'm terrified he'll think I'm a catfish. In our conversations, I feel confident and pretty, as weird as that sounds. How can texting make you feel pretty? It's just the way he talks to me, I guess. It's the way I imagine really hot girls get talked to. I'm afraid that it won't be the same if we meet in person, that we'll both disappoint each other.

She continues as if I've answered her. "Are you guys gonna be pen pals forever?"

I'm avoiding thinking about the future. While I'm happy with our current arrangement, I can't imagine this thing with 54 is going to end anywhere good. I don't think I've ever heard any stories like ours that have happy endings. Although I've probably watched too many episodes of *Catfish*.

"I just want you to experience life and have fun *offline*. You think Leo is attractive, and your dogs get along. You should go for it."

I sigh, swiveling my chair around to look out at the city lights. "He's too hot. It's so aggressive."

"You're hot."

I am not hot. If I had to describe myself, I'd say that I'm cute. Despite the fact that I'm taller than most people, people are always calling me "sweetie" or "hun." Something about the combination of my face and voice has removed me from the "sexy" category and placed me squarely with the other "cute" sweeties of the world. I suspect it's because I'm more soft than hard, with my fleshy stomach and thicker thighs. My boobs are decidedly not cute—and when they're unleashed, I get a whole other kind of attention—but I try to shield them from the public.

"I'm not going to date anyone right now."

Allison rolls her eyes, and the oven beeps like it's agreeing with her. She can't imagine anyone not wanting to be in a relationship given that she's obsessed with hers. Allison's boyfriend pulled her out of her main character's LA lifestyle, and now I imagine they'll be getting married soon, or at least sometime in the next few years.

"It's true," I insist. "I don't want to date. It just never works out, even when things seem like they're going perfectly well. I just don't have the time. I'm too focused on the store. And that's the way I want it."

"I don't know if that's true. You spend plenty of time on your phone messaging with Plant Daddy, and you still have time to run your store." She pours the mixture she'd beaten into submission into a cake pan. I've never seen anyone make baking seem so violent.

"Are you sure you're okay?"

"Don't change the subject!" she snaps, her voice loud and agitated. I wonder what's bothering her so much. Maybe she's having issues with John? Or maybe it's something with the store? She must see the worry on my face, or she knows she's gone too far, because her shoulders relax and she takes a deep breath. "I'm sorry, but we're talking about you right now."

"54 is different." He *is* different. He doesn't feel like work. When I talk to him, I don't feel like I'd rather be alone at home or with my plants. I like messaging him, and, on the rare occasions when it takes him a bit longer than usual to respond, I miss him. "I don't have to do or be anything. We just talk. I don't have to take time away from my store to do the girlfriend thing or anything like that."

"John helps me."

"Not everyone is a miracle man like John."

"You know you could find someone to help you."

Yeah, but I don't need help.

"Everyone needs help," she adds, reading my mind again. I hate how she seems to always know what I'm thinking but I have no idea what she's not telling me right now.

"I'm fine."

"I just worry. I want you to go out and have fun and live your life." She pulls the door of the oven open, and I can feel the heat even from my chair by the window. She's more delicate now, carefully placing the cake pan on the metal tray and closing the oven door as gently as possible.

"Is everything okay?" I ask again.

"Yes, I'm fine." She finally exhales and looks at me. Her smile is fake, like she's posing for a magazine. She can sense me thinking that, too, so she relaxes her face into a frown. "Okay, so I'm a little stressed with work."

I don't buy this, of course. I love Allison, but her store doesn't require much from her. Something else is up with her, but I don't want to push it. We're best friends. If and when she wants to tell me what's going on, she will. But I can't help trying to reassure her.

"Hey, you know you can tell me anything, right?" I say gently.

She stares at me for a few long moments, and I can tell something is on the tip of her tongue. It's surprisingly stressful because the look on her face is telling me that the reveal is a big one. So I hold my breath, waiting. But the longer she's silent, the more worried I become.

"Have you talked to Norma yet?" Allison asks.

Okay, she's not telling me anything. Can't everyone just be normal?

I groan, my sugar high now ruined. I don't want to tell Norma anything. It's always best to handle as much of the store stuff on my own rather than bring it to her. I also don't know why Norma and I even need to be talking about Botanical Brothers right now. There's no reason to worry . . . yet.

Allison continues her argument. "I think she should know. About the rent hike and the new store opening down the street."

I'm already shaking my head before she can even finish what she's saying.

"She'll freak out if I tell her any of that. And, besides, it's fine. I've got the costume garden party tomorrow, and that's always a big day. The store is gonna be fine. We don't have anything to worry about, and there's no reason to have a scarcity mindset. There's plenty of boutiques, right?" I continue before she has a chance to answer. "Right. And there's tons of antique stores, but it's not like you or Bill are closing up shop, so why would I? It's gonna be fine." As I say it, I'm starting to believe it myself. Maybe everything is gonna be okay. Maybe we're all gonna be just fine.

"I just want you to keep an open mind." She stops her aggressive stirring and mixing and creating, and she stares me down in a way that is just so Allison. It's almost motherly, even if it's a little intimidating. "Things don't always stay the same, Tessa. Sometimes things have to change."

God, I hope not.

chapter four

PlantDaddy54: Do you think you'd know me if you met me?

PlantDaddy13: I'd hope I would. I hope I do. Should we drop a subtle hint of some sort when we think we've met each other?

PlantDaddy54: Yeah, what should it be?

PlantDaddy13: Mention the ZZ plant at some point. That will let me know it's you.

PlantDaddy54: HAHA, okay. I'll just be like "Hey, it's a nice day. ZZ plants are great plants!"

PlantDaddy13: Exactly like that.

———

"Miss Tessa! Can we eat these?" an adorable first grader named Jamie asks. But even before I look up and see him, dressed in a perfectly cute little cabbage costume and with his mouth full of seeds, I know I'm already too late. I rush over to him and stick my hand out for him to spit the seeds into without saying anything. He does and smiles at me afterwards. Gross.

On the second Saturday of every month, I have a garden party at Plant Therapy, and people show up to the store dressed for the occasion. Usually that means they're either wearing a trendy gardening dress from ModCloth or dressing up like a fruit or vegetable or flower. Today I'm dressed up as a giant juicy red tomato. The event doubles as an educational opportunity for the elementary kids who attend the school down the street. They get to drop by and pick up little plant plugs for the community garden. Jamie comes with his class every month and always tries to eat the seeds. It's another tradition that I secretly like, even though his love of eating seeds is deeply unsettling.

"Don't eat the seeds, plant them in their pots please!" I say, scooting him back over to where the other children are planting tomatoes in little planters. Wildcat, also dressed as a tomato for the occasion, follows the two of us and plops down next to the kids to stand guard.

The store is pleasantly full, which feels good considering the looming presence of Botanical Brothers down the street.

The bell rings, and I greet another patron. It's a young man, probably in his late twenties or early thirties, very hot, and something about him seems familiar. Since when did all these hot men come to town? He gives me a nod and a quick hello while looking me up and down (oh yeah, I'm a tomato). Then he smiles, but it doesn't quite reach his eyes. When he walks in, it's with purpose, almost as if he knows exactly what he's looking for.

He heads directly over to my plant wall and studies it. Maybe he's a plant nerd. Maybe he's 54. This is a game I play a lot. Whenever I see a man, I wonder if he's 54. I watch him, silently hoping to get some sort of sign. I feel like I'd know if it was him, right? Maybe I should just scream "ZZ plant!" and see if he reacts.

Wildcat's bark interrupts my thoughts, and she rushes to the door, her adorable tomato costume swaying back and forth. Although she does usually greet everyone, she's never this enthusiastic. I hurry over to pull her off of whomever she's managed to randomly fall in love with today.

And I see it's Leo.

I close my eyes and try to suppress the knowledge that I'm currently wearing a giant tomato costume in the presence of Sexy Merman™. He's looking particularly hot in a Wu-Tang T-shirt and jeans that fit him perfectly, and he's smiling down at Wildcat, who, of course, is already lying on her back with her legs spread. Again, I can't say that I blame her.

"Hi, Wildcat," he says, his voice as sexy as ever. "How are you, good girl?"

I linger a little too long on "good girl." Perhaps that's something I'll unpack later.

He finally looks up at me, and I feel like I'm on fire. I remember having told Allison her idea was silly when she suggested I dress as a slutty tomato—because what would a slutty tomato even look like? But right now, I wish I was dressed as anything else. I could have made broccoli sexy. Or maybe cauliflower.

Leo stands up, and we're face-to-face again. I can feel his body just on the edge of my rotund tomato costume. He gives me a look over that feels agonizingly slow. "Hello, Tessa."

"Hi. It's a costume party. And a garden party. So I'm a tomato." He's smiling at me, and I want to melt, but instead my mouth keeps going. "Because, you know, tomatoes grow in gardens, for the most part. But of course there's some research into the cloning of tomatoes, which feels unnecessary, but I guess I can see the appeal of having fruit that's genetically identical, can't you?" I'm rambling, and he's just . . . watching me. "Sorry."

"No, I was listening."

Wildcat nudges his leg as though feeling ignored, and he reaches down to scratch behind her ear. She gives him the most adoring look in the world, like she's in love. I'm happy for her, really.

"Where's Alfred?"

"Not here, thank god. He's been a little terror. He needs another run."

"Well, we're always available to service you both." Slow down,

Tessa. Use your words. "I mean, *Wildcat* is always here to be of service . . . to Alfred."

He takes a step forward into my space. "Oh? And what will we do while they run around?" I think his eyes actually glint, like we're in a fucking cartoon. "I like your outfit."

He's flirting with me, right? This is flirting. He's a flirty guy. You flirt all the time, Tessa. Just channel the energy to this random man and stop flailing.

"You don't," I say, trying to maintain eye contact. I can handle a hot man. No big deal.

"It's very . . ." He gives me another once over, his mouth quirking into a half-smile.

"Sexy?" I offer. "Nothing hotter than a big red tomato." I'm going for a mock sexy voice, but I'm shocked at how convincing it actually sounds.

"Mmm, delicious," he answers, completely serious, stepping closer. "Who doesn't like juicy red tomatoes?"

I gawk at him for a moment, unsure what to say. "I . . . uh . . ." Well, shit.

"Sorry, that was a joke, but I feel like my delivery was a little intense." He laughs. "I'm so sorry, you look horrified." He gets shy, all dimpled smiles and closed eyes, and looks down at his feet and then back up at me through his eyelashes. Pretty. Eventually I laugh along with him, and I think how nice this is, how much I'm enjoying this.

"Is this plant hard to take care of? I really like the colors." A new customer wearing a bright Lilly Pulitzer-style garden dress holds up a prayer plant. Right. I'm in my store. This is what I'm supposed to be focusing on, not the hot man in front of me.

"It's definitely an advanced plant. Maybe a Chinese evergreen would be a better choice if you want something colorful and easy," Leo answers. He actually looks at me when he says it, and my customer looks at me as if she's confused. I'm confused, too. Leo knows about plants?

"Tessa?" she asks pointedly, shooting Leo a skeptical look. She holds the prayer plant up higher, so I can see it better, I guess.

"He's right," I say, watching his face. "It's not really for beginners. Try the aglaonema instead, or maybe the raven ZZ, both are good. They're over near the display out front. Or even one of the begonias! There's also a purple variety."

Leo seems to be studying me just as intently as I'm studying him, and I wonder if there's something on my face besides the red paint that goes with my tomato costume. He shakes himself out of it.

"Sorry, I shouldn't have done that." He takes in the space as if he's just realizing where he is. I'm not sure what's going on or how to answer, so we just stand there.

"This is my store," I finally offer, feeling proud. I don't have a lot to my name, but my store is one of my greatest achievements, and I'm always happy to claim it and show it off. It's especially cute today. In addition to the normal setup, every surface is covered with freshly cut flowers, and I brought in some fresh fruits and vegetables from the local market at Bluff Park to sell. It's giving a sort of cottage in the middle of the woods vibe, and I can't help but swell a little with pride as he looks around.

"I thought your name was Tessa. The owner's name is Norma, isn't it? An older woman?" Is that . . . panic in his gorgeous brown eyes? How does he know about Norma?

"It is! I'm also the owner. Norma is in a retirement home, and I've been running the store for about six years now." The color drains from his face and his dimple disappears as he takes a step back. Now I'm even more confused. "Everything okay?"

"OMG!" someone screams, and Wildcat barks in response. I turn in the direction of the outburst and see a sexy corn and sunflower, both university students from the look of it, squealing in front of the mysterious man standing in the corner next to my plant wall.

The mysterious man reminds me of Gaston from *Beauty and the*

Beast, standing there in front of a chorus of screaming girls, practically preening. "Hi, girls, thank you so much for your support! We appreciate it!"

The girls scream in unison. "Can we get a selfie? Is Leo here?"

Is Leo here? I turn to look at Leo, and when we make eye contact, it feels like something significant has changed between us. Like I'm getting broken up with before we even get a chance to know each other. That's impossible, I know, but that's how it feels.

The girls run over to the two of us and start screaming again, their phone cameras pointed at Leo like he's a celebrity. They had the right idea with their sexy costumes. Wonder what he thinks of them.

"I can't believe you're here!" the corn girl squeals.

Leo doesn't say anything, but he looks like he'd rather be anywhere else right now, which makes me feel a little better. Wait, why am I feeling anything?

"Can we get a picture?!" the sunflower begs.

"Of course!" The other guy joins us, and the sunflower gives me her phone. The guy then puts his arm around Leo, and they both pose with the girls for a photo. I'm in a daze, still processing what's happening, and I take the photo on autopilot.

"Oh my god, thank you so much!" the girls scream in unison, and they then scurry away, leaving me with the two men. There's a little bit of tension in the air, so I decide to break it.

"Can I help you with something?" I hope my throat doesn't sound as tight as it feels. "Help you find a plant or something? You aren't in a costume, but you can still take advantage of the deal."

Not-Leo looks at me and says, "You're the owner?" He gives me a once over, like Leo had, but it's not warm. Instead, it makes me feel like he's trying to figure me out, like I'm some sort of puzzle.

"Wait, why do you two keep asking me that?" I look back and forth from one man to the other, and I start to notice the similarities. The general hotness. The jet-black hair and golden eyes. The dimples. And I suddenly understand. They're brothers.

"I'm Paul Ahn. This is my brother Leo. We're your new neighbors. The Botanical Brothers," Not-Leo explains, and the world seems to stop as I glance at Leo again. His warm face now seems a little harder, a little colder. "This is a cute store. You've done some good work here. It's a well-appointed space."

Wildcat claws at Leo's leg, wanting more attention. He pets her again.

"Thanks, we've been here for almost forty years." I don't know why I feel the need to add that. It just feels appropriate, like I'm protecting the honor of the store, letting him know that we, the store and myself, aren't afraid of them. Or maybe it's the way he called the store "cute." I already hate when people call the store "cute," and I hate the way he said it even more, making it feel like an insult.

"Of course, of course," Not-Leo—Paul, his name is Paul—says, waving a hand like he wants to cut off my speech before it begins. There's something slippery about Paul. While Leo seems genuine in his niceness, with Paul it feels put on—a mask that might slip. "I know things are changing in the neighborhood, though."

I don't like where this is going.

"Some things don't change." I can't help but copy his tone, and I catch Leo trying to hide a smile that wants to erupt from the corner of his mouth.

"Sometimes we don't have a choice. Have you thought about being acquired?"

I look at Leo, feeling betrayed. "Acquired? What do you even mean?"

"I mean, this space *would* be a great location for some of our more exclusive plants. And it's set up so nicely. We could showcase our wish list plants here. The rare shit. Right, man?"

Leo won't meet my eyes now. My face feels hot, and my hands start to shake, one of my tells when I'm angry. I've been like that forever. My mom actually has VHS tapes of me shaking with rage after being run over by a barrel for the fifteenth time while playing *Donkey Kong*.

"Let me get this straight," I say, folding my arms across my tomato costume and trying to ignore how ridiculous I look. "You want to buy me out and turn this store into your second location? What makes you think I'd let you do that?"

"He's not saying that," Leo interjects. "It's more of a collaboration." His voice is soft and soothing, but it feels like a trap. I ignore it.

"This store is just so . . . *cute*." Paul walks away from me again, wandering to the plant wall, a clear fixation of his. And of course there's that word again. Has "cute" ever sounded more condescending? He continues. "But once our store opens, I imagine things might get a little difficult for you, and I just wanted to reach out now. We're prepared to pay handsomely."

"You just come in here, look around my store, and decide you're gonna buy me out? Am I supposed to be afraid of you? How do you even know what's going on with me or the store?"

I'm getting loud now, and even though I'm trying not to make a scene, I know I'm failing miserably. When I look around, everyone is staring at me and Allison and Wildcat are by my side, although I don't remember when they got there.

"He's just trying to provide you with options," Leo argues, his voice still soft. But now I'm even more enraged because it's bullshit and we both know it. I can't believe he was the star of my merman fantasies just a little while ago.

I glare at him. "Oh yeah? And what are *you* trying to do? Were you spying on me at the beach? Was all that sexy merman stuff just a trick or a scam or something?" I probably could have left that "sexy merman" part inside my head, but I hope my anger lands.

"Spying?" Leo has the nerve to look offended. "We were just looking to connect with people in the neighborhood."

I want to take off my tomato hat and smack him across the face with it. I want to yell some more too. Let him know just how angry

I am. But nothing comes out. That's probably for the best given that the store is filled with customers and young children.

In true Gaston fashion, Paul walks away from me, throwing back a "If you change your mind, you know where to find us."

When Paul leaves, the store is silent, and everyone is still watching me. The absurdity of it all—everyone dressed in colorful plant costumes, their expressions frozen with disbelief—makes it feel like some type of *Alice in Wonderland* fever dream.

"Okay, okay. Are you not entertained? I thought we were shopping for plants. Mind your business. Let's go. Let's go." Allison distracts everyone, and eventually people settle back into what they were doing, though I still see a few worried glances thrown my way.

Leo is rubbing the back of his neck in a way that is both sheepish and annoyingly hot. Despite myself, my eyes drift to his tanned tricep, and I'm even more irritated. Sure, hot men can get away with a lot, but I'm not going to let him off the hook so easily.

"My brother . . ." Leo trails off, a line appearing between his eyebrows. He shakes his head. "Paul can be a little straightforward, but he means well." His voice is back to its smooth tone again, but it doesn't sound sexy to me anymore.

"He seems like an asshole."

"Seriously? That interaction was only like five minutes." Now he seems to be pleading, and it nearly breaks me, but I catch the reflection of my "cute" plant wall and refocus.

"Your asshole brother came in here, looked around my store, called it 'cute,' and then . . ." I feel my voice becoming louder again and sense people trying to pretend like they aren't listening to me. I take a step closer to Leo, trying to ignore how mortifying it is that my tomato suit is slightly in the way, and lower my voice to a whisper.

"How could you even have leftover plants?" I hiss. "That space is huge. I thought it was going to be a fucking grocery store."

"Paul's passionate about the plant store."

"He's passionate about being a dick."

Leo takes off his hat, and I'm momentarily distracted as he rakes his hand through his hair a few times before slipping his hat back on. It's like he's straight out of a '90s centerfold. Sexy asshole. Why can't he look a little busted? It would make my life easier.

"Now *you're* being a dick," he mutters.

"*Me?*" It comes out as a shriek. Sensing eyes on me again, I plaster a smile on my face and wave at my worried customers. "I'm good."

Once they look away again, I turn back to Leo.

"I'm here dressed like a freaking tomato for *my* store's garden party for *my* clients, and you both waltz in here like big, bad, mustache-twirling villains, but *I'm* the dick?"

"He should have taken you to lunch or something," Leo says, shaking his head. He's staring towards the door like he can't even look at me. "He's not a bad guy, he just gets . . . tunnel vision about some things."

"Do you defend him often?"

He goes still and gives me a strange look. Something in his gaze makes me pause, and I wonder if there's something deeper to it than just Leo defending his brother. Then I remember the screaming girls. "And how did those girls know who you are? Are you guys in some type of boy band or something?"

Leo smiles at that, and he looks at me again, his eyes sliding up and down my body like he's seeing me for the first time. I wonder if I'm blushing at first, but then, for the millionth time in the past ten minutes, I remember that my face is painted red and I'm dressed as a tomato.

"That's right, this shop isn't on social media at all. Makes sense that you wouldn't be either. Hmm . . . interesting."

So Leo's been stalking my store? For how long? I try to hide my concern.

"Social media is . . . Okay, well, it's a lot of things. I personally think my life is better without it."

I cross my arms over my tomato, or at least I attempt to. It's awkward, and Leo chuckles a little. I hate that I don't know if he's laughing with me or at me. Maybe he senses that, because he cuts himself off when he sees my face.

"I should go," he says. He closes his eyes and then opens them, like he's trying to reset himself.

"You absolutely should go." I try to sound stern, even though I'm a tomato.

"Fine."

"Fine."

Neither of us move. We both stare at each other, and I wonder if he's thinking what I'm thinking—that this is all so stupid, that it would be so nice if we could just forget everything and go back to the beach. Instead, I turn away first, pretending that the pothos nearby desperately needs my attention.

I hear the bell ring as Leo leaves the store, and I'm left there holding my pothos for dear life. Allison wanders over from where she was likely spying. She gently takes the plant out of my hands and places it on the countertop. I walk behind the cash register and slump down into my seat, covering my face with my hands. A moment later, someone comes up to buy her plant, and I do my best to put on a smile and ring up her stuff.

"Sorry about all that drama," I say, bagging up her hoya.

"Don't worry about it, Tessa. It was the most memorable garden party ever." She gives me a sympathetic look and puts a dollar in the tip jar. Wonderful.

chapter five

PlantDaddy54: Did you see that new dracaena they found? The leaves are beautiful. Here's the photo. Do you see the little touch of orange? Do you think it will become a part of the hobby or no? I'm gonna see if I can get my hands on one. If you do, you have to let me know. Also—and this is gonna be a little off topic—how do you know if you're a good person? I have someone in my life who I love but sometimes I worry isn't the best person but they think everything they do is good or for a good reason. I worry that I might be doing the same thing? What if I think I'm a good person and I'm really not? I just walk around thinking I'm good, when actually I'm a shitty human being. And as I'm writing this, I'm wondering why I'd ever say this to you. If we ever do meet in person, I promise we'll talk about normal things and not my inherent goodness. I also worry that by asking you this I'm exposing myself as a bad person? That dracaena has me in a reflective mood, I guess. I'm also kind of drunk but in a normal social way and not a worrying way. I don't know why you bring out all the anxious parts of me I always try to hide?

PlantDaddy13: I totally see the orange and it could totally be a contender for the hobby, but this variety looks kind of slow growing so I'm not sure. I don't know if bad people ask themselves if they are bad people in the way you're asking. I also don't think that anyone is completely bad or good. We have gray areas! Does being good mean being nice? For example, I have this person in my life who is good but not nice at all. They are actually kind of mean, but beneath the grouchy exterior, they are a really good person. I also know people who seem nice but have this ugliness about them. I don't know if that answers your question. I guess I don't think of myself as a good person or a bad person. I just think of myself as a person who is doing the best they can. Maybe you should, too. I guess the real question is—do you feel good about the things you're doing? I found this photo of a bonsai that looks like an ass if that will make you feel better?

PlantDaddy54: Why are we like this?

PlantDaddy13: I don't know.

―――――

"That was something," Allison says, looking at her phone a little later in the day.

The rest of the garden party went off without incident, and although we sold more plants than expected, I don't feel great.

"The audacity!" I'm still furious, even hours later, and I'm channeling my anger by rearranging my plants and cleaning the store.

"Well, I found them online. The Botanical Brothers. They even have a description on Google. 'The Botanical Brothers—Paul and Leo Ahn—are plant influencers who have amassed over four million followers in the last three years.' "

"What the hell is a plant influencer? Four million? For plants? That's a lot. Oh god, do you think they are going to the Plant Expo? God, I'm sure they're going." The Plant Expo takes place at the Long Beach Convention Center every year. We attend along with all of the other local plant-related businesses, including nurseries and wholesalers.

Allison continues reading. " 'The brothers have developed a loyal following by creating educational content about house plants and flowers. Viewers enjoy their contrasting styles, with Leo being the calm, thoughtful brother and Paul being more of a lady-killer. In the last two years, the Ahn family has expanded beyond just YouTube and Instagram to a brick-and-mortar location in Redondo Beach and released a line of branded products—including soil and pots. And . . .' " She pauses, biting her lip.

"What? Just tell me."

" 'And they're opening a second superstore in Long Beach as well as an exclusive third location just for their rare plants.' "

"What the hell?"

"It looks like they've made some pretty popular videos. Look at their Instagram."

I lean in to look over Allison's shoulder as she scrolls through photos of the two of them holding a variety of plants. Sometimes they're shirtless. Each photo and video has millions of views.

"Is he holding a pink princess without a shirt on? That feels wrong somehow. Can you do that?" I don't want to admit that the pink princess actually has some nice variegation, which is hard to get. I wonder what he uses for his light set up. I try not to linger too much on Leo's bare chest and his biceps. The gold skin and the . . . I shake my head to focus. See, this is bad. Why is he so disruptive?

"Wow, I didn't think a man holding a plant would do it for me, but this is . . . doing something for sure." Allison goes quiet, and when I look back at her, she's scrolling in silence, fully engrossed.

This is absurd. Who cares if he's a "plant influencer"? I grab my broom and start sweeping.

"Why would I be afraid of a dude who doesn't even have the decency to put on his shirt when he's handling a pink princess?" I'm sweeping quite aggressively, but it's not really doing much except making the dirt fly in all directions. Wildcat, who is on the floor trying to take a nap, sneezes. "We'll figure it out. We always do. And we aren't going anywhere."

Allison doesn't say anything for a moment too long, so I stop my sweeping and look up at her. She's staring into the void of her phone, frozen.

"Allison?" My voice sounds small coming out of my mouth. Suddenly, my stomach hurts.

When Allison finally looks up from her phone, she can't hold my gaze. Instead, she looks just past me, beyond me.

"I didn't want to tell you like this," she begins with a sigh.

I think back to her frustrated baking. The way she beat the batter like she was torturing it for answers. Whatever she's about to tell me, she's been holding onto it for a long time.

"I was going to sit you down over dinner and ease you into it, but with this happening, I feel like I should just tell you because if I don't . . ." She trails off, sighing again.

"Jesus, Allison, WHAT IS IT?!?" My voice shakes a little, so the question comes out more like an exasperated yelp.

She flinches at my outburst and then finally looks up at me. "I'm moving."

"Like to another building?" I know that's not it because she wouldn't be telling me like this, but part of me still hopes.

She shakes her head. "Riverside."

"RIVERSIDE?!?!?!?" I scream. Allison winces.

If you had to pick the farthest point from Long Beach that's still in the greater Los Angeles area, you'd pick Riverside. It's practically on the other side of the world. A good hour-long drive *without* traffic and almost two hours during peak commuting times. She might as well be moving to San Diego.

"You're leaving Long Beach . . . for Riverside?" It doesn't seem real. "What about your store?"

"My store is boring. I'm not interested in running it anymore, and with the increasing rent and everything else going on, it feels like a good time. John and I are pretty serious, and we've been struggling with the back and forth. We can get more for our money there." I snort a little at this, and she glares at me. It's just funny to hear her like this when a year ago she didn't even want to sign her lease because it felt like too much of a commitment.

"But this is our life and Long Beach is our home and we've been here forever and—" I stop as she gently pats my arm.

"I'm ready for the next adventure. I don't want to be on this block forever."

I find myself thinking about astrology, wondering if I should have paid better attention to the random phrases I've heard from Lizzy, the owner of A Little Witchy. Is it Mercury's axial tilt? Or the moon in retrograde? What else could explain this sudden chaos?

"You should think about it, too," Allison is saying. "Your next adventure."

Definitely a full blood moon or something. The sun is in retrograde.

"Plant Therapy is my life."

It's dramatic, sad, and true all at the same time. The store *is* my life and has been for years. The one solid thing that gives me purpose. Allison might be ready to let go of her store, but I already know there's no way I'm giving up on mine. I blink away a few tears, although one somehow escapes down my cheek. I wipe it away, and it smears red, like blood. How appropriate.

"Maybe your life can be something else," she says carefully. She knows what she's suggesting, so why is she making me think about this?

"Jesus Christ, Allison, can you just . . ." I sniffle, hoping it's enough to build my defenses up again and bring me back. "Can I have some time on my own? It's been a long day."

I see Allison bite her tongue, but she nods and makes her way out the door.

"I'm here if you need me," she says before she leaves. Except she won't be here, right?

I look down at Wildcat lying near my feet. She must have moved closer when she heard me getting upset. She lifts her head for a moment as though to check on me and then goes back to sleep.

"Is there anything *you* need to tell me?" I ask Wildcat. But she just stares at me and goes back to sleep.

With Allison gone, the store is empty. It's just me and Wildcat. And really, it's exactly the same as it always has been. But something about it feels different now that it's under threat. The store has been the one thing I've always been able to rely on, the one thing that I've known will never change. There's no way I'm gonna let it go that easily.

It's finally time to talk to Norma.

———

The next morning, I drive down the Pacific Coast Highway to Norma's retirement home. The highway is faster, but I love the view of the water on my way.

I check again on the prized orchid securely strapped into the passenger seat. Norma is obsessed with orchids, so I decided to bring her one to put her in a good mood. It's a flowering *Habenaria rhodocheila*, which is expensive and notoriously difficult to care for, so of course it's her favorite. Norma ran the store for thirty-two years and would probably have run it for another decade if not for her bad hip and the fact that she's well into her eighties. At one point, she was trying to stock shelves from her wheelchair with an extendable claw. That's when we knew it was time for her to retire. Even then, I was still surprised when she left the store to me to run.

People who hear this story think that Norma must be some sweet, generous woman, the kind of loving presence you see in movies. Norma is not that. When I arrive at her retirement home, a nice mansion overlooking the water, her nurse tells me she's in a particularly bad mood today. This could mean she either refused to eat breakfast . . . or had set the community room on fire. This is the fourth retirement home she's lived in since leaving me the store.

She keeps claiming she left the last three homes because she didn't like the nurses or the food, but I suspect she was kicked out of all of them.

When I find her in her room, she's in her rocking chair, looking out the window at the ocean. It's a nice enough room, but even though she's been here for months now, she still hasn't decorated it. The orchid will add some color. It's a bright pink, speckled variety.

Instead of saying "hello," I place the orchid on the windowsill so Norma can see it, and me. She grunts in approval. Then it's time for business.

"How's the store?"

This is the first question she always asks me when I visit.

"The store is good," I answer, and it's true. The store *is* good . . . for now. Maybe I'm delaying the inevitable by not immediately mentioning the rent hike, or the Big Bad Botanical Brothers, but I want a little space without that information in the room.

She nods, not saying anything. She looks a little sad today, and I can't help but wonder why.

"You know we used to provide plants to some of the Kennedys?"

I do know that. This is a story she tells a lot. Next she's gonna talk about that bastard DeNiro . . . .

"And Bobby! He wanted to feel like he was living in a jungle, him and his wife. That bastard ran me ragged tracking down philodendrons." She shakes her head, but she's got a hint of a smile on her wrinkled face now. "I miss it."

"I know you do."

Nearly ten years ago, my RV broke down in front of Norma's house. It was a crazy coincidence—the type of thing that makes you believe in fate. I couldn't afford to fix it or move it, so the RV just sat in front of her house for weeks with me living inside. She kept calling the cops on me, and they kept writing me tickets I couldn't pay. I had nowhere else to go.

Back then, I was on a cross-country adventure. My plan was to create a documentary and write a blog that would become a book. I yearned for my own version of *Wild* because, like most girls at the time who were reading *Wild* and *Eat, Pray, Love*, I was hoping to find purpose somewhere. Looking back, I guess I just didn't really know what to do with myself, with my life. And if those women could find themselves through travel, why couldn't I?

My mom is a bit of a shut-in and afraid of the world, so of course she was terrified of me leaving. After my parents got divorced and my grandmother died, her fears got worse, and I was starting to think I'd be stuck forever in the glass bubble she'd created for me.

I'd been planning for years, but I didn't have the money for an RV. So, when I graduated college, I went straight into a corporate job and started saving. I wanted to put together a nice nest egg for myself so I wouldn't wind up stranded and broke. And when the moment came, and I finally had enough money, I put in my two weeks' notice. I was so excited to live out my own adventure. I couldn't wait to meet Oprah.

But that's not what happened. I failed. Spectacularly.

I ran through the money quickly. A lot of my equipment stopped working and needed replacing. I took L after L, which was how I wound up on Norma's doorstep with a broken down RV, no money to pay for it, and too much shame to reach out to my parents, who seemed to be spending all of their time breaking up and getting back together.

One morning, when she finally got tired of calling the police on me, Norma banged on the door to yell at me, and I fell apart. I cried because I'd been holding it in so long. I cried because I was humiliated that everything I'd planned and created was a bust and everyone knew it. And, instead of calling the cops on me again, Norma took me in, gave me a job at her store, and let me keep my RV in front of her house, where it still lives to this day. I've also been renting a room in her house.

I settle into a chair across from her, and she perks up right away.

"What is it?" she asks, finally looking up at me. She rolls her eyes like she's annoyed that I have the nerve to show up here, even though she also yells at me if I go too long between visits.

"What do you mean?" I try to keep my tone light and friendly.

"You're acting weird. I can feel it. Also, it's Sunday, and you usually visit me on Mondays."

That's another thing about Norma. She's never been one for small talk.

"A plant store is opening on our street. It's huge. I just felt like I should tell you."

Norma's face doesn't even twitch.

"So what? There's always something new in the area."

"Yeah, but this store is huge. I feel like it's gonna be a pretty big deal, and I mean, I met the owners. They have this huge following on social media, and"—I suck in a deep breath—"I don't know how we're supposed to compete with that."

I feel like I'm starting to sweat, and I fan myself with my hand, which of course does absolutely nothing. Norma narrows her eyes at me.

"In almost forty years of business, have we *ever* needed social media? Do you think I was using 'social media' in the '80s or '90s?"

I want to roll my eyes and remind her that "social media" didn't exist in the '80s and most of the '90s, but I suppress the urge and just say nothing.

"Exactly," Norma continues. "Do they know plants like you know plants?"

"I don't know." It's not the right answer, but I'm not sure what else to say. "But it's not just the new store. Elliot is also raising the rent. Like . . . by *a lot*."

Norma scowls. "This isn't you. Since when are you like this? So timid? We've dealt with plant stores and rent raises before."

It's true. This isn't the first plant store that's tried to open on the street. There have been three in the last few years, and none of them lasted for very long. We've managed to stick around, probably because our connection with the community has kept us afloat. But this time feels different. None of those stores had nearly the same amount of hype—or square footage—as the new Botanical Brothers spot. And something else seems to have changed as well. I'm not sure what it is, but everything feels different.

"Is there something else?" Norma slides her glasses down the bridge of her nose to get a better look at me. "You seem distracted. What is it about this situation that makes things different?"

I think of dimples and black hair. I see the rare dracaena in my head.

"Nothing!" I say a little too quickly, and Norma clocks it and shifts in her seat. "It's just . . . there's a lot going on all at once. Maybe I've been a bit distracted, but I'm focused now. You're right. Everything will be fine."

Norma touches my arm, a rare bit of warmth from her that makes me feel emotional.

"Just do what you do, Tessa. People come and go, and things change, but Plant Therapy is forever, right?"

I nod because this is something I absolutely believe. "You got it. Of course. Don't worry. I got it."

She nods and gives me her version of a smile, which is more like a grimace. I smile back.

"That lipstick is the wrong color." She shakes her head at me and looks back out at the water.

Right.

chapter six

PlantDaddy13: Tell me a secret.

PlantDaddy54: How am I supposed to tell you a secret with our rules? (You still want our rules, right?) Should I tell you something general? I fantasize about leaving my life all the time. It makes me feel selfish, but I want to be left alone. Not by you, of course. Never by you. Sometimes I just want to go into the woods and be by myself and create things. I know we aren't giving details, but I have this family business that requires so much of me all the time and sometimes I fantasize about walking away from it all . . . but I can't. Is that a good secret? I guess another secret is that I don't like cheese. I feel like that's the biggest red flag about me. Who doesn't like cheese? Okay—you tell me a secret.

PlantDaddy13: I don't know you, but I feel like you're always giving yourself such a hard time. I don't think anyone who asks the questions you ask me could be selfish, you know? Fantasizing about going into the woods just seems natural. If you're selfish, I'm also selfish because I have walked away. I don't have a family business or anything like that but I know what it's like to be over-whelmed by family. I sort of escaped my family in a way? I guess "escaped" isn't the right word. I just felt pressured and overwhelmed because of this thing that happened and I couldn't handle being there anymore so I moved. I'm actually from the East Coast. (I think that's okay to say, right? There are plenty of states there.) I think it's amazing that you feel this sense of loyalty to your family and choose not to escape. It's not about what you think, it's about what you do, and if you are there for your family, that's all that matters, right? My secret is that I don't really fantasize about anything anymore. Is that weird? I used to but now I don't really have dreams. That sounds really pathetic but it's not. I know we're supposed to have these big ambitions but I just kind of want to just be. What kind of psychopath doesn't like cheese?!?!

———

"Maybe we can sabotage the store," Allison muses.

She, Bill, and I are sitting and eating ramen on Bill's vintage garden furniture outside his store. The first event of the grand opening week of Botanical Brothers is happening just down the street, and we can hear the loud music all the way from here. The event is huge—practically a block party taking over the whole street. While Allison's and Bill's stores get the occasional visitor from the crowd, no foot traffic flows through Plant Therapy.

Allison and I are talking, but not the way we usually do. I think we're both trying to ignore the elephant on the patio—her leaving. I do my best not to stare at the big sale sign in her window claiming "Everything must go!"

Instead, I look into my store. It feels so empty. I left my phone in the store to help myself keep my social media stalking of the Botanical Brothers to a minimum. I've already spent way more time than I'd care to admit scrolling through their Instagram feed. I kind of get the appeal. Their videos are entertaining. Leo and his brother have this really fun dynamic, with Leo being the serious one and Paul acting as the playful one with a sort of "himbo" energy. So I guess I can see why their schtick works. Still, it's bizarre to see all of the comments and attention Leo gets.

Leo, marry me!!!!

Leo, I love you!!!!!!

I want him biblically!!!!

It's depressing—sitting here and watching the relentless waves of people making their way down the street towards the party. Parking closer to Botanical Brothers ran out hours ago, so people are getting desperate. But I'll admit there's nothing more discouraging than seeing someone park their car in front of your store, head down the street, and come back with a plant that's not from you.

"Here's the thing," Bill says, setting down his spoon. "You just need a little buzz around Plant Therapy. I know Norma built it to be more of a hidden gem, best-kept-secret kind of business, but it's time to go online."

The irony of my eighty-two-year-old friend telling me to get back on Instagram is not lost on me. But there's no way I'm going back. Been there, done that. Never again. I'd made the mistake of announcing my massive failure, hoping for support from those who read my blog, but what I got instead was a bunch of comments about how I should have known better and how I was in over my head and how I'd wasted my money. It was humiliating. And although it's unlikely anyone from all those years ago even remembers, I don't want to be seen online like that again.

"He's right," Allison ventures. She's being careful because she knows how I feel. "We need to figure out a way to make you stand out more. Maybe if you just did a few videos . . . ."

I want to puke. "No, no, no way," I say.

Someone screams as they walk by. It's like Leo and his brother are the Beatles.

Bob, a reporter from the *Long Beach Post*, stops in front of us, and we all collectively groan.

"Hello, I'm Bob with the LBP," he says as if we don't know who he is, as if I didn't just grab his favorite fancy pickles from the top shelf at Ralph's earlier that day because he couldn't reach them.

"We know that, Bob," I say, distracted as I watch a woman make her way up the street to Botanical Brothers. She's *literally* wearing a wedding dress, holding the hem in her arms.

"Do you have any comments about the recent addition of the very large and impressive plant store opening in your neighborhood?" Bob takes his job very seriously, despite the fact that he doesn't get to cover many stories beyond the opening and closing of things.

"No comment," I say, slurping up my ramen. It's not as good as I thought, although maybe it's the hot sun making the eating experience slightly uncomfortable.

"Are you worried at all about the store's presence here? So close to your small business?"

"Not at all, there's room for more than one plant store on 4th Street."

"Okay," Bob says, scribbling something in his notebook. "And do you have any comments about Jupiter Plants?"

I look at him then. "What about Jupiter Plants?"

He seems excited to tell me something I don't already know. "Apparently, the Botanical Brothers have recently acquired Jupiter Plants downtown."

Jupiter Plants is a small shop that only opened about three years ago. The owner is nice—a thirty-something designer who creates gorgeous bouquets. So I guess Botanical Brothers is also going to be selling flowers? Fantastic.

"Go away, Bob," Bill says, saving me.

"Is that your official statement?" Bob asks, writing more notes down in his tiny notebook that seems much too small to be useful. I didn't even know they still sold notebooks that size.

"No comment," we all say in unison.

Bob shrugs and walks away, heading down the street to the party.

"Since when does the *Post* care about plant store openings? I feel like they only cover big restaurants?" I stand up and peek down the street at the crowd that seems to keep growing. My store has never been that packed before. Ugh.

"It is kind of a big thing," Allison says quietly. She takes a sip of her tea but doesn't look me in the eye.

"And he's got nothing else to report on," Bill suggests. "It's been quiet this summer."

"I can't believe they've already absorbed Jupiter Plants. I wonder what they offered him," Allison says.

I give her a look like "don't even think about it," and she rolls her eyes.

"I should get back to the store," she says, standing up and clearing her bowl.

I wonder how long things will be weird between us, how long it will take me to get over the fact that she's leaving.

"You know, maybe I can get an article written or something to drum up some excitement about the store," I say, almost to myself.

"Should I grab Bob?" Bill asks, already starting to stand up, but I shake my head and put a hand on his arm to keep him in his seat.

"We need something bigger. What's bigger than the *Post*?"

Allison sits back down in her chair, back in the conversation. I try not to notice. We're quiet for a second, all thinking. I scroll through my mental rolodex of clients, trying to remember whether any of them might have ties to the media. There's a client who is an editor for *Playboy*, although maybe that's not the best platform. I also know a bunch of movie producers and film industry people . . . . That's when it hits me. So obvious.

"Oh! Adeline!"

Adeline is a longtime reporter for the *Los Angeles Times*. She usually covers serious subjects, like politics and corruption, but maybe she'd make an exception.

Bill and Allison are both groaning.

"What?" I ask. "She's great."

"Isn't she a bit . . . *intense* for this?" Allison asks.

Bill, however, seems to be in a world of his own, a far-off, haunted look in his eyes. In addition to being a badass reporter, Adeline is also one of Bill's many ex-girlfriends. He's gotten around over the years and has a type—strong women. Alphas. It's admirable, but also probably why he's still single.

"She's just passionate," I say in Adeline's defense. "She feels deeply for her subjects! She's exactly who we need!"

I might be downplaying her enthusiasm just a little here. After all, there was that time Adeline doused herself in gasoline and lay down on the beach to protest the BP oil spill. And that time she covered herself in paint and walked across Broadway.

"Are you sure?" Bill asks, eyebrows knit in worry. "Once you let Adeline out of the bag, you can't really put her back in. Believe me, I know."

"Well, maybe it's not that bad yet," I say, settling back into my seat. "It makes total sense that the store wouldn't be super packed right now. There's nowhere to park."

"Totally," Bill says.

"I could barely find a spot," Allison adds.

"I'm going to the nursery tomorrow to get some stuff for the weekend, and it'll all be fine." I try my best to believe it.

chapter seven

PlantDaddy54: So what did you want to be when you grew up? Like in middle school or elementary school? When I was younger I was obsessed with Keanu Reeves and so I just knew I wanted to be Keanu Reeves. At one point I thought that meant I wanted to be an actor. In fact, when I was in high school I took a few classes to see if I liked being an actor but I could never do it. I'm too much myself to pretend to be another person which might be kind of hard to believe, given how we talk to each other here. But to be honest I often feel like I'm more "me" here than anywhere else, despite all of these little invisible barriers we've put up between us. Acting feels kind of unsafe, like I'm walking away from myself. As I got older I developed other interests and some other stuff happened and . . . that led me here. I'd say more but I think that breaks the rules. That's my answer. I wanted to be Keanu Reeves growing up but to be honest I still kind of want to be him. He seems so self-assured and cool. I was kind of a weird kid.

PlantDaddy13: Okay, that has to be the coolest answer I've ever heard to this question. I have this client who impersonates Keanu Reeves for money. The way I say client makes it sound like I'm some type of sex worker or something but I'm actually not.

Anyways, he goes to birthday parties dressed as Neo and other events and stuff dressed as John Wick. When you talk about being too much of yourself—that's exactly who I thought of. I wonder what looking so much like Keanu Reeves and taking on his identity makes you feel about yourself and how people view and think about you. I also really struggle with being someone I'm not. It comes up all the time. People ask me to do something or try something, and it just doesn't feel like me so I have the hardest time actually doing it. When I was growing up I never knew what I wanted to do. I remember meeting a cousin of mine for the first time, and when I asked her what she did, she said her job was to look cute and have fun. That's what I wanted to be for a long time but then my mom told me my cousin was a sugar baby. I think she thought that would turn me off of it, but then I just started going around calling myself a sugar baby until I got in trouble for it.

PlantDaddy54: Wow. Me as Keanu Reeves and you as a sugar baby. We were weird kids. Do you think we'd be friends?

PlantDaddy13: 100%

———

There are two ways to get plants. You can either go through a dealer, who brings plants to you and you choose which ones you want, or you can go to a wholesale nursery and pick for yourself. These nurseries are everywhere, but my favorite is just east of Long Beach. It's called Felipe's Nursery, and it's run by Felipe and his daughters. I also like Felipe's because the process is pretty simple. I just walk around the nursery, pick out which plants I want for the store, load them in my truck, and leave. Anything that can't fit in the truck gets delivered the next day.

Given the stress I'm under with the opening of Botanical Brothers, I really want to get the best plants I can. The store also did fairly well during the garden party sale, and I need new inventory. So early the next morning, I jump in my car and make the drive.

The nursery is right off the highway in the middle of a stretch of farmland. To get up to the greenhouses, you have to drive down a dirt path and up a hill. I'm there early, as usual, hoping it's pretty empty so I can get the best plants. But as I turn the corner on my way up the hill, I notice a bunch of cars and what looks like a Hollywood film set. There are lights and cameras and a bunch of people wearing black shirts, swarming around like ants.

I park my car among the mass of other cars that aren't supposed to be there and then make my way to the closest greenhouse. The floor is covered in brown bags, a clear signal that someone else is already shopping. Lupe, one of Felipe's daughters, scribbles furiously in her notebook, looking concerned. She's dressed nicely, wearing a blouse instead of her typical T-shirt/sweatpants combo, and she's also applied lipstick. I can't remember ever having seen her wear lipstick before.

"Sorry, Tessa, there's a big order," she tells me.

"What's going on?"

"Someone brought a crew to film the process and showcase us."

" 'Film the process'?" I ask, although I'm not sure I really expect an answer because she's already turning away.

She holds her hands up defensively, obviously flustered. "Don't ask me. They talked to my sister. I don't know. She just told me to come in a nice outfit today."

She strides away from me in the direction of the greenhouses, where a group of men in black shirts have formed an assembly line. I follow the flow of men into the greenhouse, and a familiar blast of warm, humid heat hits my face. Now that I'm closer, I can see the words "Botanical Brothers" clearly printed on their shirts. Great. That has to mean Paul and Leo are here buying plants.

When I reach the beginning of the assembly line, I find Leo talking to a camera. I can't help noticing he's wearing a tight tank top that shows off everything, including the plant sleeve wrapped around his biceps. I've seen the tattoo in videos before, and it's even more incredible when I'm not viewing it on a phone screen.

Even from where I'm standing, I can get a sense of the detail, all the rare plants carefully inked. I find myself comparing it to my own thigh piece—a collection of monsteras, birds of paradise, and pothos.

Maria, Lupe's sister, stands next to him in a sundress and with her face all made up. I try to forget that I'm wearing a pair of gym shorts and a tank top with a menudo stain on it. I didn't realize we were dressing up. The look on her face when she gazes at Leo reminds me of Wildcat rolling on her back and spreading her legs. He has that effect on people. I wonder if he flirts with her. Probably. Not that I care . . . not really.

"And we look forward to having a great relationship with this nursery," he's saying, all smiles and dimples.

"Yes, of course," Maria mumbles, nodding. Then she seems to find her voice. "We really look forward to working with you and your brother. Let us know if you need anything." She stares at the camera awkwardly, a fake smile plastered on her face until someone yells "Cut!" Leo puts a soothing hand on Maria's back—at least I imagine it's soothing—and she finally exhales. They say a few more words and then shake hands.

Once their interaction is over, Maria sees me, and she promptly takes off in the other direction as if she's escaping, but Leo still hasn't noticed me. This gives me a good chance to actually watch him in action. Everything seems so organized, and I imagine the plant-buying process must be so much faster with his employees there helping him. He follows the line as it wraps through the set of greenhouses and out back, and I trail closely behind just out of view. It feels a little like stalking, and I know I should say something to announce my presence, but nothing comes out. Once we're out of the maze of greenhouses, I watch him jump into the bed of a brand-new truck, like the kind you see in commercials. It's a bright red color, almost reflective. I try not to compare it to my own transportation and the old beat-up truck I'm driving, but I can't help it.

My whole situation feels even more dire. How do you compete with big plants?

When the worker hands Leo a philodendron that doesn't meet his standards, he hands it back and points at the greenhouse, which means he's pointing at me. And . . . oh, shit, he sees me. Do I run? No, I shouldn't run. He's just a dude! Just a guy. Just a guy who is walking towards me. I feel my body growing tense, and I will it to relax. I decide to cut down on the awkward wait time by walking towards him. We meet halfway.

"Tessa," he says. He pulls out a towel from his back pocket and wipes off his hands. I'm already in trouble.

"Leo."

"Were you spying on me?" he asks, his tone somewhere between sarcastic and playful.

"Spying on you? How? Do you mean standing in plain sight?" Someone hands him a Hawaiian pothos, and he examines the leaves. I look at it, too. It's slightly dehydrated. Without realizing what I'm doing, I shake my head "no," and he actually smiles at me when handing the pothos back.

"No. Not that one," Leo says, still looking at me. Why is he so big on eye contact? Is there a seminar on it or something? Why am I helping the enemy?

I look over at the greenhouse longingly. Is there going to be anything left?

"I don't have time for this," I say, trying my best to not look at the small bead of sweat snaking its way down his neck. "Do you really need to clean out the whole nursery? What about everyone else?"

"Our store's big. Gotta keep the shelves stocked. You know we're still in our grand opening week. You're welcome to come and check it out."

Another worker brings him a gorgeous alocasia black velvet with perfect leaves and coloring. God, it's pretty. I want to touch it.

He smiles at it and nods while feeling the biggest leaf. I bet it's soft. I'm so jealous. He catches me looking.

I tear my eyes away from the plant and try to refocus. "Why would I go to the grand opening of the store that's trying to put me out of business?"

He places the black velvet on the ground, next to his feet. I don't blame him for keeping that one for himself. Leo grabs a fresh towel from inside the truck and dabs at the sweat on his neck and his temple. My eyes follow his movements because I have no self-control.

Do I have a sweat kink? I think I have a sweat kink.

"You know, we don't have to be enemies," he says, and that snaps me out of my daze.

"Is it your turn to feed me more bullshit about collaboration? Are you going to tell me how you want to use my store as a parking ground for what I'm sure are overpriced, trendy plants that rich people are just gonna kill?"

"Paul's overzealous, and yeah, that was rude of him. I own that," Leo says, sweeping the towel in a perfect arc over his shoulder in a way that seems fake, like he's in a movie. I want to mention that it's not something he should have to own, and it's really a Paul thing, but I decide not to push it. "And you know, the store isn't even officially open yet," he continues. "All of these grand opening events . . . We don't *really* open until this weekend. We don't even know if the store will be successful."

"I've seen your videos," I blurt out. It's a mistake as soon as it leaves my mouth. Now he knows.

"Oh?" His lips curl up into a smirk. "Have you? Didn't know you were a fan."

Someone hands him a dracaena. Great leaves. Strong base. Nice genetics. In the back of my mind, I wonder if 54 has seen the rare dracaena in person yet.

"I just don't understand why you have to deliver your plant education without a shirt. And are there no other plants out there besides monsteras? Every other video is about monsteras. You know there are other plants."

"Monsteras are popular for a reason. Easy to care for and perfect intro plants. And people are looking for them."

"There are other beginner plants. Philodendrons? Aglaonemas?"

"Ah yeah, I saw your setup. Lots of *unique* plants."

The way he says "unique" almost makes it sound like an insult. But it could be a compliment instead. I'm a little off right now.

"And why are you telling people to use self-watering pots? You know those things are just root rot waiting to happen—"

"Oh, so you're a superfan!" Leo interrupts, his smile in full bloom. Reminds me of us on the beach, and again I wonder where we'd be if we were just two people who met on the beach. "You're kind of mean to be a superfan. Like Helga Pataki."

I want to laugh at the randomly specific pop culture reference, but then I remember this guy is threatening my business. "You don't deserve Helga levels of disturbing obsession from me."

"Sounds like you have a crush on Arnold. What was it? The football head? Or was it just because he had a cool room?"

"Arnold's a family guy. Living with his grandparents and a bunch of stray animals."

"You like family guys?" He looks at me through long eyelashes when he says it.

I want to ask him what he likes, but instead I redirect. "I also liked Gerald, but he was always more of a cool older brother in my eyes."

"I was partial to Phoebe, myself. I loved her glasses, and she was so smart. She deserved better," Leo says, shaking his head as if remembering.

I try to hide how charmed I am by this detail and refocus on the monstera he's examining. One of the leaves matches the one wrapped around his shoulder, and I let this distract me. I'm quiet for a little too long.

"Do you really not have any social media at all?"

The question surprises me, and I stare up at him, now standing up on the truck bed. I want to say something clever, but my mind can't conjure anything. I'm still reeling from the Phoebe revelation.

"No, I don't," I manage to get out.

We are presented with a hoya and both nod. It's nice. Shit, I say to myself. Stop helping him.

"That's impressive," he says, loading the hoya into the back of the truck.

"Impressive?"

Usually, people think it's weird.

"Yeah, it must be nice."

"Nice?" I ask.

"Are you just gonna repeat everything I say?"

His tone isn't mean, more amused. I'm not trying to amuse him, though. This banter is clearly just a game for him, fun and low stress. And yes, there are moments where it feels fun. But I can't really sexy my way out of my current situation. And I'm the one who's likely going to have to navigate an empty greenhouse. It's frustrating.

"God, why are you so . . . ?" I grow still, horrified because I'm again speaking my inner dialogue out loud.

"What am I?" he says it softly, and he's closer to me now.

He looks at me so directly that I'm pretty sure I've got goosebumps. There's something so vulnerable and familiar about his gaze. His lips look soft. I wonder what lip balm he uses. I decide to keep eye contact with him this time, which feels like a mistake. I actually want to answer him, but then someone presents him a philodendron micans. One of my favorites for the store. I always try to get at least one when I'm here. He nods at that one and is presented with another one, also good.

"We done here?" I ask, taking a step away from his truck.

"Yeah, I guess so."

We're interrupted by one of his employees loading a pair of

giant money trees into the back of the truck. Leo stops to help them, jumping back down to the ground.

When they're finished, the man wipes his brow and says, "I think that's everything, boss."

"Thanks, Victor."

Leo actually bows to me, picks the black velvet up off the ground, and hops back onto the truck.

"Thank you, Marie and Lupe!" he calls out toward the greenhouse. "I look forward to working with you!"

They both wave, clearly exhausted.

"You cleaned out the nursery," I say, staring numbly at the greenhouse. There are barely any plants left. I feel dazed again.

"I didn't. There's plenty of options left. Maybe if we collaborate, we could figure out something—"

"You know the word 'collaboration' doesn't absolve you from your actions, right? You can't just do something that's harmful to me and my business, intentionally or not, and then be like, 'Well, maybe if we collaborate?' Every time you and your brother say 'collaborate,' you're really saying, 'just give up and maybe we'll help your little store.' I'm not a charity case. Did you get that from Paul?"

Leo's eyes narrow at me, all the light gone. For the second time, I realize how protective he is of Paul. I wonder how many times he's defended his brother, even when Paul's clearly being an asshole.

"You don't know anything about me or my brother." Icy. All warmth gone from his eyes. He looks more like his brother now, the same stare.

"Well, you both give care instructions without shirts on, and you both use 'cute' as a derogatory term, and you both like to bully smaller businesses."

"Cute isn't derogatory!" His voice goes an octave higher than usual, and I'm not the only one who notices. A few of the workers turn to the two of us and stare. I even catch Victor mouthing a silent "oh boy." I kind of like this though. It's his turn to be embarrassed in front of everyone. "And we aren't bullying you," he adds, his voice smoothing out into something more familiar. But it's too late now.

I try to model his effortless eat-shit grin. "I'm not going to make it easy for you."

He closes his eyes for a moment and rubs the back of his head. Then, as he opens his eyes again, he plasters on an Instagram-ready smile. Transformation complete. It's jarring how much he looks just like Paul.

"Alright, Tessa. Then let the best shop win. Nothing wrong with a little healthy competition."

He even sounds like his brother now.

"Nothing wrong at all."

We hold each other's gazes for a long moment, and he breaks first, laughing a little as if shaking himself out of a trance. He slaps the side of the truck, and it roars to life.

He then reaches down and hands me the alocasia black velvet like it's a gift. "I'll see you around."

"What's this?" I ask.

"An alocasia velvet." Wide grin. He's making fun of me.

"Yeah, Leo, I know that, but why are you giving it to me?"

Despite myself, my hand reaches for the biggest leaf, the tip of my finger running over the velvety surface. God, it *is* soft.

"Because . . ." he says, as if that explains it.

Before I can respond or react, he hits the side of the truck one more time, and the truck starts moving. He settles into the back of the truck and gives me a little wave as it pulls away. I look down at the alocasia velvet, and I'm pretty sure I'm smiling.

When the truck is out of sight, I turn and walk back to the greenhouse to assess the damage. It's as bad as I thought. Whole rows are empty or nearly empty, with only a few plants left behind. They've cleaned Felipe's out.

"I'm sorry, Tessa," Lupe says, looking around. "I stashed a few away for you, so I'll go get those. Their space is just so big."

"Thanks, Lupe," I say, smiling at her even though I want to puke. When she heads to the back, I start combing through the plants, grabbing three *Monstera deliciosa* plants to sell. I was wrong. It's as bad as I thought.

It's time to bring in Adeline.

chapter eight

PlantDaddy13: I've been thinking about how we met. How did you know I wasn't some random old dude? I feel like you were flirty pretty early. I mean I know you saw what my profile said but you didn't really know who I was. I guess I didn't know who you were either.

PlantDaddy54: I thought you were cool and it didn't really matter to me who you were at that point. It still doesn't matter. I know you're a woman now but I don't think I would stop talking to you if you weren't. Is that weird? I didn't expect it but that's how I felt at the time.

PlantDaddy13: Of course it's not weird.

PlantDaddy54: That's not what I'm really asking. I guess what I want to know is . . . does that bother you?

PlantDaddy13: Why would it bother me?

PlantDaddy54: I don't know. Some girls don't like that.

PlantDaddy13: Well, I like you, so it doesn't matter to me.

———

Adeline has lived in the same loft apartment since the '90s. It feels very New York, like one of those documentaries you see about people who still pay only $400 a month in rent. Nobody has the energy to gentrify just north of the more exciting part of downtown Long Beach. The area is still a little rough around the edges, but her place is cool.

Every client has their kryptonite. Some love ferns. Some, like Norma, adore orchids. But only the truly unhinged love hoyas the way that Adeline loves hoyas. Hoyas can be frustrating plants. They can either be needy or completely hands-off, and they always grow infuriatingly slowly. They are picky, but if you do exactly what a hoya likes, it might bloom. You have to enjoy the drama, and that seems to work perfectly well for Adeline. Maybe that comes from her being a journalist. I'm not sure. But she collects them, and so I order rare varieties from overseas for her. The hoya in my hands is the variegated *Hoya callistophylla*. I hope it brings me luck.

I swing the doors to her loft open to let myself in since it's never locked.

"Adeline! I'm here!" I yell out.

Her loft is one big room, but it feels full because there's stuff *everywhere*. There are the hoyas, of course—possibly a hundred of them, courtesy of Plant Therapy—but there are also papers and books everywhere, stacked haphazardly on random, mismatched pieces of vintage furniture and knickknacks, relics from her travels or from her relationship with Bill.

I set down the hoya and take off my shoes at the door.

"Hi, Tessa!" I can hear her voice echo from somewhere inside the huge space. "Come in!"

Working my way towards her voice feels like tracing a path through a maze. As I navigate my way through the chaos, I see a nice spot—one with good light but enough shade to not scorch the leaves—and set the hoya down there.

When I find Adeline, she's hunched over her laptop in a chair shaped like a giant cat. Her computer fan is loud, which isn't that surprising I guess given that her computer is a Dell from the early 2000s.

"You don't have this variety, so I think you'll enjoy it," I say, pointing the hoya out to her.

"Perfect," she says, not looking up.

There's an awkward silence then. I'm not really sure how to go from "hello" to "hey, can you help me save my business?" And of course she's not making any moves either.

Sensing my presence, she looks up at me. "Is there something else?"

I sit across from her in a chair shaped like a dinosaur. Bernie, her huge orange tabby, jumps from out of nowhere and settles onto my lap. I try not to wince at his claws digging through my pants.

"So, I don't know if you know this, but there's this shop that opened up down the street from mine. And . . . it's a plant shop."

Of course Adeline probably didn't know this, but she nods as if she did. And maybe she did. Adeline does always seem to know everything.

Feeling nervous, I keep rambling. "It's kind of a big store. They took over the community center. You know the community center, right? It is crazy because it's so big."

"Who owns it?" Adeline interjects.

This is good. Her asking questions is a good sign. She grabs a reporter's notebook from a nearby tower of old issues of *The New Yorker*, and I wonder if she and Bob from the *Post* ever had a thing.

"These brothers Leo and Paul. I don't know if they're local or not, but they're very popular online. They're Instagram famous."

"Instagram," she says it like a curse, shaking her head. "The death of society."

We are in agreement about the awfulness of social media. I don't mention I've been stalking Leo and Paul online.

"So I was thinking if maybe you'd like to write a story about my store to help me promote it and let people know we're a local Black-owned plant shop."

I don't mention the fact that Leo and Paul are also people of color because that doesn't help my story.

"Well, what's the angle?"

I pet Bernie absently while I look out the window.

"They're taking over. Putting a lot of local businesses out of business."

This feels like an overreaction since so far the only business that they've acquired is Jupiter Plants. But Adeline seems to find it interesting, her eyes narrowing as she listens to me speak. So I go with it, doubling down.

"There's so many people working there, and it's so big that they clean out local nurseries"—okay, one nursery, but I'm sure there are others—"and other smaller plant stores just can't compete, ya know?"

"YES!" Adeline leaps out of the cat chair and starts pacing around amidst the clutter.

Her excitement shocks me, but I try to nod along with her as she works herself into a fury. At least she's on my side.

"Yes, it's a classic story with the big bad corporation coming to town, but the attention industry and the corporate social media give it a new angle."

I nod, not fully following but thrilled with her fresh enthusiasm.

"And it's part of the new row of businesses on 4th Street," I add, ready to drop the final bomb. "You know the kinds of places I'm talking about. All fancy and . . . gentrified."

I say the last word like a whisper, like a curse, and Adeline rounds on me, a disgusted look on her face. I don't want to smile because it might deflate the situation a bit, so I nod vigorously in agreement.

"Fucking gentrifiers," Adeline mutters. "Oat milk-drinking colonizers." She spits. I love oat milk because it's easier on my stomach, but I don't mention it.

"YEAH!" I say.

"Okay, you've got my interest, I'll look into it."

She strides over to the window, stretches like she's about to enter a battle, and starts to crack it open. I hurry to help her, nearly tripping over Bernie on the way. I hear the joints in her elbows crack as if she hasn't moved in ages, but together, we manage to shove the window open, letting fresh air flow into the room. It smells a bit like the trash from the street, but Adeline seems energized. New mission, new energy.

"You did a good thing coming to me, Tessa. Us working girls need to stick together."

Us? I look around the loft and try to imagine myself living like Adeline. Wildcat sleeping under a tower of books. Plants everywhere. Alone with my store. Maybe that wouldn't be so bad?

"Oh, um . . . How's Bill?" She says it quietly, so quietly I barely hear her. As far as I know, Adeline doesn't really date. Bill was the last one. There are other plant stores closer to her apartment, so I sometimes wonder if she only really comes to my store to see him.

"He's okay," I say.

She nods. As independent women, we aren't supposed to want anyone, but I think Adeline sometimes does. Maybe I do, too. But I have other interests and so does Adeline. Nobody has time. That's why I love talking to Plant Daddy. He never gets in the way. I do wonder if this life is what she's always wanted. Not just about the men but the devotion to her work. I've always thought we were similar in our passion for work, but I'm not sure if this is where I want to end up. I decide to put away that thought. I can open that door another time.

chapter nine

PlantDaddy13: Wish me luck today. I have something kind of big happening.
PlantDaddy54: Good luck. Remember you can do anything.

———

Adeline works quickly, so two days later, I'm preparing for her to arrive at my store to take photos and interview me. I decide to wear a floral maxi dress and a pair of boots to give me more of an earth mother vibe, but the top is a little more fitted than I remembered. So instead of "earth mother," it's making me look more like a milkmaid in a bad porno. Maybe having my boobs on display will help people actually pay attention to my story. I can't be shirtless like the Botanical Brothers, but I can do this.

Bill and I walk silently down the street toward the coffee shop. It's a weekly tradition—one that usually includes Allison. I try not to think about that part. But Bill has been oddly quiet the whole way, and I wonder what's on his mind.

It's a cloudy day. June gloom has arrived a little earlier than it usually does. I was hoping the weather would be nicer today. The store looks best when you can see the plants bathed in light. Everything looks fresher and healthier that way. I'm trying to not view the light gray skies as an omen.

"Are you going on a date?" Bill asks. Ahh, there is it. He must have been teeing up for this statement.

"It's nine o'clock in the morning."

"Then are you coming back from a date last night?"

He does a dramatic old-man eyebrow raise, and I laugh at the implication that I'd ever be on a date, but that little pocket of lightness dies when we walk past Botanical Brothers. The sign on their window is still flipped to "Closed," but you can see a bunch of employees in green shirts inside the store, preparing to open for the day. Botanical Brothers opens at 10:00 a.m., about an hour after Plant Therapy. I can tell because the street fills up around that time, and that's when the social media posts start. I hate that I've watched so many of their videos. I'd never say this out loud, but I might be a bit addicted to their content. I like it best when Paul makes Leo laugh. It's the best thing. All dimples and closed eyes. He laughs with his whole body, like he's surrendering to it. Somehow that fact makes him even more attractive, though I didn't think that was possible.

"Maybe we should throw a rock!" Bill says.

"Bill!" I shake my head, but I'm secretly enjoying laughing at his protectiveness. He opens the door to the coffee shop for me, and I'm immediately comforted by the smells of roasted coffee beans and freshly baked croissants. As soon as we walk through the door, one of Bill's bandmates pulls him away to his table in the corner, leaving me to brave the line alone.

When I get to the front, Blaze—yes, that's really their name— gives me a look over.

"Wowwwww," Blaze drags out. "You look *different*. Are you going on a date?"

Even stoned hipster baristas are noticing the new look? I briefly make a mental note to start putting more effort into my appearance.

"No! Why do people keep saying that?"

"I—"

"Can I just have my matcha latte please?"

They shrug, pulling down a jar of matcha and turning their back to make my drink. I feel bad for snapping and pull a few dollars out of my pocket to put in the tip jar as an apology. I'm way too tense.

I'm about to actually apologize when I feel him again. My Leo spidey-sense is very annoying. I wonder if it has anything to do with me, or if it's just him. He's the type of guy who lights up every room, so maybe there's nothing special about how I just seem to know when he's around. Yeah, let's just go with that. It may be bad for my business situation because that presence is why he has a million followers on Instagram. But for me personally, thinking of it in this way may soften the blow, at least a little.

So even though I'm going to tell myself that my Leo spidey-sense really isn't that special, I still find myself staring at him. The hair is out today, and it looks like he got a haircut because it's shorter, which makes his jawline even sharper. Must help with sales. He's also wearing a black T-shirt with a Botanical Brothers logo and a pair of cargo shorts that shouldn't work on anyone but he can somehow pull off. As soon as he enters, he heads to talk to another worker from Botanical Brothers who is sitting at the table near the window. The other guy seems happy to see him. He must be a good boss.

"Oh, is *that* your date?" Blaze asks. I face them, and they're still whisking the latte while staring at Leo. "Juicy. I love the drama. I mean I get it, look at him."

I do, and as soon as I do, he makes momentary eye contact with me before giving his employee a handshake and a hug in the way hot confident men do. Secure and warm. I wonder how he hugs people who don't work for him.

"No, that's not my date," I say, finally tearing my eyes away from them.

"Uh-huh," Blaze says, handing me my drink.

God, where is Bill? I need to get out of here. I scan the too-small cafe and realize there's no escape. Shit. Leo's coming in this direction. His eyes drift down to my dress before returning to my face.

I wheel back around towards the counter.

"Do you need anything else?" Blaze says sweetly, barely containing their laughter as though they're enjoying watching me squirm. I don't say anything, stalling.

Sick of the tension, I'm just about to open my mouth when Blaze speaks. "Enjoy your not-a-date." Maybe I should take my tip money back.

When I spin around, Leo is right there. I almost bump into him, but he braces me with his hand on my arm. I'm choosing to ignore some of the other places I'm also feeling it.

Leo looks confused for some reason. A small line forms between his eyebrows.

"What was that about?" he asks. "Are you going on a date or something? You look like you are."

At that moment, I silently swear to dress better.

"I didn't know we were close enough to talk about our dating lives," I deflect.

He doesn't miss a beat. "I'm happy to share if you want. Not much to tell."

"I doubt that. I saw a woman wearing a wedding dress on her way to your store opening." I regret saying this because it's proof I've been watching, proof that I'm keeping an eye on what's happening at Botanical Brothers. But he doesn't gloat. Instead, he gets shy again, smiling at his feet. Those goddamn dimples.

"That's different. She just likes Botanical Brothers."

"Aren't *you* Botanical Brothers?"

I glance over at Bill, but he's deep in conversation with his bandmate again so he doesn't notice my pained "help me" look. I miss Allison. She would have noticed.

When I look back at Leo, he's biting his lip and shifting from one foot to the other. Did I actually hit a nerve or something?

"I mean . . . kind of?" Leo shrugs. Leo makes absolutely no sense to me. "I am a Botanical Brother, but I'm not . . ." He trails off without finishing his thought. Instead of looking me in the eye, he seems to be staring at a spot just over my shoulder.

"You're not . . . what? What does that mean?"

"The version of me she wants to marry isn't really *me*. It's someone she's made up in her head. It's not like she knows who I am, not really."

I think about 54 and how it's totally possible to feel like you know someone online, even if you don't. Suddenly I feel sad for the girl in the wedding dress, chasing after a dream. Boy, do I get it. I nod, and we're quiet again.

"Next!" Blaze interrupts, pointedly glaring at Leo, who's next in line.

Leo doesn't move. I'm not sure what he wants, what he's waiting for. He's still looking at me like he's trying to figure something out.

"You going to order?" I ask, nodding towards Blaze.

"You know it's nothing personal, right?" Leo says.

"Of course. What's not personal about potentially putting my store out of business?" The sarcasm drips out of me like poison, but I can't help it. I thought we decided telepathically to not talk about this.

Leo looks pained. "I'm not doing any of this to you on purpose. It's just—"

"It doesn't matter, does it?" I interrupt, thinking about Adeline and the article. "It's happening anyway."

"NEXT!" Blaze basically shrieks.

Both Leo and I jump. I don't know when we started standing so close to each other.

"You should go," I tell him, stepping out of the line.

I try to make the words feel final, and he nods, but I can tell he doesn't really mean it because he hasn't moved. Instead, his eyes take another trip down the front of my dress. It's fast. My calves feel hot, which is bizarre and specific. Leo catches me catching him looking. And instead of getting shy like usual, he looks directly at me, like he's undressing me with his eyes. I bite my lip involuntarily, and he takes a step forward. His eyes go dark—which is something I've only read about in books—but here it is, happening right now.

"Tess?"

It's Bill, walking over in a huff. The spell breaks. Leo and I both take a step away from each other like we were caught doing something wrong.

"Sorry about that! You know how chatty Ted gets," Bill says, but he's chuckling fondly. Then he notices whom I'm talking to, and he looks from me to Leo. I don't know what my own face is doing, but if it's anything like Leo's, I must look panicked. Bill raises an eyebrow. "Is everything okay?" He gives Leo a fatherly look.

"Everything is fine!" I say, probably much too quickly. But I mean it. Even if things aren't fine yet, they will be soon because Adeline is going to write her story. Blaze calls for Leo again, and Leo settles back into his easy smile and demeanor, giving us both a nod and turning towards the counter.

"See you around, Tessa," he says softly, just over his shoulder.

"Yeah, okay."

I turn back towards where Bill waits at the door, but I can't help glancing over my shoulder to sneak another look at Leo's back. Bill clears his throat. When I face Bill again, he's got a big shit-eating grin on his face.

"Don't," I warn, sucking in a deep breath as I step outside into the warmth of the sun. I take another breath and almost immediately feel better. I look down at my outfit to make sure everything is in place. My boobs are the first thing I see, and I smile a little. Maybe they are already working.

———

Adeline arrives early, a little before 11:00 a.m. Her photographer is young—doesn't look to be a day over twenty-five—and is obviously terrified. I feel for the poor guy. Adeline's usual photographer, a quiet man in his seventies, died several months ago, and she's already been through four others. This guy has been with Adeline for only a few weeks but already looks traumatized.

"He's really skittish," she says with a sigh, noticing how the photographer cowers beside her. "Go take some photos of the shop," she orders, and he scampers off to the front display.

Plant Therapy feels emptier than usual today, partly because we have started carrying less stock to respond to the lack of demand but mostly because I decided to leave Wildcat at home for the day. While the store doesn't feel quite the same without her, I couldn't risk her barking or causing a scene. Adeline is also more of a cat person. No reason to make things even harder. Adeline likes me enough, but her loyalty will always be to the best story and not to me or my shop.

With the photographer snapping away in the front of the store, Adeline turns her full attention on me. She doesn't pull any punches with her questions.

How long have I run the store? Eight years.

Do I have any help? Nope.

What's my vision for the business? Survival, I guess. Not being put out of business.

Do I ever get tired of the store? Never.

Have I ever wanted to do anything else with my life? Of course.

That last question pulls me out of the interview, and I think about my dream of writing the next great *Eat, Pray, Love* and of proving my mom wrong about being adventurous and out there. My mom always told me that the world was unsafe, that my visions, my dreams were not realistic. "You can't just leave," she would say to me. It's been a while since I've caught myself lingering on the fact that she was right. I failed.

"Is that something you'd ever pursue again?" Adeline asks.

"Uh . . ." I hadn't realized I'd spoken out loud. "I haven't. No. The store is my passion now, it's my life. I don't know what I'd do without it."

She nods and writes down a bunch more notes. It takes her so long to scribble everything down, I start to wonder what exactly she's writing. I hope I haven't shared too much.

When Adeline is finally finished with poking around the shop, firing off questions, and securing her next order of hoyas, I feel exhausted but hopeful. I told her everything I wanted to, focusing on how much the store means to the community, our history in the neighborhood, the personalized attention given to our clients. The terrified photographer takes a couple of shots of me in front of my pride and joy, the live plant wall. Somehow, I manage to smile for the camera, although it feels strained.

After they are all done, I pretend to do something behind the register and hear Adeline instruct the photographer to go to "the boys up the street." She's going to visit Botanical Brothers. Of course she is. I don't know why it never occurred to me that she'd want to get their side of the story. I think about what Bill said— once you unleash Adeline, you can't take it back. I hope I haven't made a mistake.

"Have you been looking into Botanical Brothers?" I ask, trying to sound casual.

Adeline just nods, giving away nothing. I know that if I push the issue, she'll say something about "journalistic integrity." It's all about the story.

Before I can say anything else, she's already out the door and moving on to the next thing, throwing back an "I'll be in touch!" as she leaves. Her photographer, who was waiting outside, struggles to keep up with her brisk pace as they start off down the street.

With the two of them gone, the store is quiet again. For the first time all morning, I have a chance to think, and I think, of course, about Leo and how he looked at me during our conversation in the café. Successfully filed away for safekeeping, I can pull out the memory and look at it whenever I want. My calves itch.

I scan the empty store and feel, for the first time in a long time, like things are going to work out. I can't wait to read the article.

chapter ten

PlantDaddy54: How did the thing go?

PlantDaddy13: It went okay, I guess? I'll know soon if your good luck actually worked.

PlantDaddy54: Well, send some luck my way, too. I'm a little afraid of what this day will bring.

PlantDaddy13: Hey, remember you can handle anything. Be like a snake plant!

PlantDaddy54: Indestructible.

PlantDaddy13: Jesus, we are such nerds.

———

The article is called "A Tale of Two Stores" because Adeline loves drama, but it works. Within a day of its publication, Plant Therapy is getting more customers. By the next day, that number has doubled. And while it took a little time, I've managed to work around the Botanical Brothers nursery-visiting schedule. I go on Tuesdays instead of Wednesdays and spread my shopping over a few places rather than just shopping at one. Norma was right, maybe we will be okay.

For the rest of the week, it seems that way. There's just one thing . . . . I haven't actually read the article yet. It remains unread, the tab pulled up on my phone. Part of me is terrified to read what Adeline actually wrote.

"I won't kill it, will I?" A woman in her early thirties stares at me hopefully, her eyes and nose red from crying, as I hold up the giant Hawaiian pothos she just bought. Huge leaves. Easy care. Perfect plant for a broken heart. She hasn't told me she has a broken heart, but that's what the angsty music playing from the headphones in her pocket is telling me.

"No. You definitely won't kill it," I assure her. "It grows fast and big and is super forgiving. If you want, it can trail around the house. It's a very reliable plant, won't let you down."

She nods, a small smile threatening to escape from her chapped lips. "Okay." She sniffs and heads to the door.

"Have a good night."

Once she reaches the door, she stops and turns around. "And you say water once a week?" She suddenly looks panicked, like she's carrying a baby.

"Yes." I smile encouragingly.

"Okay, but like . . . how much? I just don't want to mess it up. I can't ruin another thing, I can't." She's crying now, and I come out from around the counter and put my hands on her shoulders.

"You won't ruin it. You can't mess it up. It's okay. You're doing great."

She takes a few shaky breaths and seems to relax. "Thanks," she says, her nose a little runny. She takes a deep breath as I smile and open the door for her. When she's gone, I close the door behind her and put the closed sign up.

"Okay, we're done today, Wildcat!" I say enthusiastically, turning back to where Wildcat is resting in her corner. She's worked hard today, greeting all of our customers, so she's tired too, but she jumps up from her corner when I say her name.

I move to my seat behind the counter and settle down to relax as I pull out my phone. Maybe it's time for me to finally read the article.

Wildcat feels him first this time, swinging her head around towards the door, her ears raised and at attention. Her tail wags so aggressively I can feel it knocking against my chair. Before I can guess what she's so excited about, Leo busts through the door without his usual ease. He's more clumsy than normal as well, and he sort of fumbles with the door behind him. His face is also a deeper pink, and he's not smiling. Is this Leo anger? Wildcat doesn't get it at first, bounding over to him like usual and waiting eagerly to be greeted. When Leo only gives her a noncommittal pat, she whimpers a little. I see some of the heat drain from Leo's face as he looks down at her. He pats Wildcat again, this time with more intention.

I take the opportunity to assess him. I'm guessing he's here because of the article. The article I still haven't read. His hair isn't as perfect as usual. His infuriatingly easy, laid-back manner is gone, but he's still pretty. His expression is soft as he pets Wildcat, and he mumbles something in low tones to her while she wags her tail aggressively. He's not mad at her.

But all that softness disappears when he looks back up at me.

The street is dead since all the shops are closed for the day. It's just me and Leo and Wildcat in the middle of my empty store. It feels oddly intimate. We haven't been alone like this since we met on the beach.

"Hi, Leo, how are you?" I'm aiming for a casual tone, but I feel a flutter in my stomach.

"Don't use your sexy schoolteacher voice on me."

Is that a growl? Did he just growl at me? Sexy schoolteacher?

I don't have time to unpack *that* before he slams his phone down on the counter. Without even looking, I know it's open to Adeline's article.

"Oh that," I say, feeling like I'm in trouble, even though I'm not sure why.

"Oh yes, *that*," Leo responds. "Let me do you the honor of reading you some choice passages from the piece."

Wildcat, temporarily satisfied, settles down next to his feet, totally oblivious to the confrontation about to happen.

" 'The Botanical Brothers are brothers Paul and Leo Ahn, who are well-known for their wildly popular videos in which they titillate the masses with their bare, muscled chests and *passable knowledge of plant care.'* " He starts pacing around the store as he rants. "What does this reporter know about plants anyway?"

"She's actually a hoya collector, and she—"

"Oh, I'm not done," Leo cuts in. I shut up while he continues reading. " 'After scrolling through the Botanical Brothers Instagram channel, I soon found my favorite video. Paul, the eldest Botanical Brother, holds a money tree in the shower and discusses the horticultural benefits of bathing with your plants. And, yes, he is naked.' " Leo combs a hand through his hair, frustration radiating from him. "That was a *joke* video."

I want to laugh at him, but I can't because he does look tortured. Maybe part of the reason why I picked Adeline to write this story was because she hates men. (Thanks, Bill.) I suppose that might have colored her writing a little.

Leo starts reading again. " 'At first glance, the Botanical Brothers seem harmless. A couple of charismatic ladies' men whose love for plants is only rivaled by their love of showing off their abs. But a deep dive of their social media presence paints a slightly different picture. The two party bros randomly decided to get into plants for fun and have used their abs to build their following. Now, with millions of followers and access to resources the average shop can't match, they're building an empire, and it might spell the end for a small Black-owned and -operated plant store, just two blocks down the street.' "

Leo is quiet now. He's just staring at his phone like that will somehow change Adeline's words.

I decide to break the silence. "Is any of that untrue?"

Leo sighs.

"I'm just asking!"

"I. Do. Not. Titillate," he says.

"You don't?" I ask, giving him a once over. I catch a tiny smirk tugging at the corner of his mouth, but he shakes it off and gets serious again.

"Where did this come from?" he asks.

"Well, Leo," I start, trying to keep my tone as neutral as possible, which only seems to make him madder. "Adeline is a legendary local reporter! A shining beacon in the field. She was just following the story."

"It's a hit piece."

"It's not." I look him right in the eyes. "It's accurate."

He gives me a dramatic eye roll that feels almost like it belongs in the '90s. I relish the feeling of finally, *finally*, being the calm one. It's the first time I've interacted with him without feeling like I'm fighting against his annoyingly constant serenity.

"It's not accurate because *I'm* not like that," Leo insists. "I'm not some party guy or some plant influencer. Where did she even get this information from?"

"No idea," I shrug. But I can't help but soften a little at the way he frowns, the corners of his mouth turned down in a perfect way.

"Do you really see me this way?" His voice is low, and I lean in closer to hear him. "The way she described me in the article?"

I don't want to admit that I actually haven't read the article yet. I feel it ruins the impact.

"Why do you even care? It can't be *that* bad."

I know I've made a mistake as soon as the words leave my mouth.

"You haven't read it?"

Shit.

"I didn't say that!" I rush to say.

But he's already grabbed my hand, placing his phone into my palm. Our fingers brush against each other's for a split second. We must both feel the spark between us because we pause a breath before I pull away.

"Just read it," he insists, fidgeting a little.

It feels weird to hold his phone. There's something too intimate about it, too close. I start to read but immediately feel self-conscious with him looming there, so I give him a look that I hope communicates a desire for space. He sighs but starts wandering around the store, Wildcat following him.

Adeline's article is well written, and she tells the story of the store and my involvement with it faithfully. A little *too* faithfully. I don't remember telling her that I was lost and broke and didn't know anything about plants. I don't recall giving her any details about my epic cross-country failure and my old blog and my old life. There's even a paragraph about how I was taken in by Norma, the neighborhood grouch, and how I haven't been online since. I suddenly feel my face heat up and a lump forming in my throat. This article is even more detailed than I imagined. Thank goodness she didn't find out about my Reddit account or Plant Daddy . . . me or 54.

I'm relieved to see that, despite all of my unnecessary backstory, Adeline did do the job. She made the store look great, declaring Plant Therapy a neighborhood establishment and one of the last vestiges of historic Long Beach, before all of the gentrification. Botanical Brothers, both the store and the brothers themselves, are portrayed as ravenous big-business types who destroy local businesses and dilute the unique flavor of the neighborhood. They are the big bad we all have to worry about, Adeline writes. Corporate types who try to pretend they're not. She presents Leo and Paul as new-school sex symbols, frat boy thirst trappers who think plants are a good way to meet women. The article is dramatic, like Adeline always is, but effective. I owe her another hoya. Although I'm not entirely sure I agreed with her take—I've seen way too many of their videos, and while Paul definitely fits her description, Leo just seems like a plant nerd caught without his shirt on.

When I finish reading, I peek back up at Leo. He's busy with Wildcat, who is giving him a tour of the space, showing him some of her favorite places to nap. The two of them are cute together, somehow already old friends, and it feels natural in a way I don't want to dwell on.

"It's very well researched," I say, waiting for his response.

He's holding one of my rare cacti, not a part of the tour. Wildcat sits patiently at his feet.

"This is gorgeous."

There he is using that word again. His voice drips with wonder, and it's the kind of wonder I recognize. Only plant nerds talk about and look at plants like that.

"Never seen one bloom in person," he adds, delicately stroking the petals.

He doesn't look at me when I walk over to him. The plant is a *Stapelia grandiflora*. The flower is fuzzy and star-shaped, making it look like a cactus with starfish attached. Bizarre, as though it could be from another planet.

"Oh yeah, we don't usually carry a ton of cacti, but I'm holding it for a client who's in Vancouver shooting a movie right now. I'll take it to him when he returns."

Leo nods, turning the plant around in his hands, examining the leaves. "You travel around LA a lot?"

"Yeah. Norma used to hand deliver a lot of plants to her legacy clients in the industry. I try to do the same when I can."

"Shipping is a nightmare. That's smart," he says.

"Yeah, especially for rare plants like these that come from overseas. Don't want a plant to go through any more trauma than necessary. If I could afford it, I'd go get the plants myself."

"I know what you mean. I've been dying to go to Indonesia and get some plants on my own."

"Me too!"

We catch ourselves smiling at each other before we both scowl again. His is funny because it looks so unnatural on his face. It's clear Leo does not frown often. I hold his phone out to him, and he stares at it a second before taking it back. Then he looks at me and asks the last thing I expected him to say.

"Do you still have the RV?"

I fight a cringe. I guess he also learned a lot about me from Adeline's article—information I'd rather him not know. The realization makes me feel uncomfortable.

I open my mouth to answer him but then close it again. Is this breaking the rules? The unspoken protocol for speaking to someone who is, technically, the enemy? What if I tell him something he can use against me?

But his face is just so open, his eyes so curious, and I feel compelled to speak.

"Yeah, it's sitting in my driveway. It's been there for . . . a long time. I haven't gotten around to fixing it, because, well, you know. Life. The shop."

Again, I'm not sure if Leo is just like this—that he has this ability to make me feel so understood without saying anything or if he does actually get me. For sure it's the first option, right? Totally.

"Are you done harassing me for an article I didn't even write?"

He bristles at the abrupt subject change but shakes his head, stepping back.

"I hope it's everything you wanted." He pauses for dramatic effect, and he almost succeeds, but then he can't seem to manage to keep his thoughts to himself. "Do you ever think about repairing the RV? Going back on the road?"

I'm perplexed. My bad attitude was supposed to get us fully off this subject. Why is he so interested in the freaking RV?

"I don't think about it much. It was a long time ago, and I don't have any reason to fix it now." I shrug, hoping this is the end of it. It's true that I have no need for the RV anymore. What I don't say is that I also can't bring myself to sell it, which is why it's been gathering dust in the driveway for eight years.

He's listening intently, and even though I can't see his eyes, I know he's looking right at me. It's been years since I went on a date, but I still remember how hard it was to get men to listen to me and really hear what I was saying. Usually, in my experience, men only want to talk about themselves, and if they do let you speak, they're waiting for their next opportunity to talk instead of focusing on what you're saying. But Leo isn't like that. He's clearly listening.

I don't understand how we got from him storming in here complaining about the article to me comparing Leo to my past dates. Maybe it's because this feels like a date with all the questions he's asking me.

"I'm happy with my life the way it is." I sound unconvincing, even to myself. *Am I happy with my life?* I am, right? I would know if I was *un*happy. Right?

If Leo senses my uncertainty, he doesn't show it. Instead, he simply nods, as if that's all the information he needs to know. The awkward, uncomfortable feeling returns, and I decide to ask my own question. One about a detail I learned from the article.

"Why did you leave New York?"

His expression shifts to one that seems oddly similar to the expression I had—shock at being really seen. I admit the article only briefly mentioned it—just a few sentences about his short stint at art school in New York before he'd come back home to California.

"I thought it was something I should be doing but I was wrong. It wasn't what I thought so I came home . . . ." He trails off and shuffles his feet, looking uncomfortable. I hit something unexpected, but I feel like I can relate. I wonder if he'd been trying to prove himself, like me, and found himself failing in a similar spot. "It just wasn't a good fit. I really shouldn't have been that far away from my family. I'm needed at home."

"You did the Botanical Brothers art, I'm assuming?" The Botanical Brothers logo is hipster, but it's pretty. The letters all lead into flowers and plants in interesting arches and lines. It looks like art. He nods, his mouth slightly open. "It's good." I can't stop myself from saying it, even though I don't want to compliment him. But I need to stop because I feel so many questions, right there on the tip of my tongue, waiting to come out. It feels dangerous, and when I look at him, his gaze feels dangerous. He's looking at me like he's peeling off my skin but not in a bad way. My skin prickles. That's enough. Time to end this.

"Is that all, Leo? I'm sure your store is missing your presence."

I walk away from him and back to the register area, but not before I notice how he seems to deflate, his square shoulders rounding as if he's tired. The change seems to trigger a small pang of regret in me, and for a moment, I almost regret asking Adeline to write the article. While I liked most of what Adeline wrote, I can't get on board with the idea that Leo is a party bro pretending to be a plant expert. I don't need to have watched his videos—even if I've now seen them all—to see that Leo knows his stuff. His brother on the other hand? Adeline nailed him.

"You have no idea. Want to come help?" He's joking, but I notice a hint of desperation in his tone.

"I have a job," I remind him. "But if you ever want to help out here, I can always find a way to put you to work."

I'm totally kidding, of course. I've always rejected the idea of hiring any additional help. Norma ran the shop on her own until she brought me under her wing, and she did it for years, opening six days a week. She only ever closed for three reasons: deliveries, illness, and lunch. I follow the same model. Every day, I wake up and it's just me, Wildcat, and the store.

"Don't tempt me."

I almost want to ask him what he means by that, but then he actually smiles when he looks around my shop, and I feel a bit of pride. Plant Therapy can never compete with the sheer size of Leo's store, which can hold far, far, far more plants, but I think my store is nicer. It's cozy. It's home. And I'll do anything to keep it. I have to remember that.

"I better get back to work," I say, clearing my throat.

He immediately gets the hint and nods, taking a step back towards the door. We shift back to our normal dynamic, the tension returning now that it's time for him to go. But when Wildcat whines a little, Leo gets on his knees and gives her a few pats.

"Okay," he says, rubbing behind Wildcat's ears before standing back up.

He's close to me again, and there seems to be an extra layer of intensity as we stand there, eye to eye. I'm surprised again at the fact that Leo and I are nearly the same height. Given how tall I am, it's rare for me to be looking someone in the eye like this. And when we're standing this close and talking like this, it's like we can't really hide from each other, like I can't escape him.

"Is it always going to be like this?" Leo asks quietly.

"Like what?" I'm holding my breath. I really should breathe. Oxygen is good.

"Like this," he says as he gestures at the space between us. "Is it always gonna be a fight?"

I stammer over my words until I stumble into something that feels like it touches the truth, even if it's just slightly.

"Your business and my business are competitors. And *you*—"

"I know, I know." He stares up at the ceiling as if he's looking for something up there. But there are just more plants. "What if I apologize?"

My laugh is humorless. "Apologize for what?"

All of a sudden, the air between us feels different. *He* feels different, intense. I wonder if this is the quality in Leo I keep noticing, how he's able to adapt according to his audience and where he is. Leo is a bit of a changeling. I'm not like that. I'm always the same.

"For building my shop down the street from yours? For buying all the plants in the nursery and having more followers and I don't know."

My eyes drift out the door, and I'm thinking about Botanical Brothers down the street. When I look back at Leo, I find something else, something darker in his eyes. Too late, I notice that he's standing closer to me and his hand is right next to mine, resting on the side of the counter. I know I should look into his eyes, but I'm afraid of what I'll find there. He's not looking at me, but his index finger reaches out and strokes the inside of my wrist. It's barely there, barely the lightest of touches, but somehow I feel it everywhere, and a small noise escapes me. It's stupid. Has it been that long? It feels nice to be touched. The air feels thicker around us, the space smaller.

"Are you . . . ?" I feel like I want to ask him if this thing between us is real. If he's actually attracted to me, or if it's just my imagination. I always have to check. "Um . . ."

"Sorry. Sorry. Sorry." He pulls back out of my space, and I don't actually know if I wanted him to do that.

I realize that I'm pressed against the counter, and I quickly straighten up. "Yeah, of course, I just . . . sorry." I shake my head. What am I even apologizing for?

"No, it's okay. You don't have to apologize. I was just . . . I . . ." He's shaking his head now, and he's not looking at me anymore. It's almost charming how he goes from hot to shy and almost sweet.

The impact is there, though. I feel flushed. My whole body is tense. Everything feels overwhelming, and I don't understand why. I mean, he barely touched me!

I want to say something else but he's already leaving.

"You win this round, Tessa." He's already halfway out the door when he says it.

I don't know how he moves so fast. The door whooshes shut behind him, but I walk over and open it back up, letting the cool ocean breeze drift over my skin. Why am I so worked up? He's just a dude. A dude with kind eyes and dumb dimples and really soft hands.

chapter eleven

PlantDaddy54: So I got to check out this new variation of the anthurium clarinervium. It's a cross with the gigas and the color was great. The most interesting part was the leaves. The texture was slightly different from either variation, it was almost skin-like. The leaves were soft but slightly bumpy like the feeling of lips kissing soft goose-bumped skin. I wish you could have felt it. The photo doesn't really do it justice, it's something you have to feel yourself. It's slightly different.

PlantDaddy13: That's a great description of the feeling and I think I can envision the feel of it but I may need some clarification. These lips on goose-bumped skin. There's a few places you can get goose bumps, right? I'm trying to get a clearer picture. Are you talking about the skin on the back of my arm? Maybe my neck? Somewhere else?

PlantDaddy54: Sorry I didn't clarify! That's my mistake. How can you get a full picture if I'm not specific? I'd say those places can give you some idea, but it's more like my mouth between your breasts and moving down your body, it's more like that. Think of it like my lips against the inside of your thighs.

PlantDaddy13: Oh, that clears things up a bit but I'd love more clarification. Is it just a brush of lips against your stomach, like that spot right below your belly button, or is it like more of a kiss? Is there tongue involved? I just want to be sure. A kiss behind your ear or your neck?

PlantDaddy54: Yes, that's exactly it. It's like a kiss.

PlantDaddy13: What else is it like? Describe it to me.

———

The problem with old-school media is that the results do not last for long. While we get a temporary boost from the article, we don't sell enough to make up for the lost business since Botanical Brothers opened. People soon forget about the article. By the following, Friday I'm staring at a bunch of unsold plants trying to figure out what to do next.

The article has another unintended effect—now everyone is worried about me.

Are you sure you're okay?!

That's so sad about the RV, are you okay?

What ever happened to your blog? Is this why you're not on social media?

Nobody has asked me these questions in years. I have not missed them.

My mom, who it turns out has Google alerts set to notify her if my name pops up, considered the article a cry for help. Her solution is to FaceTime me as often as possible, and it's starting to grate on me. This morning, I have her propped up on the counter while I mist the plants. It's hot and dry, and each of the plants has different needs and is on a different schedule.

"You should be here," Mom repeats for the tenth time this week.

Her latest goal is getting me to come back home to Georgia, as if that will somehow save me from my tragic existence. I've only taken a few vacations from the store since taking over for Norma. The last time was for my sister Cece's wedding.

Cece and I took opposite paths. While my goal was to get as far away as I could, Cece stayed close to home. And while my parent's divorce felt like an explosion I needed to run away from, for Cece, it was a call to action. She became even closer to my mom and practically lived with her until she met her husband, who managed to get her to move five miles away. It's good for her to have some space, I think. We play phone games together and talk on the phone about once a month. She's currently a resident at a veterinary hospital, so she's really busy, but we catch up when we can.

As if she's reading my thoughts, Mom adds, "Your sister is going to start a family soon. And what exactly is *your* goal? Do you want to run the store forever? It's time to come home."

My mom doesn't mean to make me feel like a failure, but everything I do is framed as one. I've not successfully run my store for eight years, I'm escaping and avoiding figuring out what I really want to do, I'm not going around the country in my RV, I'm being reckless and irresponsible like my dad. It's exhausting. I can never be safe or secure enough, even though I've been running the same store for years without any major failures or incidents along the way.

I'm glad when a customer comes in and I have an excuse to hang up. "Gotta go," I say, picking my phone up from the counter as I watch Wildcat jump up in greeting. "I'll talk to you later, Mom."

She wants to protest—after all, she hasn't yet convinced me to move back home—but I give her a little wave and hang up before any more words can be said. Then I pocket my phone and smile at my customer. Time to get back to work.

After the article came out, Norma also requested a visit. So once I'm finished at the store that day, I lock up and head out. I can only assume she's read the article and wants to give me notes on how she was portrayed. When you read Adeline's account of the role Norma played in my life, it's tempting to view her as a kind mother figure who took me in at my darkest hour. I guess that's kind of true, but she's also kind of an asshole. She's grumpy and obsessive. My mom and Norma are kind of opposites in that way. Norma expects the world of me and wants me to have supernatural powers, and my mom would prefer me not do anything, ever. For years, I wasn't even sure if I liked Norma or if she liked me. Her mood would change on a dime, going from caring to mean in an instant. I have no idea what I'm going to get today.

When I arrive, she's in the garden, reading a book and staring out at the water.

"Hi, Norma," I say.

She looks up at me without saying anything, giving me a once over from my head to my dirty Adidas Superstars. I knew I should have worn something else. I settle in the seat across from her.

"How's the store?" she asks, still staring at the horizon.

"Fine, I guess."

She turns her full attention to me then, and it works like a truth serum. I wish I had that ability.

"Okay, actually, we're struggling right now," I confess. "I'm trying my best."

"I read the article. Did that not make a difference?"

I shake my head. Neither one of us says anything. Both of us are thinking.

Finally, I muster the courage to tell her what our accountant told me.

"I say we have a few months. Maybe less if things keep going in the direction they're going now."

It's the first time I've said that out loud. I don't tell Norma the other thing the accountant said during our meeting. He told me to "explore my options." I still don't even know what that means. What options?

I remember that the first weeks at the store were just awful. I didn't know what I was doing, and I'd cry all the time. It was so bad that Norma actually kept me in the back and wouldn't let me see the customers. Again, you'd think some type of motherly or sisterly instinct would take over and she'd comfort me, but it was the opposite. My sadness only seemed to make her angry, as if it was somehow offensive to her.

Somewhere along the way, it became offensive to me too, and that's when my life truly started.

I can still remember the exact moment. I was clearing some dirt off the countertops. Dirt is a huge part of the plant experience. It's always everywhere. Under my nails and all over the floor. I was feeling sorry for myself, thinking about my many failures. I couldn't even make it to Oregon, I moaned. I caught a glimpse of myself in the mirror hanging on the opposite wall, surrounded by a thirteen-year-old pothos. I felt grossed out for the first time, and I was tired. Tired of being sad, tired of feeling like a failure, tired of crying. I wiped my eyes and swept up the dirt and decided I wasn't going to let my failures control me anymore.

And I haven't looked back.

Norma's expression now is something like a disappointed scowl. Her usual. "You know, when I first took you in, you looked so sad. I felt so bad for you because it was clear you were someone with heaps of passion, but you'd failed for the first time. And you were letting it destroy you."

I feel this odd combination of frustration, rage, and comfort in the words. She's mean, but there's something comforting about her talking to me like this. It's almost as if things are back to normal.

"You can't give up at the first sign of problems or trouble," Norma adds.

I want to tell her that I'm not giving up, that I'm being realistic. The rage takes over when I fully realize she's bringing up the past, trying to unpack the biggest mistake of my life for the sake of her argument.

"You know," Norma continues, "a couple of years ago, maybe ten years ago, there was this flower shop that opened where the old laundromat used to be. We had issues too. I'll never forget the orchid incident. But everything turned out fine."

I want to remind her that ten years ago, she didn't have to compete with plant influencers or hot men holding money trees in the shower.

"My point is that the store needs to survive," Norma finishes. "It's my legacy, and it's our life. If we don't have the store, what else is there?"

I nod. She's right. I don't have anything else.

"I'll figure it out. Don't worry."

I stand up to leave, but she grabs my wrist, her grip surprisingly strong.

"Are you having any doubts?" she asks, her eyes boring holes into me.

I shake my head, but she keeps going. "Is the store still what you want? Is this still the life you want?"

The article did make me sound tragic, as if I was a martyr to Plant Therapy. As if managing the store is a runner up to what I really want to be doing. But that's not true. If this is really my second choice, why am I willing to fight so hard to keep it?

chapter twelve

PlantDaddy54: I just wanted to apologize about the thing we did. I didn't mean for it to go that far. I know that we're friends and that conversation moved way past the friend boundary really quickly. I have no clue why I let it get that far or what came over me? I don't want to make you feel uncomfortable. I just . . . want. I think that's the best word for it. I've always been fine with what we are, but lately I've just found myself yearning for you more? I do . . . want to touch you.

PlantDaddy13: No, it was okay. I liked it.

———

"Okay, I'm doing it. It's happening." I feel uncomfortable, my face hot, like I'm in front of an audience about to give the speech of my life.

"You're just opening the account," Allison says calmly. She's talking to me like she's trying to coax a cat down from a tree. "Just starting a social media account for the store and posting one thing."

It's not that creating an Instagram for the shop is difficult, but for me . . . it feels *huge*. At this point, I have a username and a profile, and there's nothing left for me to do but click "create account." Easy, right? Nope. Not at all.

The account was Lisa's idea. When Allison said she had a friend who was a self-proclaimed business coach and brand consultant, I was skeptical. And when I called Lisa to schedule our consultation and she told me she needed to get a sense of the aura of the building and the vibe of the space, I wanted to cancel our meeting altogether. But, after looking at the store's bank account again, I decided to go through with it. At this point, I'm willing to try just about anything.

When we met, Lisa told me I HAD to be online if I had a chance of winning this fight. I was hesitant, but she gave what felt like a TED Talk-level performance. Her leather jacket and hat made her seem trustworthy.

"You're so close. All you have to do is click the button." Allison's voice pulls me back to reality.

I think about what Lisa said about no longer hiding and suck in a deep breath. Then I hit submit.

The page congratulates me and welcomes me . . . to hell, I guess.

"Okay," Allison says, letting out a deep breath. "That's step one. Now, let's create some content."

I smile at Allison, happy she's here. Maybe the move isn't gonna be as big of a deal as I thought. We're still here, and everything feels fine.

Then I lower my eyes back to my phone and stare at the store's new Instagram account. It feels empty, zero followers and zero following. This is a mistake.

I remember that at one point, my old blog was getting close to thirty thousand views a month. And then when Instagram came around, it felt like a natural extension of my blog, and I quickly turned it into a visual diary of my life, a place where I posted moody photos and wrote long captions about all my desires and all the things I wanted to do. But although I shared my journey, it didn't end like Cheryl's or Elizabeth's journey. Mine ended in failure.

The emptiness of this new account—with its zero followers and lack of posts—reminds me of that, of the version of myself who was looking for something online that I never managed to find. I'm not a Luddite by any means. I talk to PlantDaddy54. I watch YouTube. I consume content all the time, but I no longer create my own. I just can't bring myself to do it.

A few minutes later, I'm staring into the tiny camera lens of Allison's phone. I'm trying to talk about the monstera in my hand, but the words feel awkward and land with a thud when I say them. I think about how natural Leo and Paul are on camera, how they look like they're meant for this. I look like I'm under duress.

"And this is the monstera, a great plant for any beginner." All thoughts leave my head, and I stare at the camera blankly.

It's awkward and not just because I can't think of basic plant care facts but also because Allison is officially moving today. She's been busy for days. I've watched people come in and out of her store to take advantage of her final sale prices. I took some plants over for her to sell, and to show her I supported her decision to leave, but it only made us both feel more sad than anything else. Now there's nothing left in her shop but boxes and dust.

"How was that?" I ask, even though I already know the answer. I'm sure it was as awkward and uncomfortable as it felt.

"Umm . . . Maybe we should take a break and try again."

I catch my reflection in the mirror. Allison styled me in what I'd call girl boss chic, complete with a ridiculous park ranger-style hat. I try to adjust it on my head, like a slight tweak will improve the situation. Then I test out another smile that looks more natural, but that only makes me think about how I was smiling in my overly edited photos ten years ago, trying to figure out a way to be seen.

The hat comes off.

"I don't know if I can do this. There has to be a different way to handle social media that's not *this*. The video's too close to what Leo and Paul do, and I just can't pull it off like they can."

I look over at Wildcat, who is lounging in the sun in her favorite spot, surrounded by snake plants. She looks so peaceful. It must be nice to not have to worry about anything. I snap a photo of her and smile at it.

"Why can't I just post photos of Wildcat?"

I say it as a joke, but then Allison tilts her head to the side, like she's thinking about something.

"Wait, can I just post pictures of Wildcat?"

Instagram is easy when you post photos of your favorite being in the world. It would almost be fun, with all of my favorite things in one place. Wildcat, the shop, the plants. Wildcat seems to understand that the store's success rests on her shoulders because she's being extra cute, and I end up snapping a bunch more pictures. I scroll through the new pictures and my old ones, and it's actually harder than I expect to pick which image to share. Ultimately, I chose one of her sleeping among the calatheas in the corner. I hit the share button, and I wait, wondering if something big is going to happen. If maybe Wildcat will go viral, and everything will change.

Wildcat does, in fact, NOT go viral. Her likes are mostly the few clients I told to follow the shop on Instagram and a smattering of family members who magically (and scarily) got the suggestion to follow me from the app itself.

"Maybe I should close the account?" I ask Allison on the phone a few days later. Allison is in the middle of moving into her new place, a huge two-story house that looks like the ones you see in typical American suburbs and that you could never find in Long Beach for less than two million dollars.

"It takes time!" Allison reminds me.

I don't have time. Money is running out. Quickly. I look around the store, and it's empty again, even though it's 4:00 p.m., one of my peak times.

"And, yes, you have time." Allison is somehow still reading my thoughts, even from Riverside. "This is gonna work out."

"How's the house?"

I change the subject, deciding this is a good time to do some plant maintenance for the third time today. The plants couldn't be more perfect, but that doesn't stop me from continuing to work on them. I keep telling myself that if they look better, they will sell better. I try not to think about how there's barely been any customers in the store to look at them.

"Big. Plenty of space."

Her words are dripping with meaning. I suspect I know what she's saying—there's a guest room for me if I want to stay there.

"Things are going to work out, but just in case they don't . . ." Yep, there it is. "You can stay here. We have the whole basement, and it's finished with a bathroom and everything. Your own little apartment."

I picture myself in the basement of a suburban palace. No light. Concrete walls. Hell.

"Thanks, but I'm good." I try to cheer up. "This account is gonna work. It's just Wildcat, plants, and stuff around the store. I'll just . . . keep doing what I'm doing."

I hear the bell, and a group of college-aged students make their way inside. Wildcat jumps up and greets them at the door. Customers! Finally!

"Hi, ladies, how can I help you?"

"Hi, sorry, we got turned around. Is Botanical Brothers this way?" I try not to look too disappointed.

"You're almost there," I say. "Just keep going down the street, you can't miss it."

chapter thirteen

PlantDaddy13: Do you know anything about business? Are you good at it?

PlantDaddy54: I'm actually not bad at it. What do you need help with?

PlantDaddy13: If you know something is wrong, how do you go about fixing it? Where do you start?

PlantDaddy54: Well, the first thing I do is call in an expert. The worst thing you can do is think you have it all figured out when you don't. But a second opinion can point you in the right direction. Don't try to be a hero and do it all on your own.

PlantDaddy13: Can I confess that I find this business version of you to be very sexy?

PlantDaddy54: I can start talking about profit margins if that will get you going?

PlantDaddy13: Go ahead.

———

It doesn't work. While my posts get some traction in the dog community, there's no real difference in sales. The only positive is that social media is slowly becoming less and less scary to me. While I always expected my past failures to loom over every post, it turns out that no one seems to care about my past life as a blogger. Logging in becomes easier, no longer filling me with a sense of dread, and I actually start taking pictures of my plants at different places around Long Beach, including Liz's Coffee Shop. When Botanical Brothers opened, I figured the shop would stop buying plants from me. But they've remained loyal, which I and my bank account both appreciate.

And really, at this point, my business seems to be completely reliant on my business clients—the other shops along 4th Street and in downtown that buy plants from me. I don't know how long this will last, of course, but I know I need this income source. I'm no longer making money from in-store sales, ever since Leo and his dumb dimples opened up shop down the street.

Today, I head down to the coffee shop with a box full of new plants for them in my arms and Wildcat at my side. Doing shop visits is one of her favorite things. I imagine that's because she gets to feel like a celebrity walking down the red carpet, everyone fawning over her. I'm a little jealous of her blissful ignorance while I'm here all nervous that I'm gonna lose my contract with the coffee shop.

Fortunately and unfortunately, I have so much extra merchandise that I can actually just give them these plants today. It's not exactly a bribe. It's showing appreciation for their business, which is part of how Plant Therapy operates. And as usual, I'll also take the time to water the plants that are already at the shop and make sure they all look healthy.

I mentally prepare myself to pass Botanical Brothers, but nothing can quite prepare me for what I see—two life-sized cardboard cutouts of Leo and Paul outside the storefront, along with a few shirtless men greeting people as they wander in, like bouncers trying to bring people into a bar. I wonder if there is some type of shirtless policy? They could really use some body diversity. Why is everyone so muscled up?

I catch a glimpse of Leo inside the store. He, at least, is not shirtless. But he is wearing a tank top that shows off his broad shoulders and the philodendron tattoo I couldn't stop staring at when I saw him at the nursery. I watch a group of women ogling him as he stretches to grab a plant off a high shelf, the muscles in his arms and back flexing. The women are completely immersed in the sight, and honestly, I am too, but then Wildcat spots Leo and starts trotting towards him.

"No, Wildcat, let's go." I whistle, and she huffs a protest but obediently follows me the last few steps to the coffee shop. I stop in my tracks just shy of the door. Out front is a huge dracaena, around six feet tall, sitting next to the "Today's Specials" sign along the curb. Usually that would be fine except that it's not my plant; I didn't give them that one. But I'm sure I know who did.

I manage somehow to keep walking, and I make my way to the door. Blaze rushes over to open the door for me and relieve me of the heavy box I'm carrying and to greet Wildcat.

"Oh, these are great!" Blaze's tone is cheery, which makes me suspicious. They aren't typically cheery. "All these for us?"

I nod, still not knowing what to say.

While Blaze places the heartleaf philodendron in a hanging basket, Wildcat takes a seat by the door, her tail wagging as she watches people come and go from Botanical Brothers across the street.

"The—the plant out front . . ." I stammer. Blaze stops me before I can get going.

"Okay, let's bring the rest of these to the back."

I warn Wildcat to stay put by the door and follow Blaze to their back office.

"Am I getting fired?" I say, my voice finally working.

"Of course not. Paul just brought the plant here. Said it was a friendly gift and we're neighbors." Paul? They're on a first-name basis now. "It's not like that."

I guess Blaze can see the frustration on my face.

"I just . . . I know it's a big store. They have a lot to offer." Shirtless men. Endless plants. A steady stream of customers into the store. I feel like crying.

"They wanted to talk about cohosting some events," Blaze says. "Nothing serious. We aren't going to stop using your plants. That's not what that means."

My face feels hot, but at the same time, I'm almost shivering. I understand the appeal. So many people stop by Botanical Brothers every day. It makes sense that the coffee shop would want to collaborate with them to get some of that business.

"I get it." I try not to sound too sad, but Blaze frowns and not in the typical way they always do. This time, they actually look sad.

"We aren't going to stop working with you. It's just neighborhood collaboration. They're our neighbors now. We can't just ignore the impact they're having on the street. That place may be big and flashy, but you're part of the community here."

I decide not to point out the irony of the owner of this particular coffee shop—one of the first signs of 4th Street's gentrification—telling me not to worry about Botanical Brothers. They mean well, and the sweat on their forehead shows that this conversation is stressing them out too. I wonder how long it will take before they officially start working with Botanical Brothers. Especially knowing that Botanical Brothers can easily afford to provide and keep up the plants for free. Another nightmare.

"Okay," I say, because I'm not sure what else there is to say. "I should water the plants and get going."

Blaze tries to say something, but I'm already making my way back to the front of the store.

When I get there, Wildcat is gone.

"She went out with purpose," says an old man sitting near the window with a newspaper and coffee. He points out the door when he sees my confused expression. "We figured she knew where she was going."

I hurry out of the shop but almost immediately stop in my tracks. Wildcat is across the street, lying on her back while Leo rubs her belly. She's surrounded by a crowd of college-aged girls all screeching at her cuteness. Where were all these people when I was posting about Wildcat and getting low double-digit likes on Instagram?

I'm not sure what to do, so I just hang back and watch the crowd for a moment. Leo is in performance mode, his smile a little too wide as he pets Wildcat. I stand there for a solid three minutes before Wildcat sees me and breaks through the crowd to jump all over me. It's almost like she's trying her best to pretend she isn't the world's biggest traitor.

When Leo does finally see me, I don't have much time to wonder if he'll come over because he's already on his way. He maintains eye contact with me, and my eyes burn as I try to avoid looking down at his arms and shoulders, showcased perfectly in the tank top he's wearing. I'm pretty sure it's see-through. Where is his decency? Should he be allowed to leave the house like that?

His smile eases into the one I'm familiar with, the one you never see in his videos, and I hate how his presence calms me, how my anxiety seems to fade. We haven't seen each other since that charged moment in my shop. The slight brush of his fingertips against my wrist is still there, lingering just beneath my skin. I don't know how it's possible that such a small touch can have this type of impact. Why is it still so intense?

"You should keep up with your dog," Leo says once he reaches me. I breathe in his scent of dirt and pine.

He sounds different, somehow, and it takes me a second to pinpoint why: he's using his "video voice," which is intentionally sexier and sterner than his normal voice. I know the difference because I once fell asleep watching his "repot with me" video on his YouTube channel. I'm confused at first—why put on the "video voice" for me?—but then I remember the small crowd he'd been with outside his store, which is now starting to gather around us. And it makes sense. Leo's casually sexy act is not for me. He's performing for his fans.

Leo's fans circle us like they're getting hyped up for a fight. I try to smile at them, but I'm just met with curious looks. I guess they probably want to know if there's anything going on between Leo and me. Which there isn't. They can have him. They can be the ones to deal with his infuriating sexiness. I try to soften my expression, to seem as nonthreatening as possible. Maybe I should roll on my back and spread my legs, like Wildcat. That's a submissive posture, right?

Leo must sense my discomfort, because he motions for the two of us to walk away from the women. Of course, as soon as the disciples see Leo move, they try to follow their savior, but all he has to do is hold up a single hand and they fall back, like he's some kind of wizard. I can't imagine having that kind of influence over people. I wonder if Leo enjoys his power. It doesn't seem like it.

"Sorry about that." I hate myself for apologizing to the person putting me out of business, but it feels like the appropriate thing to say. "She got out while I was talking to a client. You know Wildcat, she's obviously not dangerous or anything, but I still don't want her to disrupt your store."

I can see his crowded store behind him, just over his right shoulder, and the feeling of hopelessness hits me again. How the hell am I supposed to compete with a bunch of hot, shirtless men and all those plants?

"Nah, you know I love Wildcat."

He's still using his video voice. I fight the urge to tell him to cut it out.

"I took a photo with her," he continues. "I'll tag you in it. @PlantTherapy, right?"

Great. He knows about my profile. I was hoping he didn't because he isn't one of my ninety-three followers. The thought of him looking at my Instagram and my pathetically small profile makes me feel so insignificant. I wish I could just delete the page now and pretend it never happened. "Embarrassing" isn't a strong enough word to describe how I feel at the moment.

"Don't bother!" I say, trying to sound casual. "I don't think this social media thing was the best idea anyway, it's not like we're gonna be great at it. It's silly."

"It takes time," Leo says, the video voice gone. I can't stop the wave of relief that crashes down on me when I hear his regular voice come back—his soft voice, gentle and compassionate. I tear my eyes away from him and look at the girls gathered around the front door of his store. Then I look into the store full of people and then over at Liz's Coffee Shop and the dracaena sitting out front. Wildcat licks my hand, and I pat her head, hoping her presence will keep everything from boiling over in my mind. Leo just watches me, clearly waiting for whatever I'm going to say next.

"I'm going to have to close my store."

The words leave my mouth before I can stop them. Leo looks almost as shocked as I feel. It's the first time I've even entertained the possibility of closing, but now it seems like the truth is staring me in the face, in the form of Leo's glorious biceps.

"I mean, I feel like I'm going to have to close it," I add, an obvious lie. "I don't know how we can compete with that." I tilt my head towards Botanical Brothers.

Leo looks back at his store like he forgot it was there. When he turns back towards me, he looks as sad as I feel. I can't figure him out. Why is *he* upset?

"Anyways," I say, shaking my head as if that will help slow things down, "I should, uh . . ." I hate that my eyes are wet. I hate it so much that the tears finally fall. Just a few—I'm still clinging to my last shred of dignity—but he sees them. I brush them from my cheek, turning my face away from him. Ugh. This fucking sucks.

My store is the one thing that made me feel like I'd avoided failure. So predictable and simple, and I never had to worry about it.

My store could never hurt me. At least, that's what I thought. Yet here I am, right here on the edge again, and I have no clue how I'm gonna stop it. When the RV broke down and I lost all my money, I felt like my life was over. And I'd do anything to not feel that way again. I don't know what exists beyond the store, but my biggest fear is that I'll be back inside that feeling, that sticky heaviness of failure in my bones. I can feel it now, just the edges of it. I cough a little, my throat dry.

The feeling of Wildcat's tongue licking the tears off my hand brings me back to reality. I smile down at her, patting her on the head again.

"We should get going." My voice is scratchy, like I've been smoking ten packs of cigarettes a day. "And you should go back. I think those girls are still waiting for you."

Behind him, a few girls still hang around, pretending not to hear us. Paul is also there, taking a selfie with one of the girls. Where did he come from?

"Don't give up," Leo says, and my focus returns to him.

"You don't want me to give up? Why not?"

"Just . . . don't give up yet. Okay?"

His hand flexes, and for a moment I think he's going to touch me, like he'll reach for my hand. But he doesn't. He just leaves.

I watch him go. He pauses for a moment, shaking his head once, twice before walking back over to the girls. When they snap their selfies, he's all smiles.

chapter fourteen

PlantDaddy54: Did you solve your business problem?

PlantDaddy13: Not really. Want to say random business things to make me feel better?

PlantDaddy54: Do you want to talk about it?

PlantDaddy13: Not really. I feel like everyone I talk to feels a need to talk about it and I'm kind of tired of going over it so many times. If only everything was as easy as the two of us talking on here. Everything else in life is so complicated.

PlantDaddy54: It is very easy. Do you think it's easy because of all of our rules to not talk about anything specific or too personal or is it easy because it's just . . . easy?

PlantDaddy13: Maybe I should start a conversation with Hoyaluver3 and see what happens.

PlantDaddy54: No, don't do that.

PlantDaddy13: Why? Would you be jealous? Is that allowed?

PlantDaddy54: The idea of you sending photos of phallic plants to someone else does make me a little jealous, yeah.

PlantDaddy13: Well you don't have to worry about that. Those photos are just for you, for us.

PlantDaddy54: Good to know.

———

My section of 4th Street is so quiet at night, especially on weekdays. You can hear the faint sounds of people laughing and clinking glasses at the restaurants and bars farther down the street, but otherwise it's mostly quiet and peaceful. Except of course for the rare occasion when someone decides to scream and yell as they make their way down the street, but I try not to think about that too much.

Typically, I would spend this time preparing for the next day, dealing with shipments, organizing the displays, and sweeping. Instead, I'm staring at my phone and all the likes on the Instagram post of Wildcat and Leo from earlier. I've fixated on the photo for so long that I've managed to pick apart every last detail. Wildcat is smiling, her tongue lolling off to the side, almost as if she's posing. Leo is crouched next to her, his arm around her. He has a few beads of sweat running down his neck and a chain resting against his collarbone. It's a gold chain—the signature chain of the man whore —so that just makes sense. What doesn't make sense is that the post somehow already has over 50,000 likes. Low numbers for Leo, impossible numbers for me.

Just as I'm about to type and delete a response to the post for the 400th time (do I say thank you? do I tell people to come to the store? I don't know), I see a notification for a new message. It's pure instinct that makes me check it rather than retyping my response to the post yet again, and my thoughts immediately jump to Plant-Daddy54. I smile for a moment, distracted as I think about how he can manage to make even a dracaena seem sexy.

I shake myself, frustrated with my inability to focus on even the simplest task, and read the message.

plantsandlipstick: When Leo moans, what does it sound like? Does he whimper?

I groan and push the phone away. It skitters to the edge of the countertop. That's enough social media for today.

My eyes drift around the store, looking for something to do, something to get my mind off of Plant Daddy and Leo and everything else. A gnat buzzes by, and I take it as a sign from the universe, telling me that I should go through every single plant in the store and treat them all for pests, just in case. It will take all night. And since Wildcat is already home and was already walked earlier, there's really nothing stopping me from being alone with my plants for hours. Perfect. I exhale a sigh of relief, grateful to have something to do besides obsessing over likes.

I turn on my '90s playlist and slip off my shoes, preparing to settle in for the night. Blaque's "Bring It All to Me" starts playing, and I smile. I really do love plant chores. As soon as I apply the neem oil to my first alocasia leaf, I feel my shoulders relax.

My phone buzzes again with another notification, but this time I ignore it. I study the Jose Bueno for bugs and find there are none. It's not surprising, really, since I did treat all of my plants just last week. But I'll admit it still feels good to see nothing but pristine leaves.

Across the room, my phone vibrates again, followed by a chorus of several more notifications, one after the other. Another wedding proposal? More requests for me to figure out how to get a pair of his underwear? It has to be nothing, right? Nothing to be worried about. I make my way over to the phone and see that the screen is lit up with a link from Allison. I realize I haven't talked to Allison in forever. Maybe I should call her. I'll do that in the morning.

I click the link.

It's an Instagram video from the Botanical Brothers. It must have been posted within the last few minutes because I've been obsessively refreshing their page all day and have never seen this particular video before. The video shows Paul walking with the camera in his hand. In the video, it's sunny outside, so I figure it must have been shot earlier today, in the afternoon probably. He's walking along 4th Street, talking to the camera about how much they are loving the neighborhood. As he talks, I feel goosebumps on my arms, as though I know something unsettling is about to happen. And then it does.

He turns the camera to show Wildcat and Leo greeting each other. I don't see myself in the video, so he must have been recording when I was in the coffee shop. Paul's face fills the frame again.

"See? Perfect example. That's Tessa's dog from down the street at Plant Therapy. Now, Botanical Babes, let me ask you all a question. If we're so horrible, why is our so-called competitor's dog here? Does that look like the playboy the author of that bogus article described?" The camera faces Leo and Wildcat again. My eyes narrow at the close-up of Wildcat rolling on her back for belly rubs, blissfully oblivious to the fact that she's being used for such nefarious purposes.

"Dogs know," I hear Paul's voice say from behind the camera. "Dogs always know."

The screen changes suddenly, and I see myself talking to Leo on the street. It looks like the video was shot from a bit of a distance, but you can still tell that I'm upset. I watch myself wipe my tears away, my face sad. The text on the screen says *Leo talking with Tessa from Plant Therapy*. Paul's face suddenly appears again, and I jump in surprise as though this simple Instagram video is actually a horror movie.

"Nobody is against anyone else," Paul says. "We're a family here. A community. Anyone who says differently is trying to pit our communities against each other, which is a tactic used throughout history."

My face grows hot, and my hands start shaking again, the same anger from earlier burning through me. And I'm angry not only because it's an awful thing for him to do but also because it's so smart. Paul is the most dangerous kind of villain, he's a smart one.

"Don't believe me? Come visit us at Botanical Brothers and see for yourself," Paul says, winking at the camera.

I pace in circles, unsure what to do with this energy. The video is not only manipulative, it's mean-spirited. Why would he record me crying like that? How did he even know I was . . . Oh. Paul did show up during our conversation. Was this all just some type of elaborate setup?

Before I know it, I've slipped my shoes back on and I'm out the door and marching up the street to Botanical Brothers. The street is still unnaturally quiet. It should be scary, but I feel like the shadows are on my side. It typically takes me about five minutes to make it up the street, but with the anger driving me, tonight I do it in one.

I don't know what I'll say or do when I get to Botanical Brothers —I'm just going—but I know that someone will be there late because I always see their lights on when I finally leave my store every night.

When I get to the door, it's locked, but I see Leo in there, Rage Against the Machine blasting on the speakers while he sweeps the floors. His hair is growing out a little. I didn't get to fully appreciate it before, between Wildcat and the screaming fangirls. Some of his dark locks frame his face, falling perfectly as if someone planned it. He's wearing cargo shorts and another of those damn Botanical Brothers shirts again.

I hoped to have more time to ogle him, but he spots me and smiles—his real smile, not his video smile—as he hot-guy jogs to the door. He unlocks the door while I stand there awkwardly, scrambling to think of a plan. What am I going to say? Why am I here again? Now that Leo is in front of me, I'm struggling to remember what exactly I was so upset about.

"Tessa, hi. What are you doing here? Come on in."

Leo swings the door open, and somehow I'm inside, even though I don't actually remember moving my feet. I haven't been inside the store since before they opened, afraid of what I would find, but I'm mesmerized by the space. The gray stone floors and

LED lights lining the walls make it feel like a warehouse rave or a West Hollywood bar. There's even a photo booth on the far wall surrounded by plants and a kombucha bar. I'm shocked by how comfortable it feels inside. My plant store is always on the warmer side. The space is small, and with the humidifiers, everything heats up really quickly. The sheer size of this space helps with air circulation, but I do worry about the plants getting dry.

As I look around, I see that their supply, while substantial, is fairly standard. They carry the basics—snake plants, monsteras, and fiddle leaf figs—but I don't see a ton of exotic plants or anything beyond what you'd find at any garden center. The difference is that these plants are exquisitely taken care of. I don't see a single brown spot on any of the leaves. In fact, everything is thriving. My eyes land on the biggest and bushiest pilea I've ever seen. How did he do that? Why is the high quality of the plants such a turn on?

"This place is so big," I say, stalling as I wander around the room, taking everything in. "Are you here by yourself? Doesn't it get weird being alone here?"

"Yeah, it kind of does," he answers, his voice just behind me now. "But I like being here when no one else is around." *I like the quiet too*, I want to say, but I stay silent.

I walk over toward the cash register area and see a picture of him and Paul as kids, smiling with their arms around each other. Cute.

Leo clears his throat.

Then I remember why I'm here. I turn to face him.

"The video." Good. My rage is slowly coming back. "And that photo . . ."

"Yeah?"

He seems more amused than mad, which makes me feel silly. Leo must clock my mood, because he sets his broom down to give me more of his attention. And here we are again—infuriatingly face-to-face. No hiding.

"I don't understand what the problem is," Leo says carefully. "The Wildcat photo is getting a lot of traction—"

"Only because of you! And your tank top! Wildcat was just an accessory."

"Haven't you gotten more followers from it? Isn't that a good thing?" His tone is on the edge of irritation. There's no backing down now.

"I've only gotten requests for more photos of you with my dog and a few, surprisingly moving, proposals for your hand in marriage! Someone asked me if you whimper."

He looks like he's suppressing a laugh at that last part, but he continues. "But did you get more followers?" he repeats. "I know you did. I—"

He cuts himself off this time. We're so close to each other now that I can smell him. He smells fresh, like the moment after a really good, hot shower on what you know will be a really great day. I hate how much I like it, but I refuse to be thrown off.

"And what about that shitty video Paul posted? That footage he got of you and Wildcat and then of you and me."

Leo frowns. "Paul? What video are you talking about?"

I pull my phone out of my pocket, glancing at my Reddit messages for a moment before opening Instagram. I pull the video up, wincing at the thumbnail of me and Leo, and hand the phone to him.

I can't stand the idea of watching him watch us, so I turn away and continue looking around the store. I walk over to the hanging plant wall—rows of nearly identical pothos of different lengths. It's a nice feature—not as impressive as my living plant wall, but still nice. Their wall reminds me of Plantiitas, the only plant store in Long Beach that can maybe rival Botanical Brothers in size. They have a similar display, but theirs is better, warmer, with a neon sign and more varieties. It's also in North Long Beach and so doesn't have to compete with Botanical Brothers. I wish I could be far away, too. Leo's sigh brings my attention back to him.

"Paul shouldn't have done this without asking me."

"No shit," I mutter, keeping my back to him.

"But what's wrong with what he said?" Leo asked. "I mean, I wish he hadn't recorded us talking to each other, but don't we have a right to defend ourselves from the allegations in that article?"

I turn away from the display and make my way back over to him.

"Your brother used a private moment against me. And you know we aren't some big happy family, Leo."

Leo looks back down at my phone in his hand.

"I didn't know about the video," he says quietly. "All I did was post a photo with Wildcat, tag your store, and tell my followers to visit you. I was trying to help."

This isn't just about the selfie with Wildcat, and he knows why I'm upset. But he's sidestepping the issue because he's trying to protect his brother.

He sighs again and continues. "I don't always agree with what my brother does or his methods. He can be really harsh in the way he goes about things. I'll try to talk to him about this."

Somehow this makes me even madder because while Paul is an asshole, I'm not even sure Leo saying anything will help.

"That won't do anything! Nothing is going to change! It doesn't matter what I do!" I start pacing again, ranting and trying not to cry in front of him for the second time today. "This store is here and you're here and I don't think I can compete against this store and you, especially when you look like that"—I wave my arm at him— "It's too much! I can't, and Paul is like some type of evil genius or something."

"I'm not sure what you want me to do!" His voice is louder than I've ever heard it, matching my energy perfectly. "I didn't know that we'd move here and there would be you and your . . . every-thing." He motions to my whole body, and I look down at myself reflexively. What does he mean by everything? Likely the milkmaid boobs, right? "I only agreed to open this location because Paul said it was an up-and-coming area and I thought it would be simple."

"Well, I'm sorry my little shop is disrupting your plans of plant domination."

"I thought you were going to be an elderly woman close to retirement!" he yells.

"So you like putting elderly women out of business? Is that like some weird kink?"

"I love elderly ladies! They're great! It's just that I didn't expect you."

Besides the low hum of the humidifiers, it's silent. I listen to their familiar drone. We use the same ones at Plant Therapy. If I close my eyes, I can pretend I'm back there, back home.

"Paul shouldn't have done that," Leo says. "That was wrong, and you're right. He . . . he wasn't kind."

I watch his face when he speaks, and he looks so sincere I feel compelled to take a step towards him.

"We just . . ." Leo bites his lip. I could groan. "I mean, *I* just . . . I just want the store to be successful! Our employees are like our family. And Paul *is* my family."

"I want my store to be successful, too! Obviously!"

"I don't know what you expect me to do, Tessa. Am I supposed to just shut everything down? Put fifteen people out of work? Stop paying the mortgage on my mom's home?"

"No, I'm not saying that." I'm not, am I? "Just . . . stop being so good at social media and plants and being sexy and *everything*, okay? It's not fair to the rest of us when you look like that *and* know as much about plants as I do! Give me something!"

My internal monologue seems to be spilling out of my brain. Not a great development.

"You need to stop looking so hot when you're angry and stop making me feel confused about what I want! Stop having such a great eye for plants and having everyone in this neighborhood love you and stop wearing tank tops! Do you have to wear those?" Leo shoots back.

I know I'm smiling a little at his admission, but I clamp down because this is supposed to be a fight.

He's breathing a little heavily, and while it wasn't super hot before, it certainly feels hot now. It's been such a long time since I was this physically drawn to anyone. It's like the opposite of what I feel for 54. With 54, it's all about this intense mental attraction, like the way we click feels intense. With Leo, it's all physical. My body feels like it's vibrating when he's around. It doesn't help that he's doing his sexy eye contact trick where he doesn't just look at me, he actually sees me.

"Should we make out?" he whispers, staring at my lips.

I'm so shocked that I burst into laughter.

"What?" Leo asks, but he's chuckling, too. His gaze still flickers between my eyes and my lips. I guess I'm staring at him harder than I think. He's picked up on my horny energy.

"Leo . . . I . . ." I'm at a loss for words, again. I kept waiting for some type of wink, but all that I see are his eyes, deep and open and vulnerable. I take a step back. "We, uh . . . d-definitely shouldn't do *that*," I stammer. "Should we? Wait, I mean, no. Absolutely not. What the—"

As if on cue, all of the overhead lights shut off, leaving just the strips of changing LED lights along the walls. The plants are all cast in blue light. It's just bright enough for me to see Leo's face, but not bright enough for people on the street to look inside. It feels like we're in a strip club.

"You planned this!" I'm laughing again. This is all so absurd.

Leo shakes his head. "They're on a timer. Paul set it to remind me that I should go home."

The mention of his brother reminds me that Leo still has my phone in his hand. I grab his wrist so I can take it back. Another mistake. Stop touching Leo, Tessa.

"Is this like a bit? Something you do for all the girls who stumble into your plant store at 9:00 p.m.?"

"How? I didn't even know you were gonna be here!"

"Yeah, well, I was angry, and I floated here on top of my rage."

"I hate that you're always so upset when you see me," Leo says, a sad note to his voice. "I don't want it to be like that."

On the long list of things I expected him to say, this was the last thing I'd have predicted.

"And you think us making out is going to make me feel better? That's so—"

"No! I mean, maybe . . . . I don't know! It's a suggestion."

He reaches out and touches my arm, and it's the same, the sparks. It's like static, like electricity, like he shot me with something. I feel pathetic, but I don't pull away.

"Why does that feel like that?" I sound so young to myself, as if I'm not almost thirty at this point.

"What? Me touching you?" His voice drops deeper, and I shiver again. He slowly runs his hand down the length of my arm. "This okay?"

He sounds like he's in awe. My body is a traitor. His touch leaves goose bumps—actual goose bumps—in its wake. I don't get it. He's not even doing anything.

Leo studies my face, his hand still, like he's waiting for permission to move.

"I'm not sure," I say. But I take a step closer. Leo nods, running his hand up to my shoulder. When I tense, he stops.

"Oh shit, sorry. Too much."

"No! I mean it's not you!" I shrug my shoulders, noticing how tight and tense they are. I really need to get back into yoga. "Just a little stiff. I hold everything in my shoulders."

"You want a deep-tissue massage?" He delivers this ask with a straight face.

"*What?*" I'm learning that Leo is funny, more than I'd think someone like him would be.

"My minor was in exercise sports science!"

"You are such a scammer." I playfully shove him in the arm, and he dramatically staggers to the side. We both laugh. It's fun. He's fun. My brain also screams, "Yeah, fun and dangerous!" But I don't listen.

"That still didn't answer my question," he teases.

Do I want him to touch me again? I kind of do. "Fine."

Leo doesn't waste any time, jumping into action. He moves behind me so he's facing my back. I'm suddenly very conscious of the feel of my tank top and my sports bra against my skin, my skin prickling in anticipation. He starts at the base of my neck, massaging a few deep circles into my skin. He finds the knots immediately, and I sigh, feeling myself relax into his touch. He seems to take that as permission to get closer, because he braces one hand on the side of my neck so he can massage deeper into the muscle connecting the back of my neck with my shoulder.

"If only your adoring fans knew you could do this," I joke.

He continues to work my neck and upper back, tension releasing as he goes along. When he reaches a particularly tender spot, I groan. Seems like I've been carrying a lot.

"Sorry," Leo says quickly, easing off. His next touch is softer. "How's that?"

It's heaven, but I'm not quite ready to tell him that. "This is a really good apology," I say instead.

He chuckles, and I can feel his breath on my neck, leaving prickles in its wake.

"You know you have a few moles on your back that look like a constellation."

He traces a path with his fingers, his touch featherlight.

"Cassiopeia," I breathe. "That's what it looks like, right? That's what my mom used to tell me because I hated that I had moles. But they run in my family. I'm covered in them."

"Hmmmm," he murmurs, his thumb running a line up the

center of my spine to my neck. My mind starts to wander, and I wonder what his lips might feel like.

"Wait, *should* we make out?" I offer, because in this moment my curiosity is getting the best of me and his touch has chipped away at my will. His hands drop away, and I find that I already miss them.

"Yeah, why not?" His tone is infuriatingly casual, and he comes around in front of me. We're standing eye to eye again. And it's just as intense as it was before.

I open my mouth to remind him about all of the many, many reasons why kissing each other is not a good idea. The brutal reality of my situation—the store, his store, our rivalry, his asshole brother, that stupid video—peeks through the corners of my mind. He presses his thumb against my lips, lightly cradling my chin.

"Actually," he says, "don't answer that. I already know why not."

It's like he can read my mind.

My lips press against his thumb, again giving him the permission he's looking for. He steps a little closer so he's in my space, and I can hear the rhythm of his breath.

How do you make out with someone? I forget. Do I just lean in? Do I close my eyes? Have I really been stuck in my plant store for this long? The last time I kissed anyone was exactly two years ago, during the Grand Prix of Long Beach race weekend. I met a guy at a party. I was drunk, and he was on the pit crew for one of the racers and smelled faintly of gasoline. But best of all, he was French, and so I didn't really understand him, which made it all the more easier. We made out on a balcony, he felt me up, and I never saw the guy again.

But this is different now. This is Leo. I can't just kiss him and forget about it. I'll still have to see him again. And what if he does that weird fish face?

Leo licks his lips and moves his thumb from my lips and chin to wrap his hand around the nape of my neck, leaning closer.

"Wait! I'm nervous!" I blurt out.

He freezes, releasing me.

"No, don't go. I just, um . . ." The words flow out, but I'm not sure where I'm going with them. I feel so exposed. Something about how little I've dated recently, how long it's been since I've kissed anyone feels deeply humiliating. And this is why I should just stay in my store and message Plant Daddy, but I can't do that now. Leo's here. Standing in front of me. Touching me. And waiting for me to explain myself. I decide to tell the truth.

"I'm nervous." I feel so stupid.

Leo nods. "I feel kind of nervous too."

"You don't feel nervous."

"What if it's bad?" Leo says.

"Right! What if our mouths don't work together? We both have bigger-sized lips." He's looking at my lips now. "You might be a bad kisser."

"I'm not a bad kisser," he says, totally confident in a way that should turn me off but instead has the opposite effect. My stomach does a little flip. "Maybe you're a bad kisser."

He smiles in the darkness.

"How about this . . ." He gently spins me around so I'm not facing him anymore. "Mind if I start back here?"

I panic. Back here? What the hell does that mean? I search my references, cycling through my previous sexual encounters to figure out what he's talking about. Then it hits me.

"Oh, I've never done any butt stuff, so—"

"What?!? No! I'm not trying to do butt stuff. I just want to . . ."

He kisses the back of my neck, in between my shoulder blades. It's so soft, and I lean back into him. He kisses down my shoulder, and my eyes flutter closed at the sensation. Sparks. His lips are soft and a little chapped, so it's a mixture of a gentle glide and a light, barely there roughness, a dizzying combination. Again, I'm wondering if this is just how it is or if it's this way because of him.

"This good?" he asks, his low voice rumbling across my skin.

I can only manage a nod while I lean into him more. He bites me then—a sharp, quick nip at the base of my neck that he soothes with his tongue. Suddenly self-conscious, I feel the need to deflect.

"You bit me," I say, my voice breathy and a little rough.

"I did," he responds, peppering my neck with more kisses before biting my earlobe. I moan, feeling rather than seeing his smile. "I couldn't help it. Your skin is very bitable. Is the word lush? Ripe? Soft? I don't know." His teeth graze the spot below my ear.

"You a vampire?" My eyes are still closed, and I'm just . . . feeling.

"You can bite me back if you want." He chuckles into my skin.

"Oh yeah?" I feel him pull away, and I turn my head just in time to watch him pull his sweatshirt over his head, revealing the same tank top he was wearing earlier. My eyes land on his plant tattoo, arching over his shoulder and back and down his bicep. It's nice, really well done. It's in a more delicate style. Mine is all bold lines and curves. More abstract.

"You have one, too," he says, reading my mind again. "On your thigh."

"You were looking at my thigh?"

"As much as I can." He's smiling, and I can't help smiling back. "Philodendrons, right? Prayer plants?"

"Yeah," I say. "It runs down my thigh and arches over my lower back."

My hand traces the path over my jeans. I enjoy the power of watching him watch me.

"Kind of weird we both have plant tattoos, huh?" His eyes travel back up to mine.

"Is it? We're both plant people. Doesn't everyone have big plant tattoos?"

At that moment, I think about PlantDaddy54 and feel a sudden rush of guilt. Should I be here? Is this against our nonexistent rules? Do our rules say anything about biting hot men?

"I don't know," he says, mostly to himself. "I feel like there's something to it."

He clears his throat and bares his neck to me dramatically, like we're in *Twilight*. This is fun. I don't remember this being fun. I think about Plant Daddy again.

"Are we doing some kind of vampiric ritual or something?"

"You can do whatever you want to me." We both laugh at his Bella impersonation, but when I touch his arm, he shivers and stops laughing.

Before my brain can remind me why this is a bad idea, I wrap my hand around the back of his neck and pull him towards me. There's that rush of power again, a feeling I'm quickly becoming addicted to. He comes willingly, letting me give him a teasing bite near the base of his throat. Unlike me, he doesn't try to suppress his reaction. He gives a small, barely there whimper, a tease, before wrapping both of his arms around my waist to bring us closer together. Our chests are touching, and when I soothe the bite with my own suck, placing a kiss on the spot, he shudders again.

He's sensitive, like me. I wonder how long it's been for him, if it's been just as long.

"Come here," he breathes, using his right hand to tip my face back up to him. His eyes search mine, and it's like he's in awe, like he's questioning if this is just how these things go or if there's something about me, something about us. We haven't even kissed yet. I might just be projecting, though.

He must find what he's looking for, because at that moment, he finally leans in for a kiss. I reach up to meet him, my eyes closing.

A loud "VROOM!" obliterates the silence, random as a gunshot. Startled by the noise, Leo and I both jump. The look of shock on Leo's face makes me turn towards the sound.

A Corvette screeches to a stop just outside the shop's door. The deafening bass trap on the speakers makes the earth beneath us vibrate. I pull back from Leo, trying to get a better look at who's in the car, although the sinking feeling in the pit of my stomach should have tipped me off. The music cuts off. The lights go dark.

And Paul steps out of the car.

———

"Shit, I should go," I say quickly, watching through the doors as Paul paces back and forth, clearly on the phone.

Leo nods, and we both pull away from each other, although he's still holding me. I step away more, and Leo's arms drop from around me. And that's when the reality of the situation hits me again full force.

There's nowhere to hide, so I just stand there, waiting for Paul to come inside. It's like waiting for a dinosaur to break through the doors.

He finally spots me through the doors as he hangs up his phone, and he smirks like the villain he is. He unlocks the door and enters the store, still staring at both of us almost gleefully. I take another step away from Leo. Not that it matters—I'm here, and the damage is done.

"Well, well, well," he says, his eyes darting between the two of us. He crosses his arms over his chest, and I notice a Drake-style prayer hands tattoo and a lion tattoo on his biceps. Of course. "Am I interrupting something?"

"What's up, Paul?" Leo shifts to stand in front of me in a move that feels oddly protective. It's kind of nice, but I shake myself out of it. I can take care of myself.

Paul laughs, and it's slimy. I move out from behind Leo and face Paul myself.

"What's up with the video?" I ask.

Paul shrugs, walking smoothly across the room to where we're standing, not a care in the world. "Which one? We posted a few videos today."

Asshole. My eyes catch on Leo, who just covers his face with his hand, looking tortured. Must be hard to have a brother who's such a dick. I think about what he said a few minutes ago about his mom's mortgage and everyone they employ, and I soften a little.

"And do you mean Instagram or YouTube or . . ."

Never mind. Fuck this guy.

"Paul . . ." Leo sounds exhausted when he says it.

"You know which one. The one with my dog. The one with me . . ." I trail off, not wanting to mention my tears again, even though he's seen them firsthand.

"The moment between you and Leo? I thought it was a nice moment for the community to see. Show a united front. You two are close." He draws out the word close, and I feel the ghost of Leo's hands on my back and my shoulders. I shudder. He walks through the space between us and then wanders around the store, looking over everything. He stops and straightens a plant so it's aligned just perfectly. So he's the one obsessed with keeping the plants perfect. Interesting.

Then I remember I'm angry.

"That's not—we're not . . ." Paul looks back and forth dramatically between us to make a point. I wonder what would happen if I threw this nearby aglaonema at his head. I cross my arms over my chest. "It was private."

"You didn't seem to care about privacy when you let that whack job reporter loose on our store." Paul's chill demeanor immediately turns icy. It's nice to see the real him underneath all the bullshit he feeds me. "All of those lies."

"Adeline isn't a whack job. She's a veteran reporter. And she didn't report on anything that wasn't public information."

"And if I remember correctly," Paul continues, "your dog wandered straight to our store and rolled onto his back for Leo, and you were in front of our store crying for whatever reason."

I've never been in a fight before, but I find myself charging in Paul's direction with every intention of slapping the shit out of him. Before I do, I feel the light pull of Leo's hand on my arm, stopping me.

"Paul, you're being an asshole," Leo says. "You know what she means. That's fucked up."

"What she did was fucked up! You were just as pissed about the article as me! Just one look from her, and it seems like you forgot everything you told me about getting revenge and crushing the competition."

Right. There it is. This is why I shouldn't be here, and it's why I should definitely not be kissing him. I can't trust them, no matter how tingly I feel. I just needed Paul to help me remember. This is likely some weird trap, and Leo is the honeypot, there to make me reveal all my secrets.

"Okay, fuck you both," I say, turning and barreling towards the door.

"Tessa!" Leo calls from somewhere behind me, but I don't look back, and I don't answer.

When I reach the door, I turn back to face them. Leo's close, right behind me. But I'm not going to let him distract me this time. I feel the tension in my shoulders again. "And Adeline was right . . . about both of you." I look at Leo when I say the last part and ignore the disappointment on his face. It's likely fake anyways. And I won't fall for it again.

There's no way I'm letting them take away my store.

chapter fifteen

PlantDaddy54: Hey, I know that this is kind of not allowed but I'm wondering if we should meet.

Plantdaddy13: Oh, you want to meet?

PlantDaddy54: I mean, yeah. Don't you feel like we should . . . eventually? You don't have to answer right now but I just . . . This feels kind of like something, right? What do you think?

———

"What the hell are you doing biting the competition?" This is a great question and is exactly the type of feedback I'm after when I tell Allison about the whole incident. The two of us are at an LA Galaxy soccer game, not really paying attention. Allison's boyfriend John is screaming at the top of his lungs, stomping his feet, while the two of us sit calmly with our drinks in hand. Neither of us really know much about soccer, but we decided to turn her rare venture into town into a friend date.

"Babe! Babe! Did you see that? SO CRAZY! Tessa, did you see that?" He turns to us excitedly and points at the field, where all we can really see are little dots running everywhere.

I guess those are people. Kicking a soccer ball. Or something.

We both nod, even though we, in fact, did not see anything. He turns away, satisfied with our answer, and Allison looks at him and smiles as if he's the most incredible thing she's ever seen. She used to look at her favorite cocktail that way, but things are changing. They just keep changing.

"Anyways, when I said for you to get out more, this isn't what I meant," Allison says, turning her attention back to me. "Isn't this a little too much drama? I was hoping for some awkward dating app stories and not you groping the enemy at his place of employment."

"It wasn't groping." I think about his lips on my back, the whispered "Come here," and I shift in my seat, crossing my legs. She catches it and shakes her head, smacking me on the leg. I sigh. "You're right! I don't know what it is. He's just . . . We're just . . ." I'm not sure what words I'm looking for here. It's just so intense? I'm just so attracted to him? He has really soft lips? All this strife has apparently made me very horny.

"It's just the thrill of something dangerous. I remember those days. When it feels good because it's not good for you. But, Tessa . . . Is this the right time for you to go through this kind of phase?"

I don't like the way she says the word "phase." I also don't love the judgement. I was always the type of ride or die who would hold her earrings and take photos of her adventures. Why is it now a bad time? But she's also kind of right. Leo is a no-no. There are so many people in Long Beach. Why did it have to be Leo? Maybe it can be Plant Daddy? I don't even want to mention that Plant Daddy asked to meet, because it would just add to her concern. Maybe we should meet. Maybe when I meet him, it'll feel right. At least more right than Leo and his vampire games. But then . . . if it doesn't feel right, it will be another failure on the list, and I'm not sure I can take that right now.

Allison clears her throat. I must be zoning out.

I guess I should explain. "It's like . . . Plant Daddy has my brain, and we connect on this crazy level. But then, with Leo, it's like this physical . . ." I make a humping motion with my hands. It's immature, but it feels true for the moment. Allison blinks at me, and I fold my arms across my chest, remembering that this is a soccer establishment. "I don't know. It's so intense." If you combine the two guys—Plant Daddy and Leo—it would be my destruction, my total unraveling. Maybe it's for the best if I don't meet Plant Daddy. I don't need more chaos.

"He's a hot dude, but he's just a dude. What would Norma think? Aren't you meeting her tomorrow?"

Norma would absolutely *hate* the idea of me with Leo in his store late at night. In fact, she'd kill me if she knew. That's why I'm not going to tell her.

———

One of Norma's favorite activities is golf. She's not very good, but she sees it as the type of sport you play when you've "made it." Like a rich white guy sport. We spend about an hour at each hole, and it makes her happy. The best part is her outfit—a tennis skort and button-down and an adorable hat. I dress up too, wearing a skort, a polo shirt, and a visor like I'm one of those rich evil people in a Tyler Perry movie.

"We don't need social media! That's the issue. You have to go back to basics."

I'm giving Norma an update on the store's numbers and progress. I don't tell her about Leo and the vampire game or the visit to his store or the photos and the video. If she saw that video of me crying, she'd never let me live it down. She's always told me crying makes you easier for bears to find, which sounds both odd and mean.

She hits the ball in the general direction of the hole, and we move very slowly to retrieve it.

"Do you have any other ideas?" I ask, watching as she shimmies her hips behind the ball to get ready for her next swing.

"We've never needed ideas!" she says, squaring up with the ball. "We just sell our plants, and the rest takes care of itself."

I want to scream. As if it's that easy. Just sell plants. I'm trying. She must sense what I'm thinking, because she looks back at me and gives me a frown.

"Just sell the plants." She says it as if there's some secret meaning in her words, like this is some type of riddle.

The ball doesn't get anywhere near the hole, so we set up again. An old white man with a bright green T-shirt groans from behind us. We both throw up our middle fingers in unison.

I've long abandoned actually playing, and my ball has been in my pocket for several holes now. Norma hasn't even noticed. I turn her statement over and over in my mind. *Just sell the plants*. Botanical Brothers is big, and there are lots of plants, but the selection isn't great. I guess they were hoping to turn my location into a rare plant store. Maybe I should do just that.

"Maybe we can start selling more rare plants." I'm talking more to myself than to Norma. She curses when her ball flies past the hole again. We're gonna be here all night. "We can't compete with the basic plant buyers, but we can attract some of the higher-end clients. We can also go to the Plant Expo as a high-end plant seller."

With everything going on, I'm not sure if it really makes sense for us to go to the Plant Expo this year. But maybe this new angle could make the event worth it. I'm also a little afraid to get a bunch of plants when we're basically bleeding money, but the expo could be our "coming out" party.

"Sell the plants," she says again, and I wonder if she's starting to fall victim to her old age. She finally gets the ball in the hole and celebrates. *Sell the plants*. "Go see that asshole Avery."

Avery is someone I definitely don't want to see, but he might be exactly the person I need to see.

chapter sixteen

PlantDaddy54: Did I freak you out? I didn't mean to mess with this.

————

The plan comes together pretty quickly. Plant Therapy will become a rare plant shop, the type that people from all over will visit. With Avery's help, we'll have the plants that most stores don't carry.

Avery's story is legendary. He was a plant dealer who would travel all around California and even go overseas to obtain the best plants for local shops and nurseries. He has exquisite taste, an almost supernatural ability to pick the right plants with perfect genetics, which produce some of the most amazing varieties. Then, after a big trip to Thailand, he decided that instead of selling all his plants, he'd keep them and start growing himself.

Turns out he was also a bit of an artist. He developed two rare but very popular anthuriums, which sell for around $7,000 each, as well as countless other variations that are super popular with rich collectors around the world. Everyone knows about Avery and his plant collection. Getting any one of his high-end plants will bring people from all around to the store, especially if they don't have to jump through hoops to make a purchase.

Avery is picky. If you want to get a plant from him, you have to fill out an application. He needs to "know of you" and approve of your collection. Norma thought he was stuck up and elitist and refused to beg for plants.

"They just grow from dirt like any other plants," she would say.

A few years back, she fell in love with one of his syngoniums. She refused to go through his process and instead just showed up at his house. I wasn't there, but rumor has it he actually ran away from her and hid in his backyard greenhouse. He would never ever let Norma buy from him, but I'm hoping that by following his process exactly, he'll somehow find it in his heart to sell me at least one or two of his plants for the opening.

So I settle in at the coffee shop to fill out the application. My table is by the window, so I have a full view of Botanical Brothers. The steady stream of customers at all hours of the day is a good inspiration. And I get started.

The form feels like an essay because you have to convince him that the plants are going to a good home and that you'll take care of them. You have to tell him about the store and the plants you want and why. You have to talk about the history of the plants and their genera. As I fill it out, I feel like I'm applying for college. I even add references and testimonials from some of my high-end clients as further proof. I know I have a lot to do to convince him to look past his experiences with Norma and give me a chance.

I try to bare my soul sufficiently for his taste and also tell him about my plans to create the first high-end plant store in Long Beach. Lots of stores have select plants, but that's all we're gonna sell. The "essay" I end up writing makes me cry, but I don't know if that's just because I'm a bit emotional or if it's because of all the frustration and exhaustion from the last few weeks.

When I'm finished, I hit send, gather my things, and head back down the street to my store. I'm just settling in to sweep the floors

—something to keep myself occupied at least—when I get an email from Avery requesting a phone call.

Damn that was fast.

I try not to get too excited, but as I send a short response agreeing for him to call me, I can't stop myself from imagining my store filled with customers again. New customers from all around, all wanting to buy rare and unique plants from me. It's surprisingly uplifting.

I smile for the first time all day, set my phone down, and start sweeping again. Almost immediately, my phone rings, and I rush over to answer.

"Hello?" I answer on the second ring, but it still doesn't feel fast enough. Like if I'm not answering on the first ring, I'm not truly recognizing how *huge* it would be to get some of his rare plants. He's silent for a moment, but I don't lose my nerve. The man is known for his weirdness, Norma warned me. All those fertilizer fumes, I guess.

"Avery? This is Tessa. You emailed me?"

More silence.

"Sir, I just wanted to say that it would mean the world to me if I could buy some of your plants. I know I wrote that in my application, but can I just say that . . ." I take a deep breath, but I can feel my throat closing up. This feels like a moment to tell the truth, one that I haven't really said out loud yet.

"The store is my life, and it's slowly being taken away from me. I don't know what my life would look like without my plants, and I don't really want to know. I hope you understand. I'm scared. I don't know if I know how to do anything else."

It's silent for a beat, and it feels like I've failed some type of test I didn't fully know the rules for. "I . . ." I start.

"Four thirty tomorrow. Bring your own boxes."

He hangs up, and I start breathing again. Didn't even know I was holding my breath. I try not to think about the words and what they mean and what will happen if this new plan doesn't work. This is going to work. Avery is in. It's all happening.

———

Avery lives in North Long Beach in a small house with a fence around it. It looks neglected on the outside. The wood paneling is chipped and worn. The paint used to be white but now has a yellowish tint, sunburnt from facing south. It might have been by design—no one would suspect that the house contains close to a million dollars in plants.

When I knock on the door, he opens it immediately, like he's been waiting for me. I brought cookies from Allison, a form of bribery. I immediately realize this is a mistake because he rolls his eyes at the gift. I'm sure people are always bribing him with things. I wish I could tell him that Allison's cookies are actually the best and that he'll realize that if he just tries them. This whole experience might go a lot smoother if he's in a good mood.

"It's nice to meet you, Avery. I've heard a lot about you." I don't mention how Norma called him a power-tripping asshole when I called to tell her the good news. I suspect she still thinks we don't really need him, but she doesn't know how truly bad things are. Yesterday I had four sales the whole day.

"Hope you didn't believe any of it, Norma hates me." Okay, maybe he does know. There's an awkward silence between us before he abruptly opens the door and signals for me to come inside. "I'm not the biggest fan of hers either. She still alive?"

"Yes, but she's retired. I run the store now. Just me." I smile, and he doesn't quite smile back, just a slight lip quirk. I'll take it. "Thanks for seeing me."

Avery only grunts.

The house is plain and straightforward, devoid of any personality. It looks like one of those model apartments travel businessmen stay at. There are also no plants, which is kind of shocking. I'm wondering if this is some type of weird serial killer trap. I wish Wildcat was here. We stand around awkwardly for a few more moments before I make the executive decision to speak. It doesn't seem like Avery spends much time with anyone other than his plants. I try not to think about how much time I've spent with my plants over the last few weeks, especially with Allison gone. In fact, I haven't talked to many people at all outside of, well . . . Leo. I shake off the thought.

"Can I see what you have?" I ask.

"Sure," Avery shrugs. "That's why you're here."

I follow Avery out of his living room and into what looks like a bedroom turned greenhouse. There's a small twin-sized bed in the corner, but otherwise it's just plants. There are containers of prop boxes piled up with a couple of water bottles and coffee cups on top. The far wall is just rows of IKEA greenhouses and terrarium boxes. There's no rhyme or reason to the space. There are $4 Trader Joe's plants next to $600 philodendrons. Cuttings litter the ground.

He walks out of that room and into another one, which feels like it might have been an office at some point. There's a desk, but on top of the desk are rows of propagations and then displays of plants. This is where the more expensive plants live. I even notice his special monstera varieties and some strawberry shake philodendrons in the cupboard. It's both beautiful and sad, a strange love letter to the hobby. I'm trying to decide who would appreciate this more—Plant Daddy or Leo. I'm currently technically ignoring them both.

"What's the temperature of your store, on average?" Avery asks.

I jump, realizing that I'd gotten so lost in my thoughts I forgot he was there.

"Seventy-five up front and eighty-five in the back room." This is it, the big test. I turn to face him, and he comes to a stop right in front of me.

"What medium?" He crosses his arms.

"Orchid and perlite mix."

"Lighting conditions?"

"The store faces north, but we use lights everywhere."

He nods, drifting out of the room and leaving me there again, like some type of plant-knowledge ninja. A few minutes later, he returns with my box, which I left at the door when I came in.

"What you see is what's available. I'll give you a total at the end."

I try to hide my surprise as I nod. I'd been hoping to get one plant, maybe two, if I was lucky. But I'd apparently passed his notoriously impossible test, and now I get to pick what I want.

And of course he doesn't give me individual prices. I just have to use my own knowledge as a guide. I lean down and pick up a mint monstera, that's probably around $800. The *Thaumatophyllum williamsii* is around $1,000. I put them both in my box. Gotta go big if I want this to work.

When I'm done, my haul is huge—close to $40,000 worth of plants. I pay for it with a combination of my own money and what I could pull from the store. All of the plants are dream plants, the kind that people have on their wish lists for years. It's a huge financial risk, but I really believe this is a great way to make Plant Therapy stand out, to do my own thing.

After I finish loading the plants into the truck, I manage to convince Avery to eat one of the cookies I brought him. We sit on his porch together, and I watch him shrug as he takes a bite. I imagine it's because he gets a lot of cookies. I eat one myself because it feels polite, but he doesn't seem to be paying much attention to me until he speaks.

"I liked what you wrote in your application." He doesn't make eye contact with me. "I feel the same. Plants are my life. I don't need anything or anyone else."

I smile and nod, but the way he says it doesn't feel good. I always thought Avery was living the dream. He's a sought-after plant seller. He gets to choose whom he works with, and he has the best plants you can get. His plants are his life, and his life is his plants, kind of like mine. But sitting here with Avery, I get the sense that he spends a lot of time alone. I wonder if just being with your plants on your own is the best thing. I think about all of his rooms filled to the brim with plants, and it feels like a dream. But it also almost feels like the plants are keeping him hostage. He has nowhere to sit and barely has room to sleep. He has probably over a million dollars' worth of plants, but when I look out to his drive-way, I see a gorgeous truck that's dusty and yellow, covered in pollen, like it hasn't been driven in forever. I wonder when he last left home.

"I like your truck," I say.

"Thanks. It broke down a while ago, and I haven't gotten a chance to fix it. Haven't really needed to fix it. Everything I need is here."

I don't know why I decided to comment on the truck in the first place, but I suspect it was because I was hoping our stories weren't so similar. I think about my RV in the driveway at home, collecting dust.

"I hope you get to keep your store," Avery says.

"Me too," I say. "I really hope I get to keep my store." I want to keep my store. It's all I want.

"Who walks around shirtless around spider plants? It's unseemly. That one guy reminds me of this guy who used to pick on me in middle school." He noticeably relaxes, like he's used to me being here.

"Oh? Paul? Botanical Brothers?" I ask. I wonder if they've tried to get Avery's plants. I'm sure they have, everyone tries. I try to remind myself of this. Most people don't get as far as I have. And suddenly I'm curious. "Have you talked to them?"

"Yes. The other one knows his stuff though. He's not bad."

I shiver involuntarily as our moment in the store replays in my mind—Leo's lips on my neck and back. Then I think about Paul, and it's like I've been doused in cold water.

"You can drop by and see some of the new hybrids I have in a few weeks if you want," he says with something that almost resembles a smile. I notice he's missing a few teeth.

I guess I've passed the test. This is good. Everything will go back to normal. Avery at least tolerates me. I'll rebrand Plant Therapy as a premiere rare plant shop, and everything will be fine.

"That sounds great." I take another bite of my cookie.

chapter seventeen

PlantDaddy13: I'm sorry it took me so long to say something. I don't think I can. At least not right now.

PlantDaddy54: I understand, at least I think I do. Can I ask why?

PlantDaddy13: I just have a lot going on and honestly don't know if I can deal with something else bad happening.

PlantDaddy54: You think if we meet, something bad will happen?

PlantDaddy13: I mean, I don't know. We don't really know each other. What if we aren't what each other expects. I just like the way things are right now. It's safe and nothing bad can happen when we talk like this.

PlantDaddy54: You mean we can't really know each other but what if I want to know you? I'd like to know you for real and support you for real in a way that I feel like I can't do here.

PlantDaddy13: You are! I feel you support me so much! It just feels too risky. I don't want us to change. Do you get it?

PlantDaddy54: I get it. I do.

PlantDaddy54: Okay that cactus that looks like a pair of boobs is pretty funny.

———

To mark Plant Therapy's shift to a high-end rare plant shop, I decide to have an exclusive private showing that's by invitation only. I'll do a preview event for the neighborhood to start and have the big buying event the day after. I invite some of the most prominent plant collectors in the city, along with some of the more well-known societies in the region. My biggest gets are the Lakewood Botanical Society and the Hollywood Botanical Society, which have some of the richest potential clients in the city. I also invite Adeline to come and do another story on the store and the private showing.

While typically my method of showcasing my plants is more organic, I decide on a more methodical display style for the private showing. All of the plants will be lined up by price point and type, so it will be easy for my customers to find what they want.

When I'm almost finished setting up for the preview event, it's late, already around 10:00 p.m. I peek out the door of my shop and see that Botanical Brothers is still open down the street. I stop myself from having another flashback of me and Leo at his shop and close the door again so I can focus on finishing the job at hand —organizing all of my plants.

"Helllooo?"

Right. Allison. She's still on the phone, keeping me company while I work.

"Sorry, it's going okay."

"Are you thinking about Plant Daddy again?"

I don't want to tell her that it's not Plant Daddy but Leo, my mortal enemy and someone I absolutely shouldn't be thinking or talking about. Leo and I had our moment, but the facts haven't changed. Our stores are competitors, and I'm not giving up without a fight. His lips can't and won't change that. Plant Daddy and I haven't talked since I told him I didn't want to meet.

"I'm not," I say.

"Oh?" She seems to hear the truth in my words. "Trouble in paradise?"

I miss waking up to his messages, but I need to focus on other things. And I've tried to not be frustrated about him going silent now when I really need his funny photos the most, but there's no way he could know that. He doesn't actually know what's going on with me, and that's my choice. But in this moment, it feels like a bad one.

"Just . . . have a lot on my mind. What about you? Is everything okay? Are you settling in?"

Allison is quiet for a moment. "It's just all hitting me. I'm in the suburbs. I live here. We were just looking at SUVs! What is happening to my life? When will you make it up?"

I want to say never. I don't have much of a desire to go to Riverside. Yeah, it's far, but also, once I'm there, I think it'll suddenly feel real. I mean, that she's really there and I'm here . . . mostly alone. And while I know there's no actual correlation to my presence in Long Beach and bad things happening, I still don't feel like I should go anywhere. I feel anchored to this spot, like if I'm not constantly watching the store, I'll come back, and it will be gone.

"Soon," I say. "When all of this is over."

When all of this is over. I imagine me back with my plants and a full store and no stress or sexy men with plants and their evil villain brothers. Something in the back of my brain screams that it feels unlikely that will happen, but I tell my brain to shut up and focus on the show.

———

We open for the neighborhood first. It's mostly a dress rehearsal for the private showing the following day. I want to see whether I maybe need to make any tweaks to the setup. I arrange the plants in museum-quality displays and dress up for the occasion in a long dress with a colorful plant print. The dress is much more modest than the porn star dress, and I kind of look like a New York City mom.

The store feels oddly empty without Wildcat as my constant

companion, but I didn't want to risk her knocking anything over, so I left her at home.

The event does what it's supposed to do. The store is fuller than it has been in a while. Most of my regulars who can afford plants at this price point come in, and I actually make a few sales of some of the lower-priced plants. Around $6,000. It's pretty good money, a big boost considering that I haven't been selling anything lately. I also notice the shop's Instagram getting lots of photos and tags, which give us another little boost.

"I like this one." My client Nick, a thirty-something lifeguard still in his trunks and an open shirt, holds up a large, variegated *Monstera adansonii*, which is $1,000.

"Yeah, I like it too. It's $1,000."

He puts it down carefully, like it's a bomb that's going to detonate at any second, and then backs away slowly. I put my hands on his shoulders and walk him over to the more affordable plants I still have on display for the neighborhood. He picks up a regular *Monstera adansonii*, and I smile and say, "Thirty bucks." He gives me a thumbs up and takes it over to the register, where Bill is helping people check out. I'm following him over when an odd silence fills the store.

I look over towards the door and see Leo and Paul, the two people I really didn't want to see.

I guess I should have expected them to come—I did invite the neighborhood. But my brain didn't quite make the connection. Leo and I haven't seen each other since the incident at his store, but I haven't stopped thinking about it. I smooth down my dress and glance at my hair in the mirror, checking that the loose curls I spent almost two hours forcing my hair into actually still look good. When I turn back to find him, he's already heading over to me. He's wearing another hot-guy uniform—a sweater and slacks. A sexy dad. He's smiling, but his gaze is a little unsure. Despite that, my heart is beating. Hard. Shut the fuck up heart. Not now. Remember the betrayal. It's been almost two weeks since our night at the store. I still wonder what he would have said if I'd looked back and answered.

"Hi." He looks at me like he hasn't seen me in months, not weeks. I wonder if I'm looking at him the same way. "This is a really good idea."

Come on, Tessa. Tell him to go fuck himself.

"Thanks." Awesome job, Tessa.

"I can't help but think I kind of helped you with it." His eyes land on the side of my neck, where the bite used to live. There was a mark, but it's faded. You can see the faint edges of it if you squint.

"It just came to me," I say. His eyes fall to my neck again, and I wonder if he's imagining it, if he's also back there in his empty shop, late at night, just the two of us and the plants. "I can't tell how you really feel about me taking over the rare plant market. Are you actually happy? Or is this some kind of strategy? Like the video?"

"I never wanted to destroy your business, Tessa." Hearing my name from his mouth never gets old. It always feels good. I try to ignore that feeling as he continues. "That was never my goal. I had no idea about the video until you showed me. Did you notice we took it down?"

I did notice. When I lost my nerve and started stalking them again, I noticed it missing.

We're both quiet for a moment, just taking each other in. I'm still mad, but the longer I'm in his presence, the more the anger is slowly starting to melt away.

He leans in close and whispers in my ear, his lips barely touching my skin. "You look beautiful."

I take a step back and look around self-consciously. I hope nobody is watching us. It's easy to forget that we aren't alone. "You shouldn't say things like that." I lean in to whisper back. We make eye contact. It's a mistake.

"I know." The delivery of the line is buttery and warm. He can turn on the sex so quickly, and I'm never quite prepared.

"This is really impressive, Tess. I can't believe you managed to get ahold of some of these. Must have cost you a fortune." It's Paul. *Tess? Ew.* There's the rage again.

My Leo trance tricked me into thinking that Paul wasn't here, but he is, and in all his villain glory.

"Thanks. Yes, it was an investment for sure."

Paul takes in the space like he's making a copy of it in his mind. I watch in silence while he walks slowly around the store, peeking behind the curtain at my greenhouses and flicking one of the spider plants on the live wall with his hand. He is the worst.

"Oh, we have the same humidifiers and air filters," he observes.

"Are you in the market for anything?" My tone is sunshine in a way that sounds unnatural, even to my ear. I was going for passive aggression, but maybe I overshot a bit.

"Maybe that philodendron red congo over there. The variegated one. What do you think, Leo?" It's $3,000. Of course, they don't even have to think about making a plant purchase that big. "I already have one, this one will go nicely with it."

Leo only nods, still looking at me.

"We'll come back tomorrow for it. Just wanted to stop by and show our support," Paul beams, flashing a perfect smile. His words sound vaguely threatening.

"Thanks for stopping by," I say. I don't want to make a scene. Not this time.

Paul grins, clapping Leo on the shoulder. He leaves with a few admirers following behind him. Leo seems like he's thinking about something. He looks around the store a little sadly, almost guiltily. It shifts something in my gut.

"What? Is something wrong?" I wonder if he spots an infection on one of the plants or something.

"You just looked so happy, and I want you to stay that way."

"I'm happy. This will be fine. Everything is fine." He stares at his feet, and I can't help myself. "Hey, is everything okay with the store and everything?" Why am I asking him this?

He doesn't respond, and the knot in my stomach grows tighter.

"Leo?" I ask.

"I should go," he says. "I'll see you tomorrow to grab the plant."

"Okay."

"Okay."

We pull apart, and he gives me another wave when he leaves. I feel a tug in my chest.

chapter eighteen

PlantDaddy54: I'm sorry I've been absent, just a lot on my plate.

PlantDaddy13: That's okay, you don't owe me anything. I have a lot going on right now.

PlantDaddy54: Me too. Maybe we should take a little break for now?

PlantDaddy13: Yeah, maybe we should. I mean, if you want?

PlantDaddy54: I think we should. At least for now.

———

When I arrive the next day, there's already a few people waiting outside so they can be first in the store for the big showing. Yesterday was only a test run. Today is when I think all the money will be made and our reputation will be set. Today, all the clubs and societies are coming, along with all the big names in the Southern California plant scene, including Avery. Adeline has also said she'll be here. I'm hoping this will be the day everything comes together. Plant Therapy will officially be the only rare plant seller in South Bay in Long Beach. Everything will go back to normal. I try not to think too much about Plant Daddy, who I'm pretty sure just dumped me? Is that what that was?

Normal can't come soon enough.

We have about two hours before the store officially opens, so I assume the people waiting must have some special items on their wish lists. The museum display style pre-show for the neighborhood did a great job of promoting the store and making sure news about it spread. In an act of charity that I'm sure Paul didn't appreciate, Leo also posted a photo from outside the store, urging everyone to "go visit our friends down the street!" *Our friends*. I guess that's an interesting way to put it.

I've got Wildcat here with me this time, and she's already doing her job, greeting everyone outside as she follows me in.

"I just need to get everything set up!" I say to the people outside waiting, and they all cheer. I'm distracted and overwhelmed. It feels so good to see everyone so happy and excited to be here.

"Is everything okay in there?" an older woman says as I'm unlocking the door. "Sounds like something might be leaking."

I pause to listen, and my stomach drops. I hear it too. Something *is* leaking.

As soon as I open the door, I know something is wrong. The air feels thick and stale. The store looks eerily empty because I put the rare plants away last night before I left. At first glance, everything is where it should be. But as I walk through the store to my back room and greenhouse, I step into a pool of water, and it soaks through my sneakers. Horrified, I look down.

The floor is covered in water. The humidifiers are leaking.

In a daze, I continue on the path to my back room. It feels ominous, like I'm a character in a horror film about to meet my death. It's actually exactly like a horror film, because when I arrive in the greenhouse, I scream.

There's water everywhere, and the greenhouse lights spark and flicker on and off. I spot broken wires near the water and take a step back. It looks like the insulation around the wires melted off.

Not wanting to be electrocuted, I take another step backwards as I survey the mess.

It's a disaster.

The plants are in disarray and scattered around, some crushed by the weight of the falling lights. The back door is open, and a raccoon scurries away when I turn on the light. It seems so impossible, so unreal, and I feel like I'm having an out-of-body experience, like this is happening to someone else.

It's all ruined. My $40,000 in rare plants. Ruined.

"Hey, everything okay? You screamed . . . . Oh, holy shit!" Bill appears next to me and pulls me away and out of the room. He's talking, but I can't hear him. My vision goes white, and my ears feel full and heavy. Like in one of those movies. Everything feels far away. Everything is ruined. All of the plants are ruined. All of my money, all of the store's money . . . gone. Out of the corner of my eye, I can see a Thai constellation on its side, covered in water and dirt. It looks like someone smashed its nursery pot, and one of the larger cuttings is missing.

"Tessa, we need to call the fire department. This could cause a fire. It's really dangerous. Tessa! Tessa!"

I feel sick, like I'm gonna puke. In fact, I know I'm gonna puke. I rush back into the store and vomit into the trash can, slumping to the floor. From my position, I can see the crowd forming outside, peering through the window at me, searching for answers. I throw up again. I sit for a while until I eventually hear the fire trucks making their way up 4th Street. Everything goes white.

I wake up in the back of an ambulance with an oxygen mask on.

"Tessa, are you awake?" I recognize the voice. It's Jeremy, who works at the hospital and is one of my only clients who can keep a fern alive. I make a noise that I hope sounds enough like a yes. "You passed out," he says.

I hear commotion all around. Sirens going off. Somewhere far away, I hear what sounds like Leo speaking.

"Is she okay? Where is she? Holy shit. Holy shit."

"She's fine. She's fine. She's just asleep. Go home, Leo. Go home." It's Bill.

I try to lift my head to get a look at him.

"Bill! Bill!" I squeak, and he rushes over to the ambulance to me. I see Leo standing back a ways, and he looks concerned. He must have seen the commotion when walking by. The commotion. My store. The plants. I turn my attention back to Bill. "Make sure they don't throw anything away!" I might die, but maybe I can at least save the plants.

"Tessa, don't worry about that! Just . . . relax okay?"

I nod and feel my eyes start to close, and I hear Bill step out of the ambulance and the doors shut.

Bill sounds far away when I hear him next. "Hey! Don't throw that out! Leave it!"

———

I wake up at the hospital a few hours later. I wanted Plant Therapy to have more of an online presence, but this isn't the way I wanted to do it. By the time I'm fully coherent, word of the $40,000 disaster at Plant Therapy has spread. People are stopping by just to see the damage. There are rumors of a raccoon walking around with a *Monstera* 'Aurea' clutched in its front paws. I doubt that's true. Monsteras are toxic to animals. My phone is full of missed calls and messages, including a very angry message from Avery, who will likely never sell to me again. I replay it again in my mind.

"Tessa, I trusted you! You came into my home, and I gave you some of my nicest plants. You said you cared about plants. Did you hear about that raccoon? The one with the 'Albo'? I can't believe you did this. You don't deserve the plants or the store. I should have entrusted my plants to someone else. ANYONE ELSE. I was wrong. You aren't like me."

Bill tells me that while I was in the hospital, he and Allison did what they could to make sure the fire department didn't throw away any of the bags of plants they salvaged. I'm thankful for that. But I'm also scared to find out just how bad it is.

It takes hours before I can even go back and assess the damage. By then, everyone is gone, and it's just me watching people in suits toss away my plants as if they are worth nothing, as if they do not represent tens of thousands of dollars and my whole life and the future of the store. The worst part is that my plant wall had been destroyed as well. The suspended light I'd set up to point at the wall had smashed into the wall, scorching the leaves and tearing the display apart. The watering system also messed up, drowning some of the more delicate plants.

Eventually, I have to tell people what happened. I tell the Lakewood Botanical Society to turn around. Bill tells Norma to spare me her screaming. She calls and screams at me anyways.

"It's been forty years, and nothing like this has EVER HAPPENED! Tessa, what is GOING ON?! How could you let this happen?!"

Social media is buzzing in exactly the way I hate, the way I'm afraid of. Everyone has the same question: What happened? Theories run rampant. The store was old, and the pipes couldn't handle any more. I had destroyed the shop on purpose. I'd been robbed.

Willis, one of the neighborhood firemen, meets me at the store to talk to me about next steps. "Tessa, we don't know what happened exactly, but we need a bunch of people to come out before we're comfortable with you going in. An electrician needs to secure the lines, we need to check for mold damage and moisture, the insurance guy needs to come, and also . . ." He takes a meaningful pause, and I feel myself holding my breath. "We really want to have the police get a detective out here to check things out."

That snaps me out of my daze really fast. "A cop? Why?" I didn't really see this as anything but an accident—the type you hear about on Reddit forums and see on YouTube videos. Catastrophic light and humidifier destruction. It seems fitting that it would happen to me on the most important day of my career.

He hesitates and then looks at the store. "There could have been some foul play. I'm not sure, but some of the guys say it looks like someone might have broken in."

"Wait, why would anyone break into the store? Who would break in?" I ask.

"Well, you promoted it as a rare plant showing, and you said the plants would be worth a lot of money. You know there's folks at Bluff Park who break into houses sometimes or shops to grab booze or stuff to sell. Maybe someone saw it as the ultimate score."

I nod. We've had break-ins before, but they typically go for money or expensive furniture. Never the plants. Who steals plants?

Willis continues. "It's hard to tell. And you're sure there's no security footage?"

I give him a look. Seriously? None of the shops around here have security footage. The cameras are all just for show. Most of the security systems on the block broke years ago, and the landlords never got around to fixing them. It never felt that important. And whenever anyone tried to talk to the landlords, they'd just threaten to increase the rent. So, really, we all decided to just shut up. Of course, it's never been a problem until now.

"How long will I need to be closed?"

"Well, you need insurance to assess the space, and everything needs to be fixed. Your landlord needs to decide what they want to do. There's a lot that needs to happen."

I feel my stomach sink. After everything I've tried to do to keep the store open, we're closing anyways. Of course.

"But I can open again?"

"I see no reason why not. Once the investigation is completed and the insurance money comes through and you still feel like you want to pursue this, you should be able to. We just need to figure out what happened."

The way he says "feel like you want to pursue this" seems pointed, but I ignore it.

"Fuck," I say, not really intending to say it out loud.

Willis nods. "I agree."

A few firemen bring out some big black bags and put them on the side of the building. I rush over to them and open the closest bag. The first plant I see is Leo and Paul's smashed up philodendron.

chapter nineteen

Bill: Are you just going to sit across the street and stare at the store forever?

Allison: You're still sitting out there? Weren't you out there yesterday?

Tessa: Do you guys have a separate group chat about me?

Bill: Couldn't you at least bring yourself a chair?

Tessa: I like the ground.

Allison: Does she look dehydrated?

Bill: She looks kind of glazed over so yeah?

Tessa: I'm fine! I'm just . . . . . sitting.

Allison: Please go check on her.

Bill: I'm going.

Tessa: Can you bring some water please?

———

For the first time in almost eight years, I don't wake up and open the store. I don't stay all day, and I don't spend the night listening to Beyoncé and sweeping the floors. Wildcat doesn't cuddle up in the corner alongside the prayer plants. Instead, I sit across the street and stare at my store, trying to will it to open again.

Adeline did apparently come by that day, and she did write about the store. The title of her article was just as dramatic as the title of her last article: "Local Mainstay Meets a Tragic End." I was on the phone with my mom for hours the day she read it, trying to convince her that I didn't need to go home. I wasn't sure what I needed to do—I'm still not sure—but I did know that going home wasn't the right move.

"It's not the end," Bill says as he takes out a chair and settles next to me. "It's just a pause."

I nod. It's just a pause. This isn't the end.

He hands me a bottle of water, and we sit there, looking on in awe as if the store is the setting sun and not a block of concrete.

After a few minutes, I look over at him, frowning. He looks like a concerned father. And I guess Bill has been something of a dad to me, considering my own dad is off somewhere doing who knows what. I feel a momentary pang of guilt for putting him through the ringer. But he just gives me a kind, sympathetic smile.

"Maybe it can be a fruitful pause. You can explore what's next." He says the words cautiously, like I'm a cat he's trying to coax out of a tree. I feel like one. I don't know what's beyond my safe tree.

"I'm not sure," I hear myself say, and I realize I haven't heard the sound of my own voice in a while.

"Why don't you come to my show tonight? Distract yourself?"

I've never been able to go to one of Bill's shows. They're usually during the week, and so if I wanted to go, I would have to close down the shop early. I want to say no, but then I realize that I don't really have any plans beyond this—sitting around and waiting for

Plant Therapy to reopen so I can get back to my life and get back to my safe tree. If I don't go, I'll probably just hang out at home, watching *Golden Girls* reruns on my TV and trying to teach Wildcat more tricks. I really don't have anything else to do.

"Yeah, okay. Sounds good."

———

"Hey, where are you?" I say, holding my phone up to my ear as I stand outside of Reno's, the bar where Bill and his band often play. I'm not a big bar person. Occasionally, I get dragged out by Allison, but mostly I avoid it. Although it's been so long that I can't really remember why.

"I'm still in traffic," Allison says on the other end of the line. She got word that I was actually leaving the house and decided she had to come too. "Are you there yet?"

"Yeah! I'm going in now. Should I wait?"

"No," she says, and I hear a loud honk and some shouting in the background. "It's gonna be a while. Just go ahead inside."

We say goodbye and hang up. Then I push the door open and head inside.

The bar is more crowded than I expected, a mix of locals and Bill's out-of-town fans. By "out-of-town," I mean retirees from Orange County and South Bay, who have multimillion-dollar homes they once paid two hundred grand for. Still, the crowd is pretty impressive; the bar isn't small, with a capacity of around 150 people, and it's full to the brim of patrons here to watch a few aging boomers sing songs. Moving through the throng of people feels a bit like the old days when Allison and I used to have to push our way up to the front of the bar. She would typically lead the way, and I'd hold her back as we made our way through. Right now, however, it's just me, so I take a deep breath and shoulder my way into the fray, trying to avoid cocktails and beer bottles as I move towards the stage to say hi to Bill. I notice a few of my regular clients on my way, and although they all seem shocked that I'm here, they wave in greeting as I float past. I really need to get out more.

From the distance, I can see Bill with his guitar, tuning it up and getting ready to go on. I rush over to the stage to greet him. He looks like a true rock star, having exchanged his button-ups and oxfords for a plain white T-shirt, jeans, and combat boots. He looks so cool, like the kind of guy who would have groupies.

When he sees me, he crouches down, and I give him a hug.

"You made it!"

"I have a lot of time on my hands." I try for a breezy tone, but my words still sound a little pathetic coming out of my mouth.

He doesn't miss anything, though, and he nods sympathetically. "It's gonna be okay."

"Do you have a drink? Can I get you one?" I change the subject and try to anchor myself to the moment and smile because this is good. I'm happy I get to see him here.

"That would be great. A Jack Daniel's on the rocks?"

"You got it." I start to turn around, and he stops me.

"Hey, thanks for coming. Really."

I nod and then turn and make my way through the crowd to the bar.

The bartender is Mike, one of my occasional customers. Every few months, he has a big break up and buys a plant. It's tradition. Last time, he ended a six-week situationship and wanted a plant that was tough and would never break your heart or cheat on you with a DJ from West Hollywood. I suggested a ZZ plant. The thought of the ZZ plant makes me momentarily think of Plant Daddy. He doesn't know what's going on with the store and everything, but I can't help but feel abandoned by him. I shake off the feeling and smile up at Mike.

He looks shocked to see me, too. "Tessa! Is that you? Never seen you out at nighttime."

"That makes me sound like a reverse vampire or something.

Can I get a beer for me and a Jack Daniel's on the rocks for the rock star over there?"

"You got it." He gets to work on the drinks.

"How is the ZZ plant?"

"Still alive, like you said it would be."

"Yep, that's right."

"ZZ plants are great plants," a voice says from behind me, and I don't have to turn to see whom it is. I would know the voice anywhere. It's Leo. I remember him calling my name, wanting to check that I was okay when I was in the ambulance the morning of the disaster at my store. I wonder when he got there and how much he saw. I suddenly feel embarrassed, and I turn towards him slowly. He smells like Honeycrisp apples. Maybe they should jar it and sell it.

"Hi, Tessa." Why is he saying my name like that? He says my name like it tastes good to him.

"Leo." I say his name, too, because it feels like I should. He's in all black, dressed down in a T-shirt and baggy jeans. His skin looks golden and glistens beneath the harsh lights of the bar.

"Twenty-two bucks," Mike says, leaving my drinks on the bar in front of me. He looks between us and smiles. I frown at him, and it just makes him grin wider.

I move to grab my wallet, but Leo stops me with a hand on my wrist. That one touch is magic. It's like he triggers a vampire premonition. Us in his store, his lips on my neck. I remember that Mike is watching this, too.

"I got it," Leo says.

While he reaches into his back pocket to pay, I study his forearms, his fingers, and the shape of his jaw. Suddenly I'm really thirsty. It's weird to see him here, away from the plants and his adoring fans and everything else. He looks different. More normal. Not so much like Paul.

"I'm so sorry." He looks so sad when he says it. I have to admit that I'd momentarily forgotten about Leo and his shop. I've been too focused on the accident. I'm sure they've thrived even more since Plant Therapy closed, not that it makes that much of a difference.

"I really don't want to talk about it." I grab my beer and Bill's drink and take a big swig to calm my nerves a bit. I hold up the drinks and give him a slight nod. "Thanks. Bill will appreciate that." I decide it's time to get out of here before I embarrass myself. I move through the crowd, not stopping to look and see if he's following me. He is.

"Oh? Is Bill your boyfriend? You guys are together a lot."

He's behind me, so he doesn't see me bite my lip at his question. He sounds a little jealous, and I appreciate the shift in topic. It gives me the opportunity to not be Tessa with the failing store and to just be me for a bit.

"No."

I maneuver through the crowd, and he follows me wordlessly, occasionally bumping against my back so we're flush at some points. I try my best to ignore him, making eye contact with Bill as I get closer. Bill smiles and waves at me and then seems to freeze when he notices Leo. When I reach Bill, Leo stops next to me like he's supposed to be there.

"Thanks, Tess," Bill says when I hand him his drink. He looks from me to Leo and back questioningly, and I just shake my head. He shrugs, and after we clink our drinks together and both take a sip, he returns to his bandmates.

I back away, giving his fifty-something groupies their spots back right in front of him.

"Ah, so you like older men. I get it."

Leo stands next to me again, and I peek at his profile while I take a swig of my beer.

"Bill runs the antique store next to mine, and he's my friend. We've been friends for years. You know that, though. I heard you that day, asking about me when he was taking care of me."

"I just saw people rushing in the direction of your store. I got freaked out and went to go check and make sure you were okay." I can't deny that I'm more than a little charmed by the fact that he came looking for me. "Bill said you'd be fine but that you likely needed space, so . . . I wasn't sure how to even get in touch with you. I don't have your number or anything. I messaged you on Instagram."

"Yeah, I haven't been on there much."

"I get it."

We're both quiet for a minute, and I wish I could go back to when I'm not Tessa the failure again.

I turn to him so we're face-to-face. He's really close. "Are you here to see Bill's band play?"

"No, I was meeting a few coworkers for drinks, and I was actually on my way out when I . . ." He trails off and takes another sip of his drink. Then he looks down at his feet, suddenly interested in his black sneakers.

"What?" I catch myself smiling at the top of his head without even meaning to. An involuntary reaction to his dimples.

"I saw you come in on my way out."

"You saw me come in . . . so you came back in?" I say it slowly, like my brain is still processing it. "Why?"

"Because." As if that explains it. He takes another sip of his drink, making eye contact with me, and then turns to the stage.

I'm about to ask him to elaborate when Bill's bandmate Ted gets on stage and announces ACAB, the name of their group. And then they start playing "God Save The Queen." I sing along—only knowing the song because of Bill's influence. I'm not sure how you dance to music like this. Do you bounce up and down? Do you move your hips? I just start bouncing and swaying to the rhythm, but I stop when I see Bill performing. Bill looks totally in his element, his eyes closed and playing his guitar like there's no one else in the room.

How have I never seen him like this? I've known him for so long, but he's really only ever been Bill of Bill's Antiques, who sits outside his shop, fixing a clock or reading the newspaper while he sips his coffee. He acts like a grandpa, and in a lot of ways, he's my adopted one. While I've known Norma for the longest, Bill was the second person I met when I came to Long Beach. He took me under his wing, playing good cop to Norma's bad cop. Clearly, there's this other part of him that I sort of knew about but didn't ever see. The part of him that exists outside of our little block of stores on 4th Street. I didn't know he had so much of a life outside the shop. The thought makes me sad. What else have I missed?

They end the song and start another one, "London Calling" by the Clash. It's just as good. Leo does a big whoop, and I'm reminded again of his presence. I take another sip of my drink for bravery and lean over to him so I'm close.

"Why did you come back when I came in?" I ask again.

He shakes his head and cups his ear like he can't hear me. I repeat my question, and it still doesn't go through. I lean in close so that I'm speaking directly into his ear. Does that shiver come from him or me?

"Why did you come back when I came in?"

He pulls back a little to whisper in my ear, "I don't know." But as he says it, his hand wraps around my lower back, pulling me to him. It's so fast that I barely have time to react, so I put up no resistance as I'm drawn to him. An older drunk woman, probably in her sixties, stumbles behind me, spilling her drink and narrowly missing me. Everyone groans and complains. A few people clap.

"Sorry, didn't want you to get hit," Leo says, his hand still on my back.

We're infuriatingly face-to-face and getting closer. He terrifies me.

"You know they think there might have been foul play with my accident," I say, needing to interrupt the intensity.

"Who would want to sabotage your store?"

I give him a pointed look. I don't actually think he had anything to do with it, but it feels appropriate to mention it. His face suddenly turns serious.

"You don't think I'd do anything like that to you, right?"

His hand grips my arm to steady me, and he searches my eyes. No, I want to say, but there's no reason for me to actually feel that way. We only kind of know each other, but I don't think he'd intentionally hurt me. Maybe that's the vampire talking.

"There you are!" Allison appears, reaching us through a clearing in the crowd. It's like the crowd parted for her, which is her way. She's always had a huge presence. "Traffic was HELL. I left at like three thirty. Should I have left at noon? Jesus." I stand perfectly still and hope maybe she won't see Leo, but of course she does. "Oh. Shit. Um, hi, Leo."

He releases my arm and takes a step back, and I watch her follow the motion.

"Hey, Allison. Good to see you," he says casually, breezily, and it's like he's performing for his adoring fans again. I don't appreciate the switch.

"Yeah, uh . . ." she says, giving him a once over and then leveling me with a "what the hell are you doing" look.

"Let's get you a drink," I say, pulling her away. "It was nice seeing you, Leo."

We disappear into the crowd, and I don't look behind me, but she calls out, "Bye, Leo!" She gives him a little girlish wave.

"He was touching you!" She squeals and slaps me on the arm as we make our way to the bar. The crowd thins the farther we get from the stage. "Are you guys a thing now after you guys were humping at his shop? Wait, you aren't giving up on the shop, are you?"

"No! Of course not! We were just talking."

We've reached the bar, and nosy Mike chimes in.

"He bought her a drink!" Traitor. He shrugs, reading my mind. "He did!"

"Oh, really?! Just a Sprite for me, Mike. I gotta drive home." He nods and walks away. When he's gone, she turns her attention back to me. "What are you doing?" It seems like an accusation. This is weird to me because when Allison used to drag me around to the clubs with her, she'd always be talking to men even when she really shouldn't have been, and I was always really supportive.

"Nothing! We were just talking."

"I thought we talked about this. He's just a guy!" she says, shaking her head. Mike brings over the Sprite, and she takes a sip and then exhales happily, like it's the best thing she's ever tasted.

"There's nothing going on, we were just talking," I say, trying to stay calm. I feel a little overwhelmed, like it's stuffier here than usual.

"I get it, I just think you shouldn't get distracted. It's time to be serious."

That's the last straw for me.

"Nothing happened. He's just . . . We're just . . . I'm by myself down here!" I'm practically screaming, but you can't really hear me over "Rock the Casbah" playing in the background.

"He's the whole reason you're in this mess!" Allison yells, her voice matching mine. "And you can come up! I'm always asking you to come up, and you never do!"

I feel a headache coming on.

"I don't want to come up to bumfuck Riverside!" I exclaim.

"You don't want to go anywhere, Tessa! Or do anything! Just sit around and be sad about the store and not even do anything about it. You act like there's nothing else you care about."

Ouch, that one hurt. I don't know what to even say to that one because she's right. The store is the only thing I know how to do because it's the only thing I've been doing. I don't have hobbies. I don't knit or draw. I just take care of plants, and now I don't even do that.

"I'm gonna get some air," I say, already walking away. I'm not sure where I'm going—just away.

"I'm sorry, I'm just stressed. It was a long drive. So much is going on," Allison explains.

I stop and turn to her.

"What's going on?" She doesn't say anything. Of course. I start walking again, and she follows me for a step or two before I stop her. "I'll be back, okay? Go say hi to Bill."

She doesn't look convinced. I put my hand on her arm.

"I'm okay. I promise. It's okay." I'm lying, but she lets me go.

"Okay."

I head out the door and into the night. There's a slight chill, but it's still warm enough. The air smells like salt and alcohol, and it makes me slightly nauseated, so I take a few steps away from the bar.

Leo's standing outside with a group of his friends. I recognize them as Botanical Brothers employees from the videos. I roll my eyes at myself for knowing this information because of all my stalking. Truly pathetic. He frowns when he sees me, and I wonder if he can tell by my face what just happened. I keep walking, and he's following me again, but I don't have the energy to tell him to go away.

"I just want you to get wherever you're going safely," he says, staying at a good distance behind me.

"I don't need that. I'm just going to the beach." I march on, my high emotional state making the six-minute walk feel a lot shorter. He follows behind, not saying anything, and I'm grateful for the silence. As I walk farther away from the bustle of 2nd Street, everything looks darker and more ominous and quieter. I'm almost grateful for his presence.

Rosie's Dog Beach is empty, but the moon hitting the sand is beautiful. I slip off my flats and bury my feet in the sand. It feels good, the way I thought it would. A welcome sensation. I pick up my shoes and step out to the sand and in the direction of the beach. Leo is next to me, and he's still not saying anything. I find a good spot, sit down on the sand, and set my shoes down by my side.

"Hey," he says.

I don't look up at him, choosing to study his feet. Why is he always around during sad moments like this? Why can't he ever catch me in a moment of victory?

"Hi," I say to his feet.

"How about we play a game?" He settles in the sand next to me. I want to say no, but my curiosity gets the best of me.

"Okay." I look at him then, and he smiles wide, all dimples and honey skin.

"I want us to pretend for a second that I'm not Leo from Botanical Brothers and you're not Tessa from Plant Therapy. What would this moment be like?"

I want to fight him, tease him, turn this into a joke somehow. But instead, I play along.

"Okay, what happened?"

"I asked you to dance because I saw you and knew that I had to talk to you, and so we're here. I want to know all about you, so I ask."

"You're asking me? Are we starting?"

He nods.

"I'm . . ." I pause and start again. "I'm Terri." I shrug. Who the hell is Terri? Am I a mom from the Midwest?

His laugh is warm, almost sensual. "Okay, Terri. Tell me about yourself."

"I'm Terri, and I'm a . . . a writer. I'm a travel writer." I don't even know where that came from. Leo gives me a look like he wants me to continue. "I like to go on long swims and watch action movies and eat lots of pasta."

These are half-truths, or stories from another life, a different version of myself. I was never a travel writer, but I used to go on long swims. I haven't seen a movie in a long time, but when I did, I loved action movies. I realize again that I do have time now. Maybe I should see a movie.

"Your turn. Tell me about yourself."

"Okay . . . . I'm Josh. I'm a painter. I also like pasta and action movies."

"What a coincidence." I laugh. "So, you paint? Did you paint the mural on the front of your . . ." I was going to say "store," but that breaks the game.

"Yeah, I've done some murals around. It's nothing serious."

"You said you were a painter, though, so it must be a little serious. And that mural is really good, so you must be really good." He gets shy again. I had no idea he painted the store's mural. It's at this moment I realize there's not a lot I actually do know. "You're a painter. You were studying painting in New York, and you came back, but you still paint. Is that what you wanted to do? You said you felt like you needed to go home." I'm breaking character now because I want to know.

"Well, when I was gone, my dad got really sick, and it was hard for everyone. My brother got into some trouble. He was shoplifting and selling stolen phones. Things just went a little sideways when I wasn't around. I needed to be back to make sure nothing bad happened to anyone." His voice catches a little on some leftover emotion. "My dad ended up being okay. But I realized I shouldn't have left. It's not safe to leave, I have to be here. We have to stick together."

"Your family is here?" I ask, not able to stop myself from being nosy. This sense of Leo's that he needs to be here reminds me a little of my mom. She used to tell me when you leave, bad things happen, and it's always been something I've had to fight against.

"Yeah, but it doesn't matter. Everyone needs to be here. That's what family is." He looks out towards the water.

"Yeah, but what about you?" He shakes his head, and I wonder if he's scared to leave, afraid that if he does, something bad will happen. I know the feeling. I want to push a little more, to tell him he's allowed to do something else, but I don't know if we're close enough to even have that conversation.

"And what about your writing? You don't do it anymore? What did you want to do?"

I try to think of something fake I can use to fill in here to bring us back to the joke because it's getting too real, but all my mind can conjure is the truth. So I let myself talk about a time when I was someone else.

"I honestly didn't know. Writing sounds nice, but to be honest, I didn't know what I wanted. My mom was someone who was scared of everything, so she made me kind of terrified of everything, too. No job or idea was safe enough. If it was up to her, I'd just be . . . home, I guess? So it was just an idea when I left. I don't even know if that's what I wanted to do." I haven't said any of this out loud in such a long time that I feel exposed and raw, like I've revealed too much about myself.

"You seem like someone who would be good at anything you do," he says.

"As long as it's not talking about plants on video," I say, thinking about the single video I recorded talking about the differences between monsteras. I'm glad that video never saw the light of day.

"It's likely a good thing not being able to perform in front of the camera. Maybe it means you know who you are more than other people and can't pretend. But I also think you could do what we do."

"Talk about plants shirtless?"

"It would for sure get a lot of attention." He chuckles, and it sounds warm and low. "Yup, that's us. Just two strangers getting to know each other." Suddenly, something in his voice shifts from joking to a more serious tone. "Two strangers. Terri and Josh. And so we'd talk for a while, and we'd laugh, and we'd get along, and . . . and then I'd want to kiss you." He leans in close, and his eyes dart down to my lips.

"But it's too soon. We just met," I whisper back.

"It feels like longer," he counters. It's too much. The moon is so bright, and he looks lit up. "We can pretend for just a second, right?" he murmurs.

Maybe we can pretend, maybe something can feel good among all the awfulness.

I feel myself nodding, as if in a horny trance, my eyes fluttering closed when—

"You guys aren't gonna have sex, are you?"

A light flashes in our eyes, the second interruption of the night. The universe knows. It's Chris, my client who takes night shifts as coastal patrol when he's not at the fire station.

"Tessa?" He says my name with the same shocked tone as everyone else tonight.

Okay, I can take the hint. You need to get out more, Tessa.

"No." I scramble up off the sand and smooth out my clothes, brushing away the sand. "I mean, yes, it's me, but no, we're not."

"Hey . . . you okay?" Chris says, and I can tell he's about to launch into the sympathy speech—the one I really don't want to hear again. "The guys at the fire station told me. I wasn't there, but I'm so sorry. I have my plant you gave me, and it's doing great, no brown or yellow leaves." He shines the light directly in my face like I'm in trouble.

"I'm fine, Chris. That's great. We're going! We're going!" I grab my shoes, and Leo and I shuffle away in the sand, side by side.

"Would it make you feel better if I let you have sex out here? I won't tell anyone!"

"We're good!" Leo busts out laughing and then grows quiet again, and we walk in the sand in silence, side by side.

As we walk, he takes my hand and laces his fingers in mine. It's such a simple gesture, but it feels so nice to have him holding my hand. I don't fight it. We can pretend a little while longer. I expect him to say something, but he doesn't, and so neither do I as I slip my shoes on and then guide us back towards the bar. Besides the streetlights on the corners, the neighborhood is pretty dark. But with his hand in mine, the walk doesn't feel so ominous. It's like we are hiding away. It's quiet—so quiet you can hear the waves crashing behind us. The walk is longer this time, taking the full six minutes it usually does and maybe a little longer. We turn down a few side streets before heading to 2nd Street. Every few moments, his thumb runs along the side of mine, and I shiver a little at the contact. When the sign for Reno's is in view, I turn to him.

"Allison is in there. I should go talk to her." We're still awkwardly holding hands, both of us afraid to fully let go.

"Okay," he says. "This was fun, Terri."

I can't think of a less-sexy name, and I laugh at the sound of it.

"It was so fun, Josh."

He brings the back of my hand to his lips and actually kisses it, like we're characters in a Victorian novel. My lips part on contact. I feel like my knees are about to buckle. He turns my hand to the side and kisses the space between my thumb and forefinger while looking at me. It's one of the most erotic things I've ever seen.

"Okay," I say, releasing his hand. I turn and walk toward the bar, in a daze. As I reach the door, I look back, and he waves.

My time out of the tree has been eventful so far.

When I push open the door and make my way back into the bar, Bill is still playing. I eventually find Allison in the crowd. She gives me a hug.

"I'm sorry. I'm sorry. I'm sorry." She repeats into my hair, and I hold her tighter, apologizing back. I appreciate her not asking where I was, but I wonder if she already knows.

"Let's just have fun." I feel her nod into my hair as she pulls away, and we turn to the stage. I keep looking down at my hand.

chapter twenty

Allison: I'm sorry again for freaking out last night. I need to get my hormones checked or something.

Tessa: Don't worry about it. Are you sure you're okay?

Allison: Yes, just struggling to settle in. Want to come up for lunch soon?

Tessa: I can't this week. Dealing with Norma and shop stuff.

Allison: Oh, good luck. Love you.

Tessa: Love you too.

———

I meet with my landlord, Elliot, and Norma also invites herself as well. This surprises me because she usually lets me take care of the business stuff. But it's safe to say she doesn't trust me as much as she used to, and I try to avoid thinking about how much that stings.

We meet Elliot at Yard House, a bar on Pike Pier. It isn't exactly the best place for a meeting. It's got that sports-bar vibe—TVs playing the basketball game, rowdy customers drinking beer and cheering—but Elliot chose the location because he wants to watch the Lakers play, and this is the only time he has available.

We sit on the patio outside, which is pleasant. There's a nice ocean breeze, and since it's dusk, everything is bathed in pink and orange light. Elliot sits across from me, looking like a typical Wall Street guy with a suit and slicked back hair. He also wears sunglasses, so you never know exactly which direction he's looking.

It's not quite halftime yet, and so the three of us sit in silence while Elliot watches the game. I keep sneaking looks over at Norma, although she won't quite look at me. Partially because I'm pretty sure she's still mad, but also because she's smiling at her phone. I try to see the screen. Were those heart emojis? She catches me looking, and she quickly turns her phone off and clears her throat.

"So," Elliot says a few moments later. From behind me, I can hear what sounds like the beginnings of a Hyundai commercial, which means we momentarily have his attention. "It's pretty bad. They're still investigating to see if there was any foul play—which is insane, because who steals plants?—but mostly we're still waiting for that. The city is breathing down my neck about some repairs and stuff they found in the store." He scoffs as if we haven't been begging to get some of those repairs done for years now. "What do you guys want to do? Do you want to open back up again, or what?"

"Of course we're going to reopen," Norma says, not missing a beat. She says "we" like she's still active in managing the store, yet all I can picture is her playing golf and crocheting with her lovely view of the beach. "Plant Therapy is a neighborhood establishment.

We've been there for almost forty years. There's no way we're going to close now." She continues her rant, but Elliot is no longer paying attention since the game is back on. I look out at the marina, where a tiny boat sputters across the water, a tugboat surrounded by yachts.

"Well, I feel like I should sell it. It's going to cost too much to fix." He says this casually, as if he's not dropping a bomb on my life. Maybe it's a rich guy thing. "Oh, COME ON! This ref is a joke. Is he a Clippers fan or something?" A few nearby patrons, all similarly dressed, agree with his sentiment.

"No, don't sell. We'll reopen," I interject before something else in the game draws his attention and before Norma has a chance to say anything. I know it's the only option. If he sells the building, the new owners will likely either kick us all out or double or triple the rent.

"Do you have $40,000?" he asks, raising his eyebrows skeptically.

We don't. Of course we don't. Not yet, at least. But maybe when the renter's insurance comes in, which could take months. He stares at the two of us, and we are silent. I wonder if Norma has the money in her retirement fund to give, if she wants to. He shrugs and looks at the screen again.

"I can get it," I say, with no idea of how. Maybe if I rehab all the plants I saved and try to sell them, I could cobble something together, but I still owe a bunch of money to the store. It's a huge mess.

"We can get it," Norma says, totally confident. "Plant Therapy is —" She stops when her phone chimes. She looks at the screen and smiles. Did I just see an eggplant emoji of all things?

"Well, let's give it till the city is done with the investigation and everything. You get the money to help get it up to where it needs to be, you can stay open. If not, I'm gonna sell it. My dad has had that place for years now. I think it might be time to move on." He takes a long swig of his beer and shifts his seat a little so he can get a better view of the screen, ignoring us.

"Can we salvage anything?" Norma asks, finally turning to look at me. She doesn't sound hostile, so I decide to push my agenda.

"Who are you texting? I didn't even know you texted!" I say.

"Just a friend," she says, putting her phone in her pocket. "What about salvaging?"

"Maybe. I think I can start over on a few of the plants. Get some nodes in some prop boxes."

"Okay, let's try to sell them. You still have a spot at the Plant Expo. You should take it and sell as much as you can."

This is something I really don't want to do. The idea of facing the plant community is just so embarrassing. While everyone has been mostly nice, it feels like there's this dark cloud over every-thing. The Plant Expo used to be where Plant Therapy really shined. We had a huge booth that we'd decorate with Bill's antique furniture, and Allison would style the space herself. We'd sell a few thousands of dollars of plants on vibes alone. I don't know how much I can get for my little nubs now, but Norma's right. And it will be a start until the insurance money comes in.

I try not to think about the fact that even if we get the money, we still have to deal with the Botanical Brothers. The thought makes me exhausted, and I haven't even started yet.

In that moment, Norma puts her hand on my arm, a rare moment of warmth that I didn't expect, particularly considering how angry she's been.

"You can do it. I know you can," she says, her voice almost gentle.

I look over at the water and find the tiny boat. It's just adrift in the middle of the marina now, stuck there with no place to go.

"Yeah! Let's go!" Elliot screams. I'd forgotten he was even there.

The store smells different. It's like the smell of your clothes after you've been stuck in the rain—soggy and stale. I have candles and incense burning everywhere, hoping to dull the mildewy stench, but it's in my nose. It's been about six weeks since the accident, but it feels much longer. Although the investigation isn't over, I begged for them to let me in. They weren't making any progress anyways. This street is dead at night, and none of the cameras work. I suggest to them that maybe it was just an accident—a tragic one, but an accident. They say they're not done yet but I can go back inside and see what I can grab. That will allow me to start making a plan to get the money we need.

The space looks the way places do after a storm comes through. A lot of stuff is still there. My hanging plants escaped the storm and hang as a reminder of what the store used to be. The rest of the plants are piled up neatly in a corner and out of the way. I look over at my humidifiers to check and see if I can salvage them, but it looks like the water tanks busted, which likely happened during the accident or was maybe something the clean-up crew did to stop the water from going everywhere. My plant wall is a nightmare—all the plants are brown and drying out. I can smell the root rot in the air.

There's a knock on the door, and I'm relieved by the distraction.

"Come in," I say.

The door swings open, and my chest tightens up. The sound of the bell. It's been a while. My eyes feel tight and watery, but I swallow it down and put on a smile. A young couple comes in, all smiles. They look to be in their mid-twenties, alternative types.

"Hi, sorry, we aren't open right now," I say.

They ignore me, looking like they're taking in the space for a few moments. The guy takes out a measuring tape and then addresses me.

"Hi. This is the unit up for rent, right? We wanted to look. I'm thinking about taking down the walls and making it an alternative art collective space."

"It's not for rent. It's just under construction." I try my best to not sound too defensive as the guy begins measuring the walls and taking notes in his notebook.

"Really?" The guy continues what he's doing without looking at me. "Because the landlord said there was a unit up for rent. I figured with the construction, this was it."

The woman he's with takes out her phone and looks at the screen. "Oh, but you aren't Bill, are you? Sorry!" she says. "We just figured this was it since it's empty. But looks like it's the unit next door. We'll get out of your hair."

"I'm sorry?" My ears burn, and the dank smell from the space feels overwhelming. They ignore me and go about their business, leaving my store to walk next door.

Once they're gone, I make my way to the door, and the bell rings as I push it open and step out. I immediately notice boxes sitting outside of Bill's store and the for sale sign in the window. How had I missed this? I hurry next door and then look through the window. From behind the glass, I see Bill. He shakes hands with the couple and motions to the space, as if presenting it to them.

So it is true. His store is up for rent.

I finally make eye contact with Bill. He waves and smiles, but his smile quickly fades when he sees my face. He excuses himself from the couple and comes outside.

"Tessa," he says in that kind, fatherly voice that would work on the average person. But it's not going to work on me. I know him too well.

"You're leaving too?" I realize that I'm not actually breathing, so I take a long breath and cough. Too much.

"I've been trying to figure out the right time to tell you."

My cheeks are hot again.

"But why are you closing the store? Your business does fine! You can easily afford the rent with your clients." Bill provides lots of props for movies and has a bunch of high-end clients. He could go on as long as he wants.

"I just feel like with the rent increasing and the street changing, it's time for me to move on. There are other things I want to do. I've been here for decades." He sighs, as if he's tired. "I'm getting old, Tessa."

Heat rises in my throat and gets trapped there.

"I feel like there's more I could be doing with the last years of my life. It's been so long, and so when Allison told me she was leaving a while ago, I thought about what that would be like for me, too."

They must have been talking about this for a long time, I realize, and behind my back. The group chat.

"But . . . but . . . What about all the stuff?"

"I'll sell it. Live off the money."

"What will you do?" My voice cracks, and I feel like a teenager begging to go to an R-rated movie. I'm not even sure why I'm begging.

"The band is thinking of touring. A few of the guys also recently retired, but we could never actually do it because of the store."

He looks excited when he talks about his life without the store. I'm jealous. Here I am, considering whether to bleed my savings dry to save my store, and he's just perfectly fine leaving his, letting it become some type of art space. I still can't find my words.

Bill comes closer to me and puts his hands on my shoulders. The touch seems to release the valve I've kept on my tears, because they just start to flow. I've cried more in the last three months than I have in my whole life.

"I know that the only possibility you can imagine is this store and this life you built, and I know you created it for a reason, but . . ." He pulls me into a hug, and I let myself sob. "I promise there is more out there for you. There's more to life than just plants." I close my eyes and breathe in his scent, his classic cologne. "Just think about it."

But I can't think about it. I need to sell the plants, get the store together, and get my life back.

chapter twenty-one

PlantDaddy13: I hope you're doing okay. So much is happening and I kind of wish I could talk to you about it.

PlantDaddy54: You can tell me anything. I'm here. I'm sorry I didn't mean to ditch you.

PlantDaddy13: I'm sorry I freaked out on you. I just . . . I don't know. Things are crazy right now and I'm afraid that I'm going to keep losing things and I really don't want to lose you.

PlantDaddy54: Maybe we can just bring things back solidly in the friend category? That might make things easier. Friends?

PlantDaddy13: Yes, friends.

I'm standing at the crosswalk, and the light has switched to "walk now" several times, but I don't move. I just stand there, holding a large box in my arms, while people walk by.

I finally hype myself up to walk across the street alongside an old man in his wheelchair. He screams as he pushes himself across the street. I want to scream too.

The Long Beach Convention Center is gorgeous. There's a giant fountain display out front, and a bunch of people gather around it to take pictures, but I don't linger. Instead, I go straight to the big heavy doors and make my way inside. I'm running a little late, maybe because of my inability to make myself cross the street. But it's fine. I don't really have much to begin with.

Obviously, people aren't all just staring at me, but that's what it feels like. I hear the random whispers and catch people staring as I make my way through the presentation hall. I try to ignore it.

I'm here to sell as many of my plants as possible. I've been rehabbing them, and while I know I can't get full prices for any of them, they are still sellable and will be a good deal for this crowd. The $40,000 I need is pretty far away, but I really believe we can get there if I can sell these plants and combine that money with what's left of my savings.

My booth is pretty pathetic, but I do my best to make it as cute as possible. While Bill and Allison used to help me turn our little section (prime real estate when you walk in) into a mini-version of Plant Therapy, I don't have their help this year, and I don't have nearly enough plants anyways, especially since I'm not planning to buy more. My display is modest, but I try to present it well. My nodes are in neon boxes, and I set out some candles to add to the mood.

The worst part of the situation is that the Botanical Brothers display is right across from where I'm sitting. They've replicated the spirit of their store, decorating their oversized booth with LED lights and playing EDM. While I haven't seen Leo or Paul in person yet, I have the special honor of being face-to-face with cardboard cutouts of them holding a new potting mix that they apparently created. I look it up, and it actually sounds good, which makes me even madder. And as I sit in my booth, I often find myself getting lost as I stare at Leo's cutout, which showcases his signature Instagram smile and the dimple. I can't stay lost for too long, though, because I get a lot of visitors.

The conversation is always the same.

"Tessa." Anwar, the owner of one of the plant stores in downtown, says my name as if I'm already dead and he's reflecting on my life so far. He looks at my piles of cuttings, nodes, and baby plants with a sad expression. I get it. It is sad. I reduced many gorgeous plants to near rubble. It would make anyone sad.

Anwar is a large guy, so when brings me into a hug because my grief is likely showing, it feels like I'm going to cry again. Is this just what happens when you hug people? You want to cry? He pats my back a little and rubs some soothing circles along my shoulders, and I hiccup like a baby and then pull away.

"Thanks," I say, because I'm not really sure what else there is to say.

I shake it off, pulling some of the cuttings out of the box to present to them. I take a quick look around and see that a few people have stopped and are looking at me. I try to ignore them.

"This anthurium is already putting off some fresh growth, so under the tents, it will do fine, and this strawberry shake node cutting has already rooted."

"Thanks, Tessa. We'll get these set up." Anwar pauses for a moment and makes eye contact with me. "Is there anything we can do about . . . everything?"

Do they want to loan me $30,000? Do they have any ideas on how to revitalize my side of the street? The list is long.

"No, that's okay."

Linda, another plant seller, stops by my booth, and when she eyes me and my pile of plants, I feel a strong desire to run away.

"Tessa, hi," she greets. "Are you okay? I heard about . . . everything. I'll take a few of those nodes. It's just all so sad, and I'm glad you had the strength to show up in this space after that happened. It's brave."

I wince at the word "brave." I'm not brave, I'm just trying to survive.

"Thanks, Linda," I say, bagging up some nodes to give to her.

As I struggle to find something else to say, a small group is forming, all listening intently. All well-meaning. The community is surrounding me to help, and I'm trying to reach for gratitude, but I just feel smothered and overwhelmed. I just want things to be normal. I look around the semicircle.

"I'm fine," I lie. "Really." My voice squeaks at the end just to make sure people know I'm in fact not fine. "I'm fine." This time, there's a bit more balance in my delivery.

"Will the store be shutting down forever? We're going to miss Plant Therapy so much."

I'm not even sure who said that. The surrounding group is getting a little bigger. I feel on display, like a spectacle.

"I honestly don't know yet. Right now, it's just about getting the repairs done, and then I'll figure out what happens next," I say to the group.

"What about Avery's plants? Are they all destroyed? Must be close to $30,000 in plants." Another comment from the crowd. Is this a press conference? It feels that way.

"Um . . ." I feel like I'm sweating now, and my hands grip the edge of my dress.

"Just let us know if we can do anything, Tessa. Is Norma all right?"

Have the lights in here always been this bright? They feel brighter now, stinging my eyes.

I look around, and everyone stares at me with a mixture of disappointment, sympathy, and curiosity. It's hitting me now, at this moment, how the store closing isn't really about me. The store is a part of an ecosystem; it means something, and I'm the one responsible for it not being around anymore. Just like I'm responsible for bringing it back.

I start to speak, but I'm interrupted by the unmistakable notes of "Baby Got Back" starting to play. Everyone turns in the direction of the sound, and I take a deep breath, feeling some space open up. The group that surrounds me slowly disperses and moves toward the music. I hear a voice I'd know anywhere. It's

Paul. I guess they're finally here now. I was wondering when they'd arrive.

I turn toward their booth to see Paul standing on a table yelling about fertilizer, "Baby Got Back" still playing in the background. Botanical Brothers workers dance around him. Is that really necessary? Do they have to dance too?

Of course they're here. It's a nice bow on the situation, the perfect narrative representation of my failure. I want to feel upset about it, but right now I feel relieved that the attention is no longer on me, if only for a little while.

I put my hand over my heart, taking a deep breath.

"Hey, do you want to get some air?" Leo whispers from behind me. He's so close I can feel his breath on my ear. I turn to him and see that he's wearing a Botanical Brothers hat and shirt. Not exactly stealthy. I glance around at the group of people who are now distracted by Paul as he strips off his shirt and twerks with a bag of fertilizer. I do need some air.

"Yeah, that would be great."

I follow Leo out the back door and instantly exhale. It feels better, but I still have this sense that I'm up for display, that I'm being watched.

"Come on," he says, his hand on my wrist. His fingers are just as soft as they've always been. He only leaves them there for a moment to direct me towards the parking lot. He's parked across the street in the parking garage near the movie theater. We say nothing and just walk. As we get farther away, I find my breath again.

———

"I figured you'd want to get away from the crowds," Leo says.

I nod, and he unlocks the truck. It's the same truck he had at the nursery, and I think back to the alocasia velvet he gave me that day.

I open the door and jump inside, settling into the passenger seat. I lean back against the headrest and take a few deep breaths. My heart is finally not beating out of my chest anymore.

"Thanks."

"Of course. Are you okay? I was walking by, and I saw that crowd around you."

It's in this moment my feelings come back and he's no longer my savior but part of the reason I'm here to begin with.

"I think I should go? Thanks for saving me."

I reach for the door, but I hear a bunch of people making their way into the parking lot. It's around lunchtime. The idea of facing another crowd of people disturbs me more than being here, and I lie back against the seat.

"Let's go to the roof." He turns the truck on and backs out of the parking spot. Then he drives upwards, level after level, until we reach the top. It's mostly empty at the top of the garage beyond a few really expensive cars belonging to people who don't want to get hit. We're near the marina, so there's a really nice view of the shops along the pier and the boats out on the water. The two of us sit in silence for a few moments. My eyes follow an ant walking across the glass. Leo's hands tap on the steering wheel. I think about when we held hands and when he kissed my hand.

"People need to mind their own business," he says out of nowhere.

He sounds genuinely upset, and again I want to laugh, but also like why am I here? He approaches my current business situation as if he has nothing to do with it. But he does.

"Are you serious?"

"Serious about what?"

I bang my head back against the headrest in frustration.

"You don't mind your business. Why did you come save me? Why do you talk to me? Why do you act like you want to be nice to me? Why did you . . ."

I have a lot more questions I want to ask. Why did you kiss me? Why did you touch me? But I stop myself.

He shakes his head and looks out the window.

"Because." He says it in that infuriating way like he did at the club. A simple word that's meant to say everything but says nothing at all. "You looked like you needed a break."

I roll my eyes.

"Shouldn't you be working at the display or something? Playing 'Get Low'?"

He hums and shifts in his seat like he's trying to get comfortable. His left hand creates a beat on the steering wheel. I want to reach for his hand and tell him to stop.

"No, my brother has it. That . . . All that is more his thing."

"Dancing shirtless on tables, you mean?"

He rubs the back of his neck, and his eyes go a little wide. Leo just doesn't seem like the guy who gets on tables or goes shirtless at all, so it's always weird when I remember that's who he is. I think about him outside of the store, posing with his fans. His sly smile.

He clears his throat, and I realize I'm staring.

"I didn't realize that starting a store would require so much nudity."

I can't help it. I laugh, and it feels good. It's been a while since I let myself really laugh.

"Your smile is incredible."

I expect the other shoe to drop or him to finish the joke, but it never comes. We're staring at each other, and then my eyes return to the windshield. The ant has disappeared, off on whatever adventure it was on.

"What are you, even?" I ask.

"That's a big question. Very existential."

He's smiling in that specific way, the one you don't see on Instagram. Maybe this is what he does. He smiles in a way that makes you feel like it's just for you. I want to tell him he has the best smile. I shake it off and focus back on what I wanted to say.

"You put my shop out of business, but here I am in your truck."

He chews on his bottom lip a little, and he looks younger, cuter than usual. He's rubbing the leather of the steering wheel again, and then he turns to me.

"Is that what you're gonna do? Close it? It's closed for good? I didn't know you decided."

"I need a lot of money to keep it open, and I don't know if we'll get it. I also don't know if it'll even matter with your store still there. I can't do anything if Botanical Brothers is around."

Leo looks a little grossed out by the name of his own store. Sometimes I wonder if he even wants to be there.

"It's that obvious, huh?"

I didn't realize that I'd actually said it aloud.

"It's not that. It's just like I said, not what I thought. I can't say it's what I wanted to be . . . all of this."

"What did you want to be?" I shift in my seat so I'm turned towards him a little, and he shifts in his seat to match me. We're face-to-face again. "A painter?"

"You remember that, Terri?" He actually winks, the bastard. Bringing up our late night on the beach. "Maybe painting. I mean, I was a designer. I wanted to—or I want to—make graphic posters. I keep meaning to make some new ones and sell them at the store, but I just haven't had time, and also it feels like there's so much more pressure now."

"Why?"

"Because it's not just me making things anymore. I'm making things for this huge audience, and I don't really want to have all those eyes on me in that way. It's one thing for people to look at me but another . . ."

"For them to actually see your work. I get it." I interrupt him without realizing it, and I've also scooted in closer to listen to him. I pull back a little, settling into my seat. "Sorry."

My heart's beating fast, and I take a few long breaths and shut my eyes. When I peek at him, his eyes are closed, too.

"What happened ten years ago?" he asks.

I don't know if I've actually told the story before, not out loud at least. It's not something I want to remember. The article shared a little about that time but not everything.

"It's okay if you don't want to tell me."

When I open my eyes, he's staring at me.

"I googled you. A long time ago. When we first met. I just felt like I needed to know more about you. I . . . I read your blog."

I didn't even know the blog was still up; it's been so long. I can still see the page in my head. The message I left, my very last one: *"I can't wait to update you all on my trip!"* Then the RV broke down, and I never wrote another post.

I close my eyes and take a deep breath. Then I start telling him my story.

"My mom is obsessed with us being safe. It's all she's ever talked about, especially when my dad divorced her to travel around the world with a new woman every month. At one point when he was gone, he got in this terrible accident, destroyed his leg, and my mom was like, 'See, that's why you don't go do things. That's what you get when you go do stuff.' But, like, that's my dad, and so I wanted to be more like him. So it just made me want to leave more, and that made my mom hold on to me even tighter, like she didn't want me to do anything. I felt so suffocated. So I was like, okay, I'm gonna go. I'm gonna buy an RV and travel around and write, and I'm gonna go on adventures and find myself and show her that it's fine, you can go. To prove myself even more, I talked about it for months on social media, and I had that blog, and I hyped it up so much because I needed the support. Everyone was like, 'Go girl, go!' Except my mom. She did everything she could to get me to stay, so I felt like I needed the help and to prove to her I could do it, maybe? So I spent like two years planning for the trip. I did all sorts of jobs and did tons of research. I saved up for the RV and saved some money for the road. But then as soon as I started, things went wrong. I got robbed. The RV was constantly breaking down, and the money I saved for a year only lasted a few weeks. It was a mess. I broke my arm, which was weirdly ironic. And so, the last time my RV broke down, I decided not to fix it and to give up and disappear. I didn't want to go home, because I couldn't stand the idea of facing my mom again and proving her right, but I also didn't want to put myself out there because she *was* right. So that's how I ended up here and never left. The store was my safe space."

I venture to look at him, and he's watching me and listening to me in that way he does, like he's devouring everything I say.

"It's crazy. I thought that the store would protect me from this type of thing. I figured being offline and . . ."

Oh shit, I think I'm gonna cry. There it is. The quiet part I've been thinking. I've finally said it out loud. I thought I was safe from public embarrassment, from getting hurt. And now I'm gonna cry, sitting here in the truck of the guy who's putting me out of business.

"Tessa."

The way he says my voice is so caring. So sweet. So tender. It makes me want to cry more, and so I do. I cry. I cry about everything. I cry about the store. I cry about my RV. I cry about my life, the one that I've worked so hard to build, falling apart. Leo reaches out and rests his hand on my back, right below my neck. His touch is hesitant at first, but then it becomes surer and he's tracing soothing circles on my back.

The truck is silent except for the sound of my pathetic cries and the street noise. I sniffle loudly. "Why do I keep crying in front of you?"

"That's okay. I have something. Let me look." He tears open the middle console and looks through it almost frantically. He grabs a pile of Taco Bell napkins and holds them up for me.

I laugh because it's cute and he's cute, and I take the napkins and wipe the tears off my face. I actually feel better somehow, like the sobs needed to get out of my system.

"I'm so sorry, Tessa. I just want you to know that I really respect what you did with the store. I can tell you really love it and love the store and people love you, too. I'm sorry our naked chests are so distracting, and I'm sorry we picked your street and not another street, and . . ." He's rambling, and again, it's cute. He's so cute.

"You are so cute," I say between loud sniffles. His ears go red.

"Cute is not often how I'm described."

"Well, you are." I take a deep breath to steady myself. "God, what am I gonna do, Leo? I shouldn't even be asking you this."

"I really think you can do anything you want. And I don't know, maybe I can help somehow? We can think of something."

"Like before on the beach or at your store?"

And like before, I have my sort of reverse premonition and find myself standing in the middle of his store, his lips on my neck.

His gaze changes, darkens, and my throat feels tight.

"I'll help you however you need. I wish I could do more." His hand reaches for my cheek, his touch light. His thumb brushes along my cheek for a moment before grazing across my lips. "I don't want to fight with you."

I nod, and his hand moves to the back of my neck. I relax into his touch. I don't know if it's my mouth or my body that hums.

He nods too and then leans in, and I somehow meet him half-way. He searches my eyes, and I nod again, and then we're kissing. It's been so long it's shocking at first. You'd think our thing at the shop would have been more intense, but this just feels like . . . more. The kiss is simple, just lips pressed against lips. His lips are soft, like they were before. Eventually, our tongues find each other, and he groans, pulling me closer to him. It's decadent and wet, and I feel it all over, and I'm wondering why I stopped kissing along with everything else. Maybe I should have kept this part. I pull away a little, and he leans in, trying to connect our lips once more.

"You're not a bad kisser," I whisper, breathless.

"You either." He kisses me again.

It's slow, but it heats gradually, and we can't get close enough. I'm chasing the feeling of something else, escaping to a headspace where I'm not fighting so hard, where I just get to feel good. Leo isn't where I should go for that, but my body doesn't seem to agree. I wrap my arms around his neck, and his slip around my waist. He tugs at me a little, whimpering against my lips. What do you want, Leo? I'm not sure either of us knows. But in the next moment, he pulls away from me long enough to adjust his seat, leaning it back to give us room. Then his large hands move to my waist, and he draws me over onto his lap. I whimper and bite his bottom lip at the feel of him, heavy between my legs, directly against my core. I hiss into his mouth, and he answers with a bite to my lower lip and a flex of his hips.

"Can I touch you?" He pulls away to whisper into my ear and then bites my earlobe. "Please?"

I don't hear it as much as I feel his please between my legs, an intense throbbing that radiates down to my toes. I moan a "yes," and he kisses down my neck and then down my throat, gripping my hips. I pull him back to my mouth, and he tilts his head to kiss me deeper, his hands trailing up my thighs underneath my skirt. His touch is light, just the whisper of his fingertips. He traces the path of my tattoo, just like I showed him that night in his store. He kisses me slowly now, giving me just enough but not enough. He's teasing me.

"So slow." I sigh into his touch, my hips grinding down so I can feel more of him.

"I'm enjoying you, but you're right." His voice is tight, and he grips my ass and squeezes to control my movements. "It's not about me."

His lips travel down my body, and he bites at my left nipple through my dress and then soothes with a gentle suck before moving to the other side. I make a silent agreement with myself to stay present, to be here with him now and to feel it all. Every touch pulls me deeper into this universe where it's just me and him and nothing else exists. I close my eyes and just feel him.

"You look so good like this." He kisses the middle of my chest and pulls back a little. "Can you look at me?"

I open my eyes and meet his as he reaches between my legs and massages through my panties. I feel a little jolt, and I lift my hips to make it easier for him.

"Yeah? This good? Can I keep going?" he whispers into my lips.

"Yeah." I rest my forehead against his and breathe, trying to regain some type of control. I feel him tug my panties to the side a little, and the movement itself is enough sensation to elicit a noise from deep in my throat. I think he's going to touch me right where I need him most, but he doesn't, and I groan, overwhelmed. I lower my straps of my dress and grab my breasts in my hands, squeezing my nipples to get some relief.

"Let me see," he breathes. I pull down the straps of my bra and then push down the cups. My breasts fall out of my dress, and it's an instant relief. He leans forward and bites my nipple again, and in the same moment, he massages my clit and presses into me hard. "So wet."

I moan something that's like his name. I feel desperate and overwhelmed, so I bring his face up to me for another messy kiss. It's not much of a kiss, just a breath and some barely there kisses. Mostly it's just us talking complete nonsense to each other. Am I speaking elvish? I'm not sure.

He chuckles a little and repositions his hand so his thumb rubs my clit. Then he plunges two fingers snugly inside me and thrusts into me slowly. It's a tight fit—it's been a while—but it feels so good.

"You okay? You're so tight."

I shift my hips, riding his fingers as the pressure builds.

"Yes yes yes it's good." I think I threw some Spanish in there too.

"You're gonna come now, I can feel it." He's right. It's right there, the pressure is building, and my heart beats fast in my chest. I grip his shoulders in an attempt to slow the intensity down, but it's not happening. He takes a nipple into his mouth and sucks. When he bites me lightly, it shoots straight through me, and I come apart in his arms. I come so hard it jolts me forward almost violently. I'm shaking, and he wraps his arms around me in a tight hug, whispering encouragement in my ear. *"You're so hot. Thank you for letting me do that, I've been dying to see it. You're so beautiful when you come."*

He holds me for a while, and I let him. Partially because it feels good but also because I'm afraid what happens after, what this will have changed.

"I . . ." I pull back to look at him, ready to break the spell, but he stops me with a finger to my lips, just a light brush.

"How about this?" He leans in and kisses my chest, letting the kiss linger. "We can pretend to not be us."

"Terri and Josh?" I ask, and he stares at me and looks momentarily distracted by something on my face. "What?"

"God, your mouth." He closes the distance between us again and sucks on my lower lip, pulling it with a teasing bite.

"Focus." I laugh.

"Yeah, we can be Terri and Josh."

I'm suddenly aware of my surroundings—that I'm on his lap in his truck on the roof of the Pike parking lot with my breasts out and my panties wet. I pull my bra back up, awkwardly putting my boobs back in the cups. He helps me adjust myself.

"Terri and Josh are pretty bold," I say, and he chuckles, low and deep. It feels like a rumble in my body.

"Text me when you want to forget about everything." Another kiss. "When you want to forget I'm here."

"You some type of sexual mental health professional?"

"I'll be yours. Only yours."

I try to laugh it off, but his words land heavy for me so I shift.

"This is a really elaborate way to get my phone number," I say as he kisses my neck, flexing his hips against me again, clearly still hard. "I owe you one." My mouth goes dry at the thought of making him feel good, imagining his eyes closed in pleasure, the sounds he'd make.

"You don't owe me anything." He smooths my loose hair back away from my face. "Okay?"

"I want to owe you." I crawl off him, landing with a thump in the passenger seat and fixing my bra and dress. He grumbles in protest, reaching for me. I dodge his grasp and then pull my phone out of my pocket. He says his number out loud, and I save it in my phone. Then we both stare at each other for a moment before I reach for the door handle. "We need to go back. I'll go first."

At his nod, I push open the door and climb out of the truck. I shut the door and look at my reflection in the mirror. I look thoroughly fucked, but man do I look happy.

"Hey," he says before I turned around. Our eyes meet, and the sincerity in them sends another jolt through me. "I hope you get to keep your store."

"Me too."

chapter twenty-two

Tessa: Hey, it's Tessa.

Leo: Is it time? I'm ready to report for duty.

Tessa: Are you talking about sex?

Leo: I'm ready to be of service! I'm at work right now but I don't need my job.

Tessa: Haha, no. I'm talking to the insurance guy today but if it goes badly, maybe after. I just wanted to message you my number.

Leo: I hope it doesn't go badly but I also do? I'm confused.

Tessa: What do you want to happen?

Leo: I want our stores to exist alongside each other with no issues. I want to see you again. I want for them to produce more of that sexy hoya variety everyone was talking about yesterday so I can get one.

Tessa: They won't. Why charge hundreds of dollars when you can charge thousands?

Leo: It would be such a good entry level wish list plant for our clients though.

Tessa: I agree. It's hearty and grows pretty well. It's just impossible to propagate.

Leo: Is it impossible to propagate or are they just saying that because they don't want us to try it? Nothing is impossible to propagate.

Tessa: Only one way to find out.

Leo: Okay, I'll see if I can get one. Do you want one?

Tessa: . . . . . .

Leo: Okay, I'll get one and then I'll try to propagate it and let you know.

———

I wear a suit for the insurance guy. My goal is to look professional since I'm meeting him on my own. Norma canceled at the last minute because she was "busy." I'm not sure what she meant by that considering she's retired, but I wonder if it has something to do with the heart emojis on her phone. At least someone is getting to relax during all of this.

The insurance guy, a bald man in his fifties, finally arrives about twenty minutes late to our meeting, and of course, he's wearing just a normal collared shirt and slacks, making me feel a little dumb for being overdressed. He says his name is Frank.

I manage to find a couple of chairs in the back of the store, and he settles into one of them with a big sigh, which feels like a bad sign. Not that I need a bad sign to know things aren't good. The store seems even sadder than it was before. Maybe that's because the block is almost totally empty now since Bill has moved the majority of his stuff and Allison has been gone for a while. I hold my breath and wait for Frank to speak.

"So . . ." he says, looking around. "I have good news, and I have bad news."

"Okay, bad news first." I can't stop my foot from bouncing up and down, and he watches it for a moment before continuing.

"The damage to the building is coverable by your insurance." That I expected. I'm not dumb enough to think that's just it, but maybe it's enough money to also do the repairs. "But the building itself is just not up to code and will need significant work in order to make it livable. The necessary repairs are very expensive. There's stuff we found that we can't ignore. The landlord really neglected that building."

"Yeah, like $30,000? The insurance money will cover that, right?"

"Not even close to it. Your accident revealed the foundational problems with the building, more problems than your landlord is willing to pay for. It's like hundreds of thousands of dollars."

"You talked to him?" I ask.

"Yes, he can't really rent any of these units. Or he shouldn't! There's mold and a million other issues here. It makes sense he would want to sell the building. The neighborhood is going through a bit of a revitalization, and he can get decent money off of it. Plus, you're the last tenant; the rest of the building will be empty soon." I think about Elliot. I'm sure he'll get courtside Lakers seats for the season with the money. "The good news is your insurance money settlement is pretty significant." His face brightens. "Enough to start over. Around $90,000 altogether."

Wow. Not a number I was expecting.

"Just the insurance? That's more money than I thought."

"Yes, you have rental insurance, and your co-owner put out an additional insurance plan on your rare and exotic plants, and while the plants from the accident weren't insured, the plants on that wall counted to your totals. Not to mention the vintage furniture and some of the other items throughout the store.

"The insurance company also suspects that there was some foul play with regard to the origins of the accident as well, and they still think so."

"Does that even matter?"

"While the investigation is open, you can't get the total amount. You can get like one-fifth of it now and then the rest once they've finished their investigation."

"Okay."

"I imagine you can start over," he suggests. "Maybe find a new location and start fresh or do something else."

"So, no matter what, Plant Therapy in this location will no longer exist," I say, looking around at the cleared-out space. I'd stripped the plant wall earlier in the week, and now there's nothing left but tiny piles of dirt.

Seeing it like this—the store so empty—and saying the words out loud make it feel that much more final. That much more official. There will be no more Plant Therapy on 4th Street.

I thought I would be sad, but instead I feel a sense of relief, like I can rest . . . even if just for a little bit. I don't need to keep fighting for this physical space. I lean forward and put my hands on my head and take a few calming breaths.

"You're practically moved out of this location already," Frank says. "But you'll likely get a call soon about officially ending your lease or wanting to stay and wait for the repairs to happen."

I look around the store, and I'm silent for a few moments. He follows my lead.

"Do you have any questions?" he asks, standing up.

I shake my head no, pulling myself out of my daze.

"Good luck, Tessa." He heads to the door.

"Wait!" I stop him on the way out, and he pauses and turns to me. "What do people usually do in situations like this?"

"It depends. In my experience, a lot of people see it as a sign that it's time to move on. But if it's their passion, they try to figure it out. Which one are you?"

"Plants are my life."

I say the thing I've been saying this whole time, but it doesn't feel as true coming out of my mouth this time.

"Well, then you know what to do. Time to move Plant Therapy somewhere else."

The door opens to the familiar ding of the bell and then closes behind him. I look around, and I'm again overwhelmed by how empty it feels. I call Norma right away. I kind of want it to go to voicemail, but this isn't a voicemail conversation. It rings a few times before she answers. It's loud in the background.

"Hello?" The word comes out like she's mid-laugh, which is strange. I don't know the last time I heard her actually laugh. "Go away! I'm on the phone." Did she just giggle?

"Are you giggling? Who are you giggling at?"

"Yes, Tessa. What is it?" Her tone goes back to normal. Mildly irritated.

"So the store is basically condemned. It's going to cost a fortune to fix it, so the landlord is going to sell."

"So we should buy it," she says, and I deflate. Buy it with what money? Is that another mountain I have to climb? "Plant Therapy has been there for—"

"Yes, I know, forty years. It's not a little bit of money. Even with the money we get from the insurance, we'd still have to fix up the building and put down a down payment."

"There has to be a way." It's easy for Norma to say all this from her retirement home where she's still giggling for some unidentified reason. Even if I were to open the store back up, that wouldn't change the fact that Botanical Brothers is still right down the street.

"Where would we get the money?" She doesn't answer for a

moment. There's laughing in the background, and I wonder if she can even hear me. "Norma!"

"You think you can find another location that will work?"

I actually don't know if I can, but it's worth a try. Maybe we can go to a new neighborhood and start over. That thought also makes me exhausted, but it might be the fastest way for things to go back to normal.

"I'll find something."

More laughter. More giggling on the other end. Is she at some type of happy hour or something? Isn't it like eleven thirty in the morning?

"Okay, keep me updated. Remember, Plant Therapy is important. We need to reopen, and then we can put this all behind us." Someone calls Norma's name in the background, and then there's a whole chorus of people calling her. "I gotta go." The call ends.

I stare at my phone for a minute, wondering what just happened. Then I look up and let my gaze drift around the store, frowning. The space is perfect. Great light. Nice size. How will I find something else that will compare?

———

"Maybe this will be the one," Allison suggests in a much-too-cheery voice. "What do you think?"

Allison and I are touring a few buildings downtown that could be the new Plant Therapy location. The insurance money gives us a pretty good budget, plus some extra for interior design and purchasing inventory. I know I should be happy, but nowhere we've visited feels right. The building we're currently looking at is a former loft. It has huge windows and views of downtown. It's a cool place, like something out of a magazine. It's not Plant Therapy, though. The super-high ceilings are a little too high, and it doesn't feel cozy at all. It's too industrial.

"Tessa? You're zoning out again. What do you think of this place?"

"Too much light."

That's bullshit of course. How do you say the vibes are off without sounding out of your mind?

Allison rolls her eyes. "Do you even want to do this?" she mutters under her breath, but I still hear it.

"What do you mean?"

"I mean"—she adjusts her top and is fanning herself as if she's hot—"we've been looking all day, and nothing seems to be making you excited or anything. You've been fighting for it, but it feels like this is more of a burden than anything else. You seem sad."

"I'm not sad, I'm just thinking." She isn't wrong. I do feel sad and tired. The store has always been my thing, but I'm starting to wonder if all this is worth getting it back. I'm starting to wonder if there's something else I could do.

"Maybe you've changed. You can always take that money and do something else with it."

"Yeah, right." I already feel guilty enough about the fact that Plant Therapy has to move locations because of me. I can't just take the money.

"I'm serious! You don't have to run Plant Therapy."

I don't have to run Plant Therapy.

I think about Bill and how happy he was to leave his store, how excited he was for the future and the unknown. I think about Adeline and Avery and even Norma.

"You don't have to decide, but maybe just think about it," Allison says. "You've had a bunch of distractions with Plant Daddy and Leo. Maybe it's time to focus on you. You and Leo are done doing whatever it was you guys were doing, right?"

I feel a zap between my legs just at the mention of his name, like some type of dick premonition. I'm definitely not going to tell her about Leo and our little arrangement, because I don't need another lecture about it. It's under control, and he's not distracting me.

"Yeah, of course," I say. "I'm focused on this."

"Good, because I don't really trust those guys, and you shouldn't either."

"No, you're right." My phone feels heavy in my pocket, and I'm wondering if it's time to be someone else for a while.

chapter twenty-three

Tessa: What are you doing?

Leo: Why? Do you want to hang out?

Tessa: Yeah, you want to come over?

Leo: Are you propositioning me? I feel so cheap.

Tessa: Oh shit, I'm sorry.

Leo: I'm kidding. I'm a happy whore, but I can't. I'm busy.

Tessa: Oh, okay.

Leo: You can be busy with me.

Tessa: Uh ok. What are we doing?

———

I haven't been to the Long Beach Aquarium in years. It's that place you take all of your relatives when they first visit but then never go back. Leo told me to meet him at 10:00 a.m., so it's still quiet. The restaurants are still closed, and most of the activity is from families with young children and school groups on field trips.

I wasn't sure what to wear for the occasion. Is this a date? A dick appointment? Do I dress normally? I landed on wearing a tank top and jeans.

When I arrive, I see Leo standing at the entrance with two kids —a boy running circles around him and a girl clinging to his leg. They both look to be about four years old, and the girl looks adorable in all pink with her hair in ponytails. Leo's laughing, but his smile is tight, like he's at the end of his rope. I wave at him, and he waves back as he starts towards me with big, wide steps because the young girl is hanging on his leg like a spider monkey. He didn't say anything about kids.

"Hey. You look nice," he says, giving me a quick once over.

"You too." He does. He always does, even when he's dressed in a simple T-shirt and jeans, like today. His jeans always fit him so perfectly, snug on his hips, and when he moves, you can see his happy trail. Focus, Tessa. There are children around.

I'm interrupted by the boy, who pokes me in the leg with his plastic fish and giggles.

"Oh, hello," I say, looking down.

"These are Andrew and Hannah. They're my nephew and niece. Paul's kids. They're twins. He has them this week, and I'm helping out." The idea of Paul having children is a little scary, but they don't have horns. "Andrew and Hannah, this is my friend Tessa."

"Your girlllllllfriend?" Hannah says, still stuck on Leo's leg. I don't love how I smile a little at the statement, and I try to go back to a look that's more neutral.

"She's a girl who is my friend." He manages to untangle her from his leg and then picks her up.

I'm not someone who wants kids, but even I'm not immune to

the view of Leo holding a child in his arms, those biceps flexing. She also looks so happy, snuggling in his arms.

Andrew, who's still next to me, reaches up to grab my hand, and I hold it as my eyes meet Leo's. He smiles at me.

"Okay, let's go inside!" Leo shouts to a chorus of "yayyys!" from the kids. I can't help it and join in with a "yay!" of my own.

The lobby of the aquarium is a large atrium with a huge replica of a whale hanging from the center rafters. On the far edge of the space, there's a giant tank that stretches from the floor to the ceiling. It's one of my favorite things in the aquarium. Leo puts down Hannah, and Andrew releases my hand. Together, they run to the tank and press their faces against the glass.

I stand there and stare at the blue abyss, watching as giant trout swim peacefully by. I feel a hand on my lower back, warm and solid.

"Hi," he whispers to me, and we turn to look at each other.

"Hi." I know I'm smiling like an idiot, but I can't help it. I'm happy. For the first time in a while. I decide at that moment to put away everything else and just be present, like in those moments between us in his truck.

"When you said you were busy, I thought you were talking about something else," I whisper.

"Yeah, that stuff is fun, but is it more fun than walking around the aquarium and watching children scream?"

"You're right. You're right. They're so cute. They look like you."

"The Ahns have strong genes," he says. The kids run off in the direction of another section of tanks, a darker room with walls full of aquariums, and we follow them, his hand still on my lower back.

When we catch up with the kids, he releases me and bends down to be at eye level with the two of them as he points out the prickly fish and eels swimming by.

"Ewwww!" Hannah screams. "I love it!" She erupts in a fit of giggles and runs to the next tank. Leo stands up and follows along, and in the darkness, he brushes his hand against mine. It's barely a touch, but I still feel it.

"SHARKS!" Andrew yells, skipping all of the smaller displays and launching into a full run to the outdoor area. We all take off after him, calling his name. He's fast, and I haven't run in a long time, so I'm gasping for air before we catch up to him. Hannah giggles again as she races beside me.

The twins love the touch tank with the sharks. It's a lagoon with nurse sharks, which mostly sleep along the bottom of the pool in corners. They don't do much, but the two children are enraptured. They give me and Leo a bit of a break from chasing them around as they stand at the edge of the tank and reach into the water, trying to touch the sharks that happen to swim by.

"So, it's your brother Paul and who else? Do you have any other siblings?" I ask.

"No, just the two of us." I think about Plant Daddy briefly. He has just one sibling too. I wonder what he's doing right now.

"And you're the oldest?" I ask.

"Yeah. That's me. How'd you know?"

How do I say that the super-protective way Leo talks about Paul makes it so clear that Leo feels like he's in charge and a bunch of other things?

"Just a hunch." He keeps his eyes on the twins, looking a bit nervous. I reach out and touch his arm, and his shoulders relax. He puts his hand over mine on his shoulder. I love touching him. It's one of my new favorite hobbies.

"What about you?"

"Just me and my sister too. I'm the youngest, and I feel like my sister doesn't really need me much. She's in school to be a veterinarian and is one of the most pulled-together people ever," I say, thinking about my sister. We don't have a dynamic that's anything like Paul and Leo's. She's always been so busy that she's never had the time to take care of me and she's never needed me. We're more like friends who talk every few months, picking up like nothing has changed. I guess that's not the typical sister dynamic. Although when I do need her, she's always there to have my back, and she's always defending me when my mom freaks out about me leaving and assumes I'm going to fail or I'm never coming back.

"Yeah, Paul . . . He's always had a lot of problems with authority and everything else, especially when my dad eventually died. He's always up to something, and people just don't get him, but I believe he's a good person. That's my brother, and even when I don't agree with him, I have to be there for him." I'm not sure I believe that, but the fondness in his eyes makes me wish I did. He turns to me, knowing what I'm thinking. "I know he's kind of intense, but he's trying, and he's got a lot on his plate. He wants to see his kids more, so he's trying to show he has it all together. His ex lives in Sacramento with them. They don't have a great relationship because of some stuff he's done."

"Like what?" I ask.

"Dumb stuff. Stealing cars. Gambling stuff. He's never been good at keeping jobs, so Botanical Brothers is a great outlet for him. He's always been a charismatic guy, so he's able to use that, and since he's the public face of the business, he's careful to not make any bad decisions. Plus, he has the kids now. He needs to stay focused, we both do. We do it for them." He pauses for a moment and looks over at the kids, who giggle as they reach into the shark tank again. "Andrew has an autoimmune disease, and the medication costs thousands of dollars a month."

It makes more sense now, why everything about this situation so complicated. We both have so much to lose . . . . My shop is my life, but Botanical Brothers is their life, too . . . in their own way. I remember what Leo said about having to pay his mom's mortgage and support his family, and then I follow his gaze over to the twins —little Leos and Pauls.

"He's charismatic," I say, trying to edge off my sarcasm, but it's still there.

"I know, but maybe you guys will get along someday." I shrug, doubtful. I can't even believe I'm getting along with Leo now. "I'm glad we have Botanical Brothers."

We're quiet for a moment, and it's like he's trying to tee up for what he says next.

"Can I ask how things are going?" he says. When I frown, he adds, "Sorry. I'm just curious."

"The building is basically condemned. My accident made it clear that there were a lot of other things wrong with the space, so I need to move to a new location and start fresh."

"I'm sorry, that sucks."

"Yeah, it sucks. There are a few places on the street, or we might move somewhere. I don't know. Starting fresh again feels exhausting."

"If I can do anything . . ." I give him a look that tells him exactly what he can do. He grins and shakes his head. "Beyond shutting down my store and going away . . ."

I laugh a little. At least he knows.

"Thanks. It's just a lot. I'm starting to wonder if it's worth it."

"Thinking of not doing it?" He looks a little too delighted.

"Not too fast . . . . You aren't getting rid of me that easily." I shove him in the arm.

"I'd never want to get rid of you. That's my problem." His thumb runs along my thigh, a little higher than is probably appropriate given that we're surrounded by young children and marine animals.

"Be good," I say, and he takes his hand away, but I immediately miss it.

Andrew finally gets bored of what he's looking at and starts screaming for the penguins and running up the stairs. We chase after him again, and when we get to the penguin exhibit, he flattens his face against the glass to see the swimming penguins. Hannah lies on the ground, letting us know that she's tired of all this.

Leo picks her up, and she puts her head on his shoulder, his embrace instantly putting her to sleep.

"She's exhausted herself already," I say.

"Kids are great, but . . ." He leans away from Hannah, his lips close to my ear. ". . . only when you can send them back."

I file the fact that he loves his niece and nephew but doesn't want kids of his own in the back of my mind for later because it's only making me run hotter. I meet his eyes, and then I'm staring at his lips as I bite my lip. Why does childlessness also make me horny?

"Be good," he practically purrs. "I don't think we're going to get to do anything today."

"That's okay. I think I'm gonna walk around, maybe see a movie after this." I don't spend much time in this area beyond the convention center, and I'd like to walk around. I wonder if I can bring Wildcat down here.

"Sounds nice."

"NEMOOOO!!!!" Andrew takes off again, and Leo grabs my hand as we run after him, Hannah still sleeping on his shoulder.

chapter twenty-four

PlantDaddy13: Hey, you. It's been a while. Just checking on you. I feel like this has changed a lot, along with everything else. I can't tell if it's good or bad. I hope you're doing well with whatever it is you're doing, however you're navigating the world. It's just crazy how we spent so much time talking just a few months ago.

PlantDaddy54: Hey! No, it is weird and I love that we can talk about it because of who we are and what we've built together. I actually am not sure what to say. Maybe it's the natural evolution of things. Nothing really stays the same for long. Maybe we needed each other at that time and it's passed? I can't say for sure. I hope you know I'll always be here for you. Whatever you need, whenever you're ready.

PlantDaddy13: Thank you and the same for you. I'm always here.

———

Googling "what do I do with my life" while I sit with my laptop on the floor of my dank, empty store feels a little on the nose, but I type it in anyway. My surviving plants surround me. I was able to make around a few thousand at the Plant Expo, but I still have some more plants to sell and liquidate. A lot of the more common sturdy plants are still viable, and I've rehabbed a few more in my spare time. I still haven't found a new location, but I honestly haven't been looking that much. I've been spending my time doing other things instead.

The door is open, and some people wander in and buy a steeply discounted plant. I've mostly been giving them away, which isn't the best idea. Maybe I never had much of a business sense.

My Google search seems absurd, but there are actually a lot of results. There seems to be a purpose industry out there.

The first search result is a list of things to do:

- Examine your purpose in life. Find your purpose. . . .
- Evaluate your life values. . . .
- Analyze your strengths. . . .
- Examine your career choices and designation. . . .
- Assess your opportunities. . . .
- Explore your hobbies and passions. . . .
- Take field trips and observe other people. . . .
- Read, learn, and get inspired.

As if "purpose" is something I can just buy at the grocery store. Where do you even find purpose? What's a life value? My brain flickers back to my blog and back to my other life, and I bring myself back. What the hell is a field trip for thirty-year-olds?

I type in the address for my blog and don't hit enter. It just sits there for a bit, waiting for me. I wonder if my purpose can be found there. There's a knock on the door, and I don't look up from the article as I give my spiel, the same one I've given all day now.

"Just let me know if anything catches your eye. They'll need love, but I can make you a hell of an offer."

"I'm actually here to talk to you."

I know that voice. I look up, and it's Paul. He's just as gorgeous as ever. His hotness is different. It feels more like the type of guy you'd see on the cover of *Men's Health* magazine. His smile is sinister but blinding, as usual, and I wonder if he knows about me and Leo.

Leo's always defending him, so I reach for some grace and openness. I try to ignore the flush of embarrassment as I sit on the floor of my empty store, knowing I've lost the war against Botanical Brothers. It was pretty one-sided anyways.

"Hi, Paul, can I do anything for you?"

My tone is convincingly friendly, and when Paul smiles, his cheeks crinkle like Leo's. They look even more alike from this angle. This softens me a little.

"Good looking plants." He's just being nice. The plants have seen better days. "I'll take them."

"Which ones?"

"I'll take them all."

He pulls out a big wad of cash, and it hurts more than I thought it would. I feel pathetic, but I also can't turn down any money, especially if I want to get the store back to where it needs to be.

"They're not for resale," I add. My ego wouldn't be able to take him selling my plants.

"Of course not. They're for Leo. Our house."

"You sure?"

I get off the ground and grab the box I brought them in to start packing them up.

"Yeah. Leo loves rehabbing plants. It's one of his things. Bringing plants back to life, ya know?"

I try to not react to his name, but I can't stop the flash of us in his truck. "Okay," I agree.

Paul's energy feels unsettled, as if there's more he wants to say.

"You know," he starts, and I cringe. "You're still welcome to the job, and it looks like you could really use one?"

"What makes you think that?" I'm a little more forceful when I pack up one of his plants.

"I heard about what's going on with this space. The landlord is selling it. So you have to move."

My stomach drops. That would just be the icing on the cake. Plant Therapy becomes Botanical Brothers, just like he offered that first time we talked. I don't say anything, just stare at him. I hope he can't see my computer screen and what I was searching for because that won't do much to help my case.

"Look, I'm not trying to offend you. I just want to talk. How much money do you need?" I don't answer, and he continues, "Besides my brother, you're likely the person with the most plant knowledge in Long Beach. I've asked around to try to find someone to help teach the employees about plants and to take care of the plants when Leo isn't around, and you're the most qualified person. At least, that's what everyone says, despite everything."

He looks around meaningfully. "You know Leo has been kind of unsettled lately. He just doesn't seem that happy." I can't believe he's telling me this. "I think he's overworked, and if he can have some more time for himself, for his hobbies, or just for dating or anything else, I think it might help."

I'm a little shocked by this tiny act of kindness from Paul. I'm used to seeing him as a devil. I watch him for a moment, and his gaze is soft. Does he have a heart?

"Look, I know you don't want to work with me, which I get, but I know you and Leo have some kind of . . . friendship."

I can't stop my mouth from opening wide with shock. Maybe he knows about our little agreement.

"You wouldn't be working with me. I'm the marketing guy and the money guy. Leo is in the store, and he needs help. It would be nice to have someone with your level of experience on staff, and nothing would really have to change."

"What do you mean?" I ask.

"I mean we'll buy it. Leo and I. We'll do what you were trying to do, make it a rare plant shop, and you can run it." I'm not good at hiding my shock. "We'll redo it and update everything, and you can do whatever you were doing before, just with our backing. You don't have to worry about competition."

I want to be offended by the offer, but part of it sounds kind of good. I want to go back to the way things were, right? That's what I want? But instead, I say what I always say when presented with an offer by one of the Botanical Brothers.

"You guys put me out of business."

He takes a step closer, crossing his arms. The air feels heavy, and I can tell he's gonna land a pretty definitive blow.

"Tessa, I know that the accident with the store sped up the timeline, but what happened was going to happen. This street was changing, and plants are popular. If not us, someone else. How much longer do you want to fight change? Fight us? Fight Leo?"

I feel like one of those fatality graphics from *Mortal Kombat*, like my skeleton has been ripped out through my throat.

"Uh . . ." My throat closes up, and I don't actually know what to say. For real this time.

He places the money down on the wooden table I've got sitting in the middle of the store and scoops up the plants. I look up at him, and he gives me a nod. "Just think about it." His face is kind, which freaks me out, and he gives the empty store around him one final look before making his way out the door.

I look down at the wad of cash. It's twice as much as I was asking for. There's no way I can do it, right? No way that I could work with Botanical Brothers and let myself get acquired. But what other options are there? I don't have any ideas. I go back to my computer and hit the enter button to open up my blog. Then I start reading.

chapter twenty-five

PlantDaddy13: You know what's funny? I recently was somewhere with a plant I used to know. It wasn't mine anymore, I gave it to a friend, but even though it was among a bunch of other plants that were pretty much identical, I knew which one was mine. I remembered it.

PlantDaddy54: I 100% know what you mean. When you meet a plant you know it. There's always something you remember like a random bit of variegation or an awkward leaf. Maybe there's a feeling or something.

PlantDaddy13: Wouldn't it be great if we could apply that knowledge to everything? Imagine if you could know exactly what to do the way you know a plant is yours or even know what a plant needs.

PlantDaddy54: Right. If we could transfer our plant intuition into real intuition. That would be great.

The house I live in isn't big, around 900 square feet. It's got two bedrooms. One is "mine," and the other is Norma's, which I've been told many times to not touch.

Her room remains undisturbed, but the rest of the house is fair game, and I deep clean everything. I scrub the sinks and toilets. I sweep and mop. I feel like somehow cleaning the house is cleaning out my own brain and giving me some clarity. Clearing my brain of Leo and his lips and his fingers. Clearing my mind of Plant Daddy and how everything is so awkward. I miss how deep we used to go with our conversations, but I'm enjoying the physical intensity of Leo. There's just not as much there, because although we can talk, our conversations are never as deep. That's probably because we're always both on the defense. I want to forget that I'm still in limbo, that I still don't know what the hell I'm going to do, but there's an idea that's kind of there, a seed in the back of my mind.

The RV.

I can't stop staring at it.

It sits out there in the driveway. I can see it from the front window. It's crazy how big and ugly it is sitting there. I feel like I've looked through it for the last few years without really seeing it. The outside is filthy, covered with pollen from the trees and sand from the windy days. Maybe I'll just wash off the exterior, so it's not such an eyesore.

Oddly, cleaning the RV feels just as good as cleaning the house. Maybe even better. The dirt washes off easily as if it's been waiting to be released. The rags I scrub it with are filthy, so filthy I'll likely have to throw them away. That feels good, too. While I clean the windows, I venture to look inside. It's eerie and empty because it's been years since I've been in there. My throat burns when I notice that it looks exactly like it did eight years ago. Nothing has changed. The sheets in the back are still rumpled like they were the last day I slept on the bed. Even one of the cabinets is slightly ajar from when I'd forgotten to shut it. I stare for a few more moments before going back in the house to get the keys and some additional cleaning supplies.

Standing outside the RV, I look down at the keys in my hand, the Mr. Incredible keychain so familiar. The door sticks, so I have to pull it aggressively a few times for it to actually open, and when I do, the air inside is stale. I cough at the dust cloud that escapes out the door, following the breeze. The air smells old, like a neglected attic, and the sheets are full of moth holes. There's no food besides a few cans of expired beans. Wildcat comes up behind me, sneezing on her way in. She's never been in here before.

I start by airing out the space for a few hours and stripping everything down. I trash all the sheets and towels and even the few clothes that I forgot to take out once I moved in with Norma.

Next up is the scrubbing—cleaning all the surfaces and getting rid of all the dust, dirt, and grime everywhere. That takes another day. Then I replace everything—new sheets, new pillows, new covers for the seats and chairs. The seats and chairs will eventually need to be replaced, but I'll worry about that later.

When I'm done, I sit in the driver's seat with my keys in my hands. I try to turn it on, but of course it doesn't start, just like that day all those years ago. My hands run over the steering wheel, catching on the flakey leather, my heart beating fast. Suddenly I feel like I can't catch my breath, like I'm choking. I try to settle down, to take deep breaths, but it's all caught in the back of my throat. I open the door and stumble out and away from the RV. As soon as I leave the space, I feel like my breathing finally starts to stabilize, like I can finally breathe again.

I haven't had a panic attack in years, and I'm wondering if my body is trying to tell me something.

chapter twenty-six

Leo: Hey, I was thinking about you. What are you doing?

Tessa: Uhhhh . . . . well . . . . .

Leo: You okay?

Tessa: Yeah, sorry.

Leo: You busy?

Tessa: Kind of. But you can be busy with me.

Leo: Text me the address.

———

Leo looks great. He always looks great, but today it's extra great. He's been out in the sun, so his skin is a deeper shade of honey, and he's not wearing his hat, so I can get a good look at his black hair.

"Hi," he says.

"Hi," I say back.

We don't really know how to greet each other. Do we hug? Do I kiss him? Before I decide, he presents me with a small plant from behind his back. It's in a plastic bag, and I immediately recognize it as a special hoya.

"You propagated it!" It's small, with a very tiny root system, but it's there.

"I told you it was a conspiracy," he says, grinning.

"Or you're just very good." His ears turn a lovely shade of pink, and I relish in it. "Thanks, Leo. This is . . . This is really sweet."

"Of course, you're welcome."

We're silent for a moment, and it's almost awkward.

"Hi," he says again, and he takes a deep breath as if he's gathering up his courage. Then he wraps his arms around me, bringing me close, and kisses me. It's sweet at first, all giggles and sighs, but heats up quickly, and both of us quickly get lost in each other. I'm only able to take a breath when I hear Wildcat crying from the house, wanting her turn.

"Come in," I say, buzzing in anticipation. I pull on his shirt, but he's a little distracted. "What?"

"You've been in the RV." He nods at the RV. The light is on inside.

"Yeah, I've been cleaning it, or I was."

He nods, but he's still looking at it as if it's a museum exhibit.

"Do you want to see it?" I haven't been in it since my panic attack, but maybe with him here, I can do it again. He nods, and I close the front door behind me and walk across my driveway to the RV while Wildcat screams even louder from inside.

When we reach the RV, I take a deep breath, open the door, and step inside. He follows closely behind me. The space suddenly feels smaller.

"Oh, wow," he breathes.

I try to look at the familiar space through his eyes. All the surfaces are clean, and it looks brand-new—well, as brand-new as possible given that it's not. When he walks by me, he has to brace his arms on either side of me to get past. He smells like canned peaches today. Sweet and aluminum.

"Yeah, I wanted to have my *Wild* adventure. My *Eat, Pray, Love* moment. You saw my blog. It was so stupid. That's not really something people like me do."

"It's not stupid," he says, and his voice has this sharp edge, unlike anything I've heard from him before. "It's a great idea. If those blonde women can do it, why not you?" Nobody really put it like that before, or at least, nobody put it to me that way before. "The things you want aren't stupid," he adds.

"Thanks, Leo."

He nods and then wanders to the front of the RV and sits down behind the steering wheel. Like everything he does, he looks like he belongs there.

"Do you know what's wrong with it?"

I hand him the keys, and he attempts to start the engine. Nothing happens.

"I never checked. I just knew it wouldn't move, and I didn't have any money to fix it, so I left it here. It's just been sitting. For years." He nods, reaching under the steering wheel and looking at the wires. Suddenly, I realize what he's doing. "Don't tell me you know plants *and* cars? Your adoring fans wouldn't be able to take it."

"Is that you?" He winks, and I roll my eyes. "I come from a family of mechanics. I can have someone take a look if you'd like."

My chest feels heavy at the thought, remembering a few moments earlier and my panic attack. And practically living in it like I have been the last few days. If it could drive again . . . what would I do? Where would I go?

My head starts to feel fuzzy again, and there's a buzzing in my ears. I walk away from him and make my way to the bedroom, where I lie flat on my back on the bed and stare up at the ceiling. I close my eyes, trying to steady my breath. When I open my eyes again, Leo's in the doorway, hovering by the bed and looking down at me. I'm glad I took a shower. It's an enticing sight.

"Can I?"

"Yeah, sure. Of course." I close my eyes again, and I can hear him sit down, feel the weight of him on the bed when he lies down. I look over at him, and he's watching me.

"Comfortable right?"

"It's nice."

I find myself staring at the tiny strip of exposed skin on his stomach when he stretches to make himself more comfortable. I'm actually losing my mind. I decide to change the subject because he's so close.

"You know, your brother offered me a job."

He immediately turns towards me and props himself up on one elbow.

"He offered you up as bait. Said we had a, and I quote, 'relationship.' "

"Oh?" His ears turn red. "I don't know where he got that from. What's the offer?"

"He basically wants to have me run Plant Therapy as a part of Botanical Brothers. I guess I would work for you two." I hesitate a second before I ask, "He says you're unhappy. Is that true?"

He chews on his bottom lip and then settles on his back again, once more staring intently at the ceiling.

"What did you say?" he asks. I notice he doesn't answer my question.

"No, of course." He nods. "But he told me to think about it."

"*Are* you gonna think about it?"

I hadn't even considered Paul's offer, really. It was a conversation I filed away in my brain for later, a thought I didn't have any intention of returning to anytime soon. My career books all talk about being open to new opportunities, but I just can't see how this is one I can entertain. If I accept the offer, I won't own the store. I'll be working for the Botanical Brothers. Plus, there's the humiliation of it. Sure, I would be able to reopen Plant Therapy, but it wouldn't really be Plant Therapy. It would still be Botanical Brothers. On the other hand, if I do take the offer, my life wouldn't have to change completely, even though it would be quite a bit different. I'd also have help with everything, which was something I'd been desperate for towards the end when I'd been working alone at the store. And then there's Leo and Paul . . . . I don't trust Paul one bit. Not to mention, Norma would never let us get acquired.

"What do you think?" I ask Leo because I really want to know. He's quiet for a moment, and there's nothing but the sound of street traffic outside.

"I can't lie and say the idea of you being there doesn't sound really nice, but I don't feel like you would like it there. Sometimes *I* don't even want to be there. I feel like there's something better out there for you."

Because he's a boy out of a movie, he turns to look at me, and I feel something deep in my gut. Something about the way he looks at me doesn't feel like this is just about fun. It's not desire, it's something else. I wonder if I look at him the same way.

"Don't look at me like that," I say, my voice scratchy. My throat feels raw, like I've been talking all day.

"Like what?"

I don't even know how I'd describe it beyond saying it's like being cracked open, like he's looking at my insides.

"Do you want me to stop looking at you?"

"No, I don't want you to stop."

"Do you want to forget?"

I nod, and before I can speak, he leans over and he's kissing me again. This time, I'm more ready than when I was in the truck. We both are, and we get in a rhythm right away. It's slightly different, more urgent. He brings me closer, wrapping himself around me, and our legs intertwine—my bare calves against the roughness of his jeans. His arm goes up behind my neck, and he brings me closer so he can kiss me deeper. I pull a little at his hair, and he growls and rolls over so he's on top of me.

We stare at each other for a moment. I feel like I'm diving off the deep end, and I make one last attempt to resist, grasping for some sense of land. I think about Allison, and I realize she's kind of right.

"You're distracting me."

"I know," he says, his voice low. He leans down and sucks my bottom lip into his mouth, and my back starts to arch into him. "And I'm sorry," he says. It sounds sincere. "I'm so sorry." Then he leans closer to my ear and kisses the skin below my lobe. I shiver. "Let me make it up to you," he whispers.

He kisses down my neck and over my exposed shoulder before returning to my lips to kiss me again. I reach for his shirt, his jeans, everything. He stops me, grabbing both of my hands and pinning them over my head. His smile is wicked, and his eyes are dark with desire. He seems overwhelmed with everything, but then his eyes soften a little as though he's checking whether I'm okay with this. I am, I definitely am. I nod and relax into his hold, and he starts kissing down my neck again.

"Can I take this off?"

He reaches for the edge of my shirt, fingers grazing my collarbone. I nod again because I don't use words anymore. I sit up, and he pulls my T-shirt over my head so I'm just in my bra and shorts. I reach up to pull his shirt off too, and he's beautiful. I scratch my fingers down his chest, and he sighs. I think about the girls online who wondered if he whimpers, and I decide I want to find out.

We kiss again, and I maneuver him so he's on his back and I'm on top of him. When I look down at him, he looks so vulnerable, his lips swollen and his chest heaving. I feel an odd sense of power in this moment, one that I rarely have when I'm with him. Botanical Brothers always looms, powerful and overbearing. Not now, though.

"You have this look on your face . . ." he says, sitting up so we're face-to-face. "It's kinda like you want to destroy me."

"Are you afraid?" I say, wrapping my hand around his head and pulling lightly on his hair. He does whimper, and it sounds as good as I thought it would. He kisses me again, and I let it linger before pushing him on his back. I look down at him, and he smiles up at me.

"You are so gorgeous." There's that word, and he's using it for me now, and I feel like I'm glowing from the inside. I lean over him and kiss the center of his chest, my lips trailing down. He's already shivering when I hover over his nipple and take a light bite. He jerks up a little and moans.

"Tessa." He says my name like it's a plea.

"Yes?" I say, kissing his nipple as an apology while looking up at him. He nods enthusiastically, and I move to the other, give it a kitten lick and a bite. He moans again, long and slow, and I kiss down his chest before reaching his jeans. He's hard. I unbutton and unzip his pants and then pull them down along with his boxers, and he's there, hard and heavy. I hold him at his base and pump slowly, placing a light kiss on the tip. Leo was in control when we were in the truck, but now he's so overloaded, his body shakes. I lean down and pull him into my mouth with a long, deep suck. I sneak a peek up at him, and he's gripping the sheets under him, his body arching up to my mouth. I take him deeper, swirling my tongue around him and picking up speed. He relaxes a little, and in that moment, I stop, pulling off with a pop. I hover over him, looking him in the eyes, and he's pleading with me.

"You want me dead," he says, reaching down to touch my cheek. I look him in the eyes as I lick from base to tip, swirling my tongue around the head. Another delicious whimper leaves his lips, and I think I can get used to this kind of incredible power, the overwhelming feeling of it. I take him into my mouth all the way this time.

"Wait, wait, wait . . ." he says, and I release him from my mouth, concerned. He looks tortured, and his eyes are watering. He massages the back of my neck, his touch tender. "Come here."

He pulls me up to him and kisses my mouth before flipping me over on my back again. He hovers over me, still catching his breath. I'm smiling. "Evil." I reach down for him, and he's heavy in my hand, still hard. He pulls my hands away as he starts kissing down my body.

Everything lights up as he makes his way to the edge of my shorts, and he moans into my skin as he pulls them down my hips. I'm already wet, which is a little embarrassing. It's been a while. He nudges between my legs, a tentative lick at the center of my underwear. He looks up at me and kisses the inside of my thigh. "Still good?"

"Yeah, keep going." I'm breathing hard. He props himself back up on his arms and kisses me deeply as he slides a hand in my panties and rubs my clit. I grip his hair and pull him closer to me, and I moan in his mouth.

"You are . . . I just . . ." Leo can't find the words, which is nice because he always seems to have them.

"Use your words," I say, and he smirks as he makes his way back down my body.

"You use your words." He lightly bites my thigh, then kisses around my hip and back.

"Okay," I breathe, and he scoots back down my body, slips off my panties, and opens my legs again, this time wider.

I feel open and exposed, and I somehow manage to look down at him. He glances up at me before taking my clit in his mouth and sucking. I yelp again, gripping the sheets on the bed underneath me. When he nibbles on my clit and then licks my lips, I actually scream, full-throated and deep, and he whispers a "shhh" into my skin before taking my clit into his mouth and giving it a suck. I tense up because it's too much, and he eases back, pressing his lips lightly against me one more time before pulling away just enough to trail kisses along my inner thigh.

I manage to breathe at least once. Then his mouth is on me again. His tongue finds my clit, and I arch my hips up to him. He wraps his hands around my hips, holding me open for him, angling me the way he wants as he laps happily at my pussy. It feels so good I want to scream. He works me up till I'm almost there before pulling back over and over until I feel like I wanna die.

"Please," I beg shamelessly. It comes out more like a whimper than words. Maybe I'm not at all in control.

"Please what, baby?" he teases, and my whole body clenches. It's partly because he's toying with my clit but also because of the name. Baby. God, I'm so predictable.

"I'm close." I grip his hair harder. He doubles his efforts, his head going back and forth and up and down.

"God, you sound so good. It's my favorite sound in the world— hearing you moan like that." He's working hard now, like he's taking the job seriously. He pulls his mouth away from my clit, and he moves up to my side as he slips his fingers into me. Then he starts sliding them in and out with a slow rhythm. He watches my face, and it feels so intimate as he fingers me while we stare at each other. He's whispering encouragement into my ear, and then my eyes close and I try to focus on the feeling as I crash, falling apart on his fingers. It's bright and overwhelming, and my whole body shakes. He kisses me as I come down, his mouth still wet. Then he pulls back just a little, his fingers still inside of me.

"Condom," I say into his lips.

He tears himself away, and I whine a little at the lack of contact as he reaches over the side of the bed. He fumbles for his jeans and then produces a condom. I'm breathing heavily as I hear the tear of the foil and him putting it on. When he's ready, he settles over me, and everything slows down. I think it's crashing down on both of us now, the weight of the situation. It's him and me naked on the bed of my abandoned RV, in the middle of a hot summer's day.

He watches me for a moment, and he looks a little worried. I wonder if he thinks I want to dial everything back a bit, to remind him of reality. But I'm too far in. I pull him down for a filthy kiss. It's messy and unrefined, but it does the trick. He pulls back, slotting his knees under my hips and eagerly positioning himself at my entrance. I open my legs some more, arching to him. He reaches for my clit, rubbing me as he enters me agonizingly slowly. It's so slow I feel like I'm gonna scream. He watches me as he pushes into me a little deeper, and it's so intense, so overwhelming. I reach out for his arm, my nails digging into his skin.

"Tessa." My name sounds tortured coming out of his mouth. I like when he says my name on a normal day, but it's even better now. It's cliché to say I feel full, but it's like that—he's everywhere. It's so deep, it feels like he's burying himself into my skin. He leans over my body so we're face-to-face, and we moan as our hips meet and he's fully inside. He doesn't move for a moment. He's sweating, his face flushed. He's not cool, or relaxed, or calm. He looks like he's on the verge of explosion.

"You good?" I hold his face in my hands, and he turns his head to kiss my palm.

"You just feel really good." His voice is shaky. I smooth my hands down his back, bringing him closer. He pulls his hips back and thrusts slowly. I whimper, bringing him down for a kiss. We try to kiss, but it's so overwhelming, and we just end up breathing heavily, our lips not quite touching. The RV is quiet beyond the rhythmic creak of the bed and our panting breaths. After all that talk, we're so quiet in this moment, maybe quieter than we've ever been. It's a nice moment of peace, here in bed with him, everything just feeling so good, and all I can think about is how he smells like fresh peaches and how I can feel the goose bumps forming on his back and how he's looking at me.

All I can think about is how I want more.

"Harder." I mouth it because I don't have much breath left. His lips fall to my neck, kissing there as I move my hips to meet his thrusts. He picks up the pace.

"Anything you want." He breathes the words into my neck, and it makes me shiver. He slams into me over and over, hitting just the right spot inside me. Our hands find each other, holding on tight as we move together. I don't remember sex feeling like this, like I can feel everything.

"That's so good," I moan. This spurs him on, and he leans up, pulling my legs back and dragging me closer to him so he can pound into me harder, more direct jolts that have me on the verge.

He's saying something, but I can't hear it because I feel like I'm underwater, overwhelmed with the sensation of being full of him. I take the moment to watch him, and it's the most incredible thing I've ever seen. His eyes dance all over my body, his brow focused, his teeth biting his lip. His biceps and arms flex with every push and pull. He sees me watching him, and he actually smiles, the dimple back on display.

"Want you on top of me," he says, pulling me up so I'm on his lap. I'm not light, but he makes me feel that way as he settles me on top of his lap, his hands gripping my ass to reposition me. The move brings him even deeper inside of me, and when I flex my hips, my hands push on his chest and he falls back onto the bed. I swivel my hips on top of him, riding him in earnest. His hands move to my hips, and I'm momentarily distracted by the sunlight shining off his golden skin, the sweat forming little beads on his forehead, the way his mouth opens and his eyes close in total surrender.

I reach down for him and pull him up to me. He wraps his arms around me, and I hug him close to my chest as I slam down my hips. He lifts up to meet me. I'm almost there. I feel the tightness between my legs, radiating through my body, like a rubber band being pulled back, ready to snap.

"I'm gonna come again," I whisper in his hair, and he nods, pulling my nipple into his mouth with a light bite. He reaches down for my clit, and I'm done for. It feels like I'm imploding from the inside. I grip his arms so tight he might bruise. It's just so much, wave after wave that feels never-ending.

I'm breathing hard, my body still buzzing, and he rolls me onto my back again, propping himself up on his elbows and kissing me while he pounds into me fast and hard. He pulls back to stare at me, and there's that moment again—that moment of recognition we both feel. It's not usually like this, is it? Sex doesn't usually change you, does it? He buries his head in my shoulder, and I hug him close as he finally falls apart inside me. We lie there for a while, exhausted. Naked as the sun peeks in from behind the clouds and watches us. After a few minutes, he pushes himself up off me and watches me intently. He looks tortured and sweaty.

"You okay?" I ask, still out of breath, still tingling.

"I have to ask you something." His gaze is really serious in a way I've never seen before. "I feel like it's gonna sound crazy, but I need to ask." I feel scared, but he seems to sense that and he kisses me.

"It's not bad, I promise. That was incredible, you are incredible. I just can't not ask this."

"Yeah, anything," I say, my curiosity growing.

I scoot out from under him and then settle next to him. It's weird how we're sitting—as if we're talking about something as mundane as the weather, even though we're still very much naked. He looks nervous, his foot bouncing up and down against the rumpled up sheets. I try to soothe him with a hand on his thigh.

"Okay, so . . . do you . . ."

My phone rings, and a door shuts outside, and I can hear a voice. I can barely make it out, but it's getting louder. The two of us freeze. Wildcat barks, which tells me the person is for sure in the yard.

"Tessa! Are you here? Have you been murdered?" It's Allison.

chapter twenty-seven

> Allison: Tessa, I'm coming down. It's been 3 days and nobody has heard from you so I'm doing a wellness check. I'll be there in like 45 minutes.

> Allison: Okay, it'll be more like an hour and a half. I'm assuming that your phone is off and you aren't dead. Please don't be dead.

> Allison: Oh god, I can hear Wildcat in the house. You're dead. I'm calling.

> Allison: Wait, you in the RV?

———

"Tessa! I can hear your phone ringing inside! Are you in there? Wildcat is barking inside! Shit, I gotta call the cops! You've been murdered!"

"Shit, it's Allison," I say, sitting up and rushing to grab my clothes. I'm still sticky and sweaty as I put them on in a rush.

"What's going on in there?" I can hear her say.

"Tell her you aren't home." He grabs my waist and brings me to him, and I kiss him again.

"She's gonna call the cops." I giggle and throw him his shirt. "One second, Allison!" I call out so she doesn't get the authorities involved.

"She's coming in from out of town so I don't get to see her very often. It's kind of a big deal that she's here. I need to see her. I didn't know she was coming."

I stand up and fix my shirt the best I can. I can't find my bra so I decide to just go without it. He's put on his shirt and jeans already and is sitting on the edge of the bed to put on his shoes.

"How do I look?" I ask.

"Like you just fucked me." It's meant to be matter-of-fact, but the way he says it makes everything light up. I'm getting turned on again, and that's not what we need right now.

"Stop it. I need to go. Just come out when you're done and act normal."

"I don't know if I'll ever be normal again, but okay."

I look back at him, and he's sitting there with his hair all messy, trying to catch his breath. I feel a swell of pride that I'm the one who made him look like that, feel like that. I rush over to him to give him one more long, lingering kiss and then head to the door.

"Oh, what did you want to ask me?" I say, looking back at him as I hesitate by the door.

"Let's talk about it later. What are you doing Thursday?"

"Nothing."

"Okay, let's hang out then?" Big smiles and eye crinkles. I nod.

I take a deep breath before I step out of the RV. Allison's eyes go wide, and then she relaxes her shoulders.

"Oh, thank god. I thought you were dead or something. Where have you been? And why are you in the RV?"

"Um, nothing! I've just been fixing up the RV, and my friend was helping me with it!"

"Your friend?"

As if on cue, Leo opens up the door from inside the RV and comes down the steps towards us. He looks way more put together than I feel. He clears his throat.

"Oh, hi, I'm Leo. We've met before . . ."

"Yeah, Leo, like Botanical Brothers Leo. I know who you are. You put my friend out of business. What are you doing here?"

Leo looks guilty. I wish I could tell her that he partly made up for it by giving me three orgasms and counting.

"I was just leaving actually," he says, and he turns to me. "See you later to work on the RV and stuff and like . . . plants and things." I try to suppress my heart eyes as he awkwardly walks away, but I'm sure Allison can tell what's up because now she's staring at me as I watch him go.

"You lied to me about him. I asked if you were still involved with him, and you said no." She's right. I did lie. But I lied to avoid this exact conversation. I don't really have a defense. It felt good? I'm tired?

"He didn't put me out of business. The accident put me out of business."

"Wait, what? Isn't that what you always say? He's putting you out of business?" She's right. Again. That is what I always say. "So are you thinking of not reopening the store?"

"I . . ." My brain is still drunk from my multiple orgasms.

"You used to call him the enemy. You said you don't trust them. You told me that you made a huge mistake at his store, and now you two are having sex in your RV, which, by the way, is *gross*. Isn't it filthy in there?"

"Actually, I cleaned it. I've been really wrapped up in cleaning it the last few days." This is a pathetic response to the situation, but I'm at a loss of what else to say.

"That's why you weren't answering your phone? Think about what's happened, Tessa. Think about it. The video? His brother trying to buy you out the moment he saw you? They're sinister. Isn't there anyone else you can fuck to get it out of your system?"

"I don't know. He's just so easy to talk to." God, this is also pathetic.

"Have you thought maybe he's easy to talk to on purpose? Maybe he's some honeypot or something." I think about how Paul had offered me the job with Botanical Brothers, and I decide I absolutely can't mention that right now. And I think about how Leo is always defending Paul, but then I think about the moments of care, when he's reaching out, and about how he told me not to take the job.

"He's just easy to talk to."

"You can talk to me!"

"You aren't here!" I yell. She frowns, but I continue. "You aren't here, and Bill's not here, and my store isn't here. I just feel so alone. But he's here. Leo's here. And . . . I don't know." I'm trying to be angry, but when I say the words out loud, it just sounds sad. I realize for the first time just how true it all is, just how much Leo has filled this void created by the loss of my store and my friends. Maybe that's why I've struggled to say no.

"I'm here!" Allison says. "That's why I'm here with you right now. You disappeared for a few days, and I was worried about you. You can't trust him."

"Nothing is happening, we're just friends."

"Why didn't you tell me then? Why did you lie?"

"Because I knew you'd react this way!"

"That's because it's insane to be hooking up with the man whose brother has been your biggest competitor and has done several things to undermine you and your store."

I think about the video of me and Leo. I think about Paul calling the store "cute," the job offer. She has a point, but also she's not the only one who's been keeping secrets.

"So what aren't you telling me? There's something going on with you, and you don't want to talk to me either!" I think about all the moments when she's clearly been upset and overwhelmed about something and has refused to talk about it, not being honest with me.

"Because when I tell you stuff, you freak out. You're always freaking out about everything that doesn't fit in that little box you've built for yourself! You don't want anything to ever change, and the more you cling to not wanting things to change, the crazier things get. If I tell you about things that are going to change more, it'll just get harder."

"What . . . ? I . . ."

"You couldn't just accept I was moving, so you've just pretended it didn't happen. I have to reach out all the time. I have to make things happen."

"The store . . ."

"I know, the store, the store."

I suddenly feel exhausted. It's not like I wanted this to be my life, to be desperately clinging to my store, to be trying to do everything imaginable just to get a chance at staying open. I don't want to worry about this anymore.

"You've been up in Riverside living your best life, and I'm just here trying to figure things out."

"Well, do you think you're gonna figure things out having sex in your abandoned RV?"

I don't know what I think. And I didn't figure anything out yet, but at least in those moments with Leo, I did feel a little bit of relief from the constant pressing anxiety of everything I've been doing wrong.

Maybe Paul was right. I should have quit while I was ahead. And maybe Allison is right too. Maybe I need to accept what is.

None of this is going to be figured out while Allison is here, though.

"You should go." She looks shocked by me saying this. I'm surprisingly calm as I continue. "If you're so upset with how I'm living my life and the things I'm doing, you shouldn't have to watch. You don't have to be a part of it, especially if you're just going to judge me the whole time."

We're in a standoff, just staring at each other. I almost lose my nerve, but then I think about how she still hasn't told me what's going on, how she's still keeping things from me while she expects everything in return.

"Fine." She says it so softly I can barely hear her, and then she turns, walks back to her car, and gets in. She sits there for a few beats before backing up out of the driveway and driving away.

chapter twenty-eight

PlantDaddy54: How do you know when you're giving up vs. when it's just the right decision?

PlantDaddy13: I think you'll know because of how you feel. Does it feel like a relief or do you feel like you've betrayed some part of yourself? At least that's how I know. Whatever happens I know you'll be fine.

PlantDaddy54: Have you had any situations like this lately? When you feel like you're deciding between giving up and keeping going?

PlantDaddy13: Honestly, that seems to be my whole life. It's literally all I think about. Am I making the right decision? Am I doing the right thing? It never ends.

PlantDaddy54: I know this is a weird question and maybe it's off-base or something we don't talk about, especially now, but what line of work are you in?

PlantDaddy13: I guess you'd describe it as retail? I don't know. Why?

———

I decide to give Paul a call, and he tells me to come in the next day. I just want to hear what he has to say. That's all. No commitment to make a decision. I take the long way around to avoid driving by my store. I don't want anything to cloud my thinking. The route takes me through a neighborhood with cute two-to-three-bedroom houses that are actually worth millions of dollars. And as I drive, the conversation with Allison still weighs heavy on my mind. I find myself wondering if she's right. If I'm being deceived by both of the Botanical Brothers. If I need to be more careful.

I feel a bit like a failure even going, but I'm trying to explore all my options and keep an open mind. I arrive at Botanical Brothers a little after lunchtime, the midday rush still in full swing. There are people wandering through the store picking out plants and people taking pictures next to the large LED lights and cutouts of the two brothers. I do feel a little thrill when I see the cutout of Leo, my mind going back to our afternoon together in my RV. Then I'm a little bit ashamed of the delight I feel when a gorgeous woman with impossibly long legs and perfect hair takes a picture with Leo's cutout. I'm not proud of it.

I try to settle on the lightness of that instead of thinking too hard about my poor store, everything still damp and rotting. But it's difficult not to think about that when the air feels so fresh here.

A young woman in her early twenties, one of the first women I've seen working here, comes up and asks if I'd like help. She's got a bunch of necklaces and bracelets—her way of fighting the good fight against the oppressive black T-shirt of the Botanical Brothers uniform, I guess. She's cute but looks overwhelmed, as if she's hoping I don't actually need any help. I wonder if she represents some kind of diversity initiative. She reminds me a little of myself when I first started working at the store and suggested a pothos to everyone because it was the only plant I really knew. I feel a pang of betrayal for being here.

"Of course she doesn't. You could probably use her help."

I can feel Paul's presence almost like how I feel Leo's. It's different, though. Heavier. More intense. He's smiling, and I decide to smile back, settling into a grin I hope is friendly enough and doesn't show how grossed out I actually am. I'm trying to discern if he's watching me differently, if he suspects or knows. But if he senses it, he doesn't act like he does. He reaches out his hand, and I shake it cordially.

"Come on back," Paul says. "Let's talk."

We walk through the store and into the back room, and the vibe is totally different. While the store itself is picture-perfect, the back room is utter chaos. There are plants everywhere, with no discernible order. Nothing like the perfect rows of plants in the front of the store. I almost trip over a calathea.

"Be careful. We're still figuring out a system back here. Especially since Leo's out today. It makes a big difference. He's the one who knows everything."

Right. Leo's not here yet. He told me he'd be here after my meeting because he has errands to run. I wonder if he knows about all this disarray in the back room in his absence. Thousands of dollars in plants are just lying around. I cringe as I step over a priceless *Monstera adansonii* and find myself wanting to pick it up and save it from the floor.

I follow Paul through the back room to his office, and the two of us settle on opposite sides of his desk. The office is more cramped than I'd expected.

"So, what changed your mind?" he asks, opening up a notebook and scribbling something on the page.

I don't want to say the real answer, which is that I'm exhausted, slightly depressed, and desperate for purpose, so instead I say, "Just trying to keep an open mind about the future."

He hums and sends a text.

"So, the job is basically just client education and also helping Leo manage the stock and supply and take care of orders." I nod. That's what I figured it would look like. "It'll be that way until we buy and fix up that old building. We need to update it."

I feel a lump in my throat when he says "old building." He's talking about Plant Therapy. My store. I'm suddenly realizing this is a bad idea, and I've only been here for five minutes.

"Beyond that, you can do anything you want and order anything you want. We have access to a huge supply and lots of dealers, so we can get plants you might not even have heard of. I know Leo wants to start taking trips to get plants. Maybe the two of you can go." He gives me a sly smile that tells me he absolutely knows about us.

"Okay," I hear myself say, but I feel like I'm silently planning my escape. I guess this is kind of my rock bottom, interviewing for a job with a competitor.

"You don't have to worry about doing anything with social media or anything like that." I wonder if that was a shot at my less-than-stellar social media skills. "And, unfortunately, no dogs."

Yeah, I can't be here. This isn't right. None of this feels right. I gotta go look at some more spaces. I don't want to be rude, so I go through the motions, stay focused on what he's saying as much as I can.

"Makes sense." I clear my throat in order to sound a little more confident.

"And you get to work with Leo, of course, and I know the two of you have some type of thing going on."

I try to laugh that off, but I'm beginning to sweat as I think about what happened in the RV.

"Oh, uh . . ."

"It's okay!" Paul says with a wave of his hand. "It's good. You're good for him. I'd prefer him to hang out with you rather than mope around all the time being sad or glued to his phone, spending all his time on Reddit. Who uses Reddit? I didn't know Reddit was a real thing. I mean, isn't Reddit for like nazis or something? Do you have a profile there? Of course you don't. Maybe we should get one for the store. He's him, you know. My brother is a handsome guy. He doesn't need to talk to girls on Reddit."

My chest suddenly burns, and there's a buzzing in my ears. The word Reddit stirs something in me that I hope I'm hiding well, but I'm shaking. Maybe it's nothing. Maybe Leo likes Reddit.

"Oh?" I squeak, barely there.

"Yeah, some girl." He holds up his hands and makes air quotes when he says the word "girl." "He actually thought it was you at some point, and I was like, be real, man. No offense to you, of course, but you aren't exactly a social media master, wouldn't you agree? I mean, didn't you just get Instagram? How would you have Reddit of all things?" He suddenly gets serious. "It's not you, is it? Plant Daddy something?"

I shake my head no because there's no way he should know this. Him knowing feels dangerous. He nods. I cross and uncross my legs, trying to focus on Paul, who luckily has now lost his train of thought and is sending another text.

It's him.

Leo is Plant Daddy.

We met in the Southern California Reddit group. He never said anything that made me believe he was in Long Beach. And he thought it was me? Why didn't he say anything? I think about what Allison said about me again—how I'm afraid of change, that I'll freak out. I try to normalize my breathing and relax, focusing on not freaking out.

No wonder it felt so easy.

I stand up and then sit back down, not knowing what to do with my hands or my body. I think I'm stuttering, but I don't think anything is actually coming out.

"You okay?" Paul says. "Is it the air? It's so hot in here. You know we can't run the air conditioner. The plants!"

"The plants!" We both laugh, and I sound hysterical because I'm feeling hysterical. The space feels hotter and smaller, and I fan myself.

"Yeah, it's a little stuffy." He jumps up and opens the window, and I notice a row of cuttings there on the windowsill. That spot is too bright for them, but maybe they're only there temporarily. I'm sure those are the ones I sold him because I recognize the leaves on the Esmerelda spirit philodendron and the Florida ghost philodendrons.

When he turns back to me, he must see my near panic, because he shakes his head and tries to reassure me or something. "Oh my god, don't worry. They broke up or something. He definitely likes you. This girl was just a *thing* for months. So while I was not exactly thrilled when I found out he had a thing for you, part of me was relieved because, what the fuck, it's better than some rando trying to scam us out of our savings. Honestly, he would have given that girl his bank account numbers if she asked."

Paul finally puts his phone away.

"Anyways, what do you think?"

"About what?"

"The job!" He picks up where he left off as if nothing happened.

"Uhhh . . ." I'm definitely freaking out now, and he starts to frown as if he's finally realizing something is going on. "Can I think about it? I'd like to think about it, if that's okay?" I'm nodding like a madwoman.

There's a beat of silence for a moment, and I wonder if Paul has somehow figured me out. Something about his gaze feels like he sees through me, like he's taking footage of my insides. His face breaks into that easy sinister smile again.

"Of course!" he says, getting up.

I get up, too, and we shake hands as if everything is fine. Then, as I turn to leave, my eyes catch something else—the row of plants along the windowsill. One of the plants looks familiar. His body was blocking it before, but I can see it clearly now. Is that . . . my strawberry shake? I notice the little dot on the leaf, and I'm pretty sure it is. It's a plant I thought I'd lost in the accident, but . . . but now it's right here. I'm sure of it. Maybe he found it? No. It was packed away with everything else. The trash?

"The exit's down the hall and to the left," he says, and I nod, still in a daze. It's a wonder I can use my legs with everything going on. I stumble a little on my way out. "We'll be in touch. Also, if you need some cash, I'm happy to take the broken humidifiers and lights off your hands, too."

Wait, what? How did he know about the broken humidifiers? The official story to everyone else was broken pipes and an electrical fire caused by all the water. I'm the one who told the insurance guys about the humidifiers.

"How did you know about that? I didn't realize people were talking about the accident," I say, trying to sound normal.

Paul looks up at me for a moment and backtracks a little. "I think Leo mentioned it offhand? We talk about everything, you know, and he was concerned about you when it all happened. Generator accidents can be really dangerous."

Nobody knows the details of the accident or what really caused it. That information wasn't released to the public. Hell, I barely know what happened. My brain hurts from everything I'm trying to sort through, and it's too much at once.

Leo is Plant Daddy.

Paul and Leo might have sabotaged my store.

Did they set it all up? Was it some weird long game that they were both playing? Was Leo some sort of a honeypot after all?

I'm in a daze. This is everything Allison warned me about, and all at once. She was right. It was all a trap. This whole time.

As I finally make my way out of the store, I see a cutout of Leo and Paul smiling and holding up a plant next to a sign that says "Your neighborhood plant store." I stare into the eyes of cardboard-cutout Leo, with his muscles and his fake smile, and I want to scream. How could I have been so dumb?

"Tessa?" Speak of the devil.

chapter
twenty-nine

PlantDaddy54: Remember when we said we'd know each other when we met? Well, I think we've met? I think we know each other. I'm scared but also excited? I don't know. I'm gonna talk to you and if it's not you it won't matter.

———

I'm trying to stay focused, but it's hard when Leo's looking at me like that. His eyes are bright and friendly, and as if things couldn't get any worse, his dimple is out. My eyes linger on him for a long time as he comes closer, and I'm taking in everything like it's going to be the last time, because it might be. I wish I could put it off, delay the inevitable. Regardless of whatever happens, everything is going to change.

And I really didn't expect to see him so soon. I haven't had time to think, to strategize, though I'm not sure that would even help. My breath catches in my throat, and I'm hyperventilating a little.

"What's wrong?" He grabs my hand and pulls me away from the store and across the street, where there's a parking lot. I don't want to risk running into Paul again, so I grip his hand harder and drag him down the street wordlessly, in the direction of Plant Therapy. I'm silent while my brain is working through the options. He's not saying anything either. Maybe he's scared. I'm scared too.

I think about Paul. That's his brother. This is his store. I also think back to what Plant Daddy said about supporting his family no matter what. His family member who he has a complicated relationship with is his brother. It's all coming together.

We reach Plant Therapy, and I open the door and step inside. It's completely empty. There's nothing left.

"Promise me you'll tell me the truth," I say, finally letting his hand go and then crossing my arms over my chest. It's like we've been pushed back in time, to the second or third time we met. Defensive. Protective. His face falls, and he nods. He senses the difference too. I feel a huge lump in my throat—too big to swallow, so it just sits there, feeling like it's slowly choking me. "Promise me." My voice is hoarse as if I'm gonna cry, but it hasn't happened yet and I won't let it happen now. I'm never crying in front of him again.

Leo reaches out to touch my arm, and my eyes water, but I shake it off. He leans in and whispers, "Tessa, baby . . ." The sound of my name coming out of his mouth burns. I pull a little out of his grasp. "You're scaring me. Is something wrong?"

When he talks, it feels like it all makes sense. All the pieces are coming together. Of course he's Plant Daddy. Even in my imagination, he sounds like Plant Daddy. And this is why Plant Daddy wanted to stop talking to me, why he thought it was too hard. It's him. It's me. This is so messy. It's why being around him makes me crazy.

I shake those thoughts away for a moment and focus on what I need from him. "You promise me you had nothing to do with the accident at my store?"

He exhales, and there's a suggestion of an eyeroll, but he thinks better of it when he sees how serious I am.

"I promise. I wouldn't do that to you. You know I told you I've felt something for you for a while." His face looks soft, his lips plump and slightly chapped.

"What about your brother?" I say, my voice a little louder than I wanted. The resolve in his expression falters a little.

"Why would you say that?"

He looks serious again, and I'm again thinking about what he said about his brother. *That's my brother, and even when I don't agree with him, I have to be there for him.* I decide to not back off now because I really want to figure out what's going on.

"Your brother just said something that makes me think he might have had something to do with what happened to my store." I whisper the words because I feel like I should, even though we're alone. "He knew about my generator and the broken humidifiers, and I hadn't told anyone that. He said you told him about it."

Leo stands at his full height, and his gaze is unfocused, as if he's considering something. He shakes his head.

"Maybe someone else told him." His voice isn't convincing. And I know he knows it, too, because he quickly adds, "I knew about the store, and nobody told me. It's common knowledge. It was a big accident."

"Leo," I say, and it feels too similar to the way I said his name that day in the RV. I switch up my tone, reaching for something more stern. "It was so specific, Leo. He knew about the humidifiers. The exact thing that was broken."

Leo's face is momentarily tender, and I think he's going to believe me. I think maybe we'll get this out of the way, and then we can deal with the next thing—the big thing—which is that he's Plant Daddy and that all these intense feelings we've been having make sense. I take another moment to study him, and it's like I'm seeing him again for the first time. His eyes look open and vulnerable, almost scared.

"He has one of my plants." He's about to say something, but I press my fingers to his lips. "Just listen, I know it's crazy, but . . ." I decide to bring out my big guns, a conversation we've had before. I'm playing my hand a little, but I need for him to believe me. "You know how you know a plant. Once you see it, you know it. You know the leaves. It's familiar to you. You know it when you see it."

Leo gets a far-off look for a second, and I wonder if he's thinking of me, thinking of us and our conversations as the Plant Daddies. He refocuses on me.

"You're sure?"

"Leo, I . . ." I reach out for him, and he grabs my hand. "I know he's your brother, but—"

Before I can finish, he pulls away from me, his face suddenly harsh.

"It wasn't him. And this is the second time you've blamed our family for what's happened to your store. Can you prove it?"

I'm shocked by the iciness of his tone.

"Can I prove it? No, I can't prove it, but I know. I know he did this. Ask him! He'll tell you. I'm sure he will. He won't lie to you."

"My family isn't responsible for what's happening to you, Tessa. I know that you've had a hard time facing the reality of what's happening with your store, but this is just how it is." When he talks, he's someone else entirely. I wonder if this is how it's gonna be. There are three versions of him: Leo, Plant Daddy, and whomever this is.

"I'm not talking about your family, Leo. I'm just talking about your brother and you."

"Is that all? Are you just gonna accuse us of—"

"Is that why you were so nice to me? Is that why you got close to me . . . ? Is that why you . . ." I flash back to the bed in my RV and his head between my legs. "Was this all a part of some master plan to put me out of business? Get close to me? Get me to trust you so I'd work for you?"

"I didn't need a master plan to put you out of business, Tessa. It would have happened no matter what."

His tone is even, and his eyes are narrowed. And I know he's right. While I'd like to think my store could have held its own for a little while longer against his store, I know it wouldn't have lasted much longer. Their store is just so much bigger, with more plants and more customers and better social media. They're better in every single way. And they have Leo, who knows just as much about plants as I do, and now that I know he's Plant Daddy, it's even scarier because that means he also had me in a way.

I must look as pathetic as I feel, because a flash of regret crosses Leo's face.

"This was a mistake," I say, and there's that lump in my throat again, the kind that feels impossible to get rid of. The kind that lingers. His eyes soften as if he knows he's gone too far. I continue, my voice quiet. "You're right. Your store is bigger and better. But I know your brother had something to do with it, and even if you don't believe me, you know it's possible. I know you do."

Part of me wonders if that's why Paul does the things he does. He knows his brother will always have his back no matter what, and he doesn't have to worry about the consequences.

"Tessa . . . He's my brother. What do you want to happen? What do you think will happen?"

I haven't really gotten that far. But I try to play it out in that moment. I'd turn Paul in and give them my evidence, and maybe they'd investigate and put two and two together. I wonder if they have security cameras. Maybe there would be some evidence there, too.

And if I did this, if I turned Paul in, I don't know how much trouble he'd be in. But their store likely wouldn't survive the fall-out. It would have to shut down. So maybe this could fix things. Maybe things could go back to the way they were, back when everything was safe and I didn't have to think about all of this. Or maybe I could take over their space and make my own plant super-store. Leo and Paul would be a distant memory.

"We can't turn him in," Leo says, interrupting my train of thought. "I can't . . . All of those people, my employees, and . . . Maybe we can figure something out. Maybe there's an amount of money that could make this go away."

I wonder if this is something he's done before, too—paid people off to take care of his brother, to cover up whatever Paul has done. The idea of him paying me off makes me feel sick.

"You want to pay me off? Seriously? Has he done something like this before?" His guilty, pained expression gives me my answer. "He could have hurt someone, he could have hurt me, he could have . . ."

"No, I just . . . Shit, I don't know! I don't know! What do you want? Anything. We can figure something out. I promise we can figure something out. He can't get in trouble again."

We're both frantic, breathing hard and overwhelmed with the situation. This is going nowhere.

"I'm Plant Daddy." It's out of my mouth before I can try to plan a different way to say it, to smooth out the edges and make it sound better. He looks at me wide-eyed, and I know I'm not going to be able to stop the tears this time. They're coming, and I'm shaking. "It's me, and it's you, right? I figured it out. Something your brother said, and it just all came together. You asked me if I worked in retail. You suspected."

"Yeah."

I want to bottle the way he's looking at me and keep it forever, like I'm some kind of masterpiece. I'll add it to the list of Leo looks. He takes a step closer to me and touches my cheek, massaging my skin lightly with his thumb. I lean into his touch because I can't help it, and it's so light and soft. And I'm holding my breath because we're officially in uncharted territory. There's nothing I can do to prevent this change from happening to us.

"I suspected a few times, but I didn't know for sure," he whispers. "There was something so familiar about you. I knew there had to be a reason why it felt like this, why I couldn't resist you, why I felt so addicted to you. I actually messaged you today. I was gonna talk to you about it."

"I didn't know, not until Paul told me. I was just . . ." I'm talking quietly, too. I feel like the two of us are in a bubble. ". . . I wasn't paying attention, I don't think. I was too busy trying to resist you."

His lips brush my forehead, and I don't feel like it's a good sign. It feels like a goodbye, even though it's also like we're just saying hello for the first time.

"I mentioned the ZZ plant." He's laughing and looking at me again with that same sense of wonder, like he's seeing me the first time.

"I know. I wasn't paying attention. I could never think . . ." This moment feels perfect, exactly like I imagined it would be. He kisses me then, and I let him. He pulls me into a hug and kisses my forehead, his lips lingering there.

"I don't even know what to say, but I'm glad it's you," he says. "I'm so glad it's you. I'm so glad it's you." He keeps saying it like it's a prayer, and I feel it under my skin.

In that moment, I see Paul's twins in my mind. I see all of the Botanical Brothers employees. I see him—Leo, who just wants to do right by his family. That's all he's ever wanted to do.

"Tessa, please," he begs, and I know why he's pleading, who he's pleading for.

"Are you asking me to not say anything?" I pull away from him, and his eyes are watery, his face wet. He's crying.

In the middle of all this mess, we've finally circled back to the beginning. The center of everything. The thing that's always between us. Our stores. He wants what he wants, and I want what I want, and it feels like life or death for both of us. I've been fighting him for months, and now that I finally get the opportunity to actually move forward, to get back what I lost, doing it would mean I'm betraying him, too.

"This is just really complicated. You know my relationship with my family. You know how it is. Paul's kids . . ." There's another layer to this knowledge now because of our history. The conversations we've had as the Plant Daddies. I know about his insecurities, about how he feels responsible for so many things. It's not fair.

"That's not fair. Don't do that," I say, the edges of anger bubbling back up.

"For you it's just this store, Tessa. For me, it's my whole family and everything else. It's not on the same level."

And now I'm angry.

"I didn't do this!" I'm screaming now, my voice echoing through the empty room. "You moved into my neighborhood. He sabotaged my store! He tried to poach me and get me to work with you guys. You could have just left me and my store alone! You could have just left me alone. You didn't have to make me fall for you." I suck at holding things back, especially now that he knows me. He knows me well.

"I can leave you alone," he says sadly.

"Maybe you should." In the end, the Plant Daddies can't change what is, can't change what exists between us.

"Tessa . . . I don't even know . . ."

"Just go. This is over." I keep my promise to myself to not cry, even though his tears are flowing. His face threatens to pull me under. But I won't let it. "I need to think. I just need to think without you here. I need to be without you." I don't know if I mean it. His face softens a little bit, and he reaches for me, but I pull away.

"Just go," I repeat. I turn away from him, looking over at the space where my plant wall used to be. It's now just a series of wet wall stains and mold pushing through the plaster, a reminder of what I lost. I can feel him linger for a moment before leaving.

Then I'm alone again. I look around the store, and the feeling hits me more than ever. I can't call Allison. Bill wouldn't understand. There's only one person I can call, but I can't believe I'm actually doing it. I pull out my phone and dial the familiar number.

"Hey, sweetie," my mom says, and I sigh. She goes into panic mode instantly. "What's wrong? What's wrong? Do you need to come home?"

"Yeah," I say, letting the tears flow. "I think I do."

chapter thirty

Leo: I don't know if I should message you here or the other way. I feel like this way is the best way for us to talk now since we know each other so deeply. You were right. I talked to Paul and he admitted it, said he did it for us, for the shop. Said that it was necessary and you were never going to just give up, that you'd keep having ideas and keep pushing. He wanted you to work with us. You're right. I know you told me to never contact you again and I won't after this, I just wanted you to know. I'm sorry how I reacted, I'm sorry we're in this situation, I'm sorry I can't turn my brother in, that I can't betray him. But regardless of what you choose, know that I care about you so much it hurts and it's always going to hurt that I'm doing this to you, that I can't be there for you. All I wanted was to be your little break, an escape, and I couldn't do that. I continue to be this nightmare, this disruption to every part of your life. I've loved knowing you.

> Paul: Just so you know—it's not just me, it's both of us. We both own the store, we are both involved.

————

My mom buys me a plane ticket, and I'm on my way home the next day. This is her dream come true. All of the warnings and worrying, and I'm finally coming home to her.

And for the first time in a long time, I'm happy to leave Long Beach. Everything feels so heavy. My final meeting with the insurance company is in a couple of days, so I have time to think about what I want to do. Do I not say anything and still have to deal with Botanical Brothers while rebuilding my store? Do I turn Paul (and by extension Leo) in and get some version of my old life back? It's also my first time in a while without Wildcat, who's staying with Bill while I'm away. His tour isn't starting quite yet, and I didn't want to drag her here. I also figure she's a nice tether to make me return to Long Beach in case my mom is serious about keeping me here.

My mom's house is a standard suburban house like any other, the kind of house in a neighborhood that could be anywhere. When I arrive, there's a sense of comfort, as always when I come home for a visit.

"Tessa, is that you??" my mom says as she opens the door. She's wearing a bedazzled top and a pair of skinny jeans she likely got from Ross. My mom has always been slightly out of step with time, likely because she doesn't leave the house much. Regardless, her face is made up exquisitely—her lipstick the perfect shade of red, her deep brown skin giving off an inner glow that people online spend months trying to achieve. She reaches out to me and brings me into a tight hug. I allow myself to fall into it, breathing in her sweet scent. Mom loves Bath & Body Works. She squeezes me harder.

"Mom, I'm okay. I'm okay."

She pulls back a little to look me over. I wait for her assessment, and she shrugs, which means there's nothing too glaringly bad about my appearance. This is surprising, too, because I don't feel good at all. I spent most of the five-hour flight obsessively reading through the Reddit conversations Leo and I had as the Plant Daddies, on the verge of tears that didn't come because a small baby was staring at me the whole time, silently judging. Putting all the pieces together was painful because when I let myself really accept Plant Daddy and Leo as one and the same, I realized that my feelings were much deeper than I wanted to admit. His text message doesn't make things better. I can tell he's in pain, how he feels like there's no choice, like he's trapped the same way I am.

"I'm so glad you're home!" my mom says, ushering me into the house.

I feel a sense of calm as soon as I step through the doorway. The house is clean-ish—the kind of clean that's good enough for company, but where there are overflowing closets and baskets with items she'd get to putting away later. It's always been like that. My mom has been cleaning the house for the last twenty years. As I walk through the corridor to the living room, I see photos of me and my sister. There's even a photo of me in front of my RV, smiling. That one hurts a little. I can't believe she keeps it up, especially since she seemed so thrilled when I got off the road.

I follow the smell of oxtails into the kitchen. Mom moves back to the stove to put some finishing touches on the rice, and I sit across from her on a bar stool while she cooks.

"That father of yours. Did you know he's in Antarctica right now? Of all the places he could be! So irresponsible. Black folks don't go to Antarctica. What's even there? Penguins?"

This is standard. My mom is always too stressed to bring Dad up when we're on the phone because she's focused on me. But when I'm safely home, she has plenty of room to chat about it. It's one of her favorite topics, even though they've been divorced for years now. I always admired my dad's sense of adventure, and he's enthusiastically supported my own adventures, though I rarely hear from him beyond a few-word conversation once every two months or so. He's not much of a presence in my life since the divorce.

I don't say anything, just let her talk. Next, she's gonna ask if I've talked to him.

"Have you talked to him?" Yep. Right on cue. She turns away from the stove and looks at me expectantly. I shake my head, and she smiles, satisfied. Just what she thought.

"I'm glad you're here," she continues. "Now we can get back to normal. I know that you need to do some stuff with the store and that Norma woman . . . ." She's still standing at the stove, but she shakes her head. "But once you're done, you can live here and do something local. There's a Home Depot they just built in that abandoned shopping center down the street. You can work there with your plants." She's excited when she says it, and I don't really have the strength to fight her. What is my defense anyways? I actually don't know if I should be trusted with my freedom.

Before I can argue that I want to try and that I can do it, I remember that I have two strikes against me now. I look around at the living room and try to picture myself here again. The air smells divine, the smoky, almost cinnamon smell of the oxtails taking over my nose. A comfortable silence fills the kitchen for just a moment before I hear the door open, and my sister Cece's voice booms from the other room.

"Seeeeestarrrr!" Cece screams, all energy. She barrels into the room wearing her scrubs and looking a little haggard, despite her obvious enthusiasm at seeing me. She works as a vet tech at a local emergency animal hospital while she's earning her veterinary degree, so she probably just got off work. I get up and meet her when she's only halfway through the hallway, giving her a big hug. She smiles at me and then looks me over and smiles even wider. "Finally."

"Finally," I repeat, hugging her close again. I silently wonder why I don't do this more. Why I don't come home more often. Maybe it's not so bad.

"Okay, everything is done! Let's sit down for dinner," my mom says.

———

"So the store burnt down?" my sister asks. I'd just given her a general idea of what had happened. I didn't want to burden her with the details, especially knowing how busy she is with her residency rotation at the vet hospital, and I honestly don't love repeating it all anyways. Each time I have to, it chips away at me. It's just so unbelievable to talk about it.

"No, it didn't burn down," I say, sighing. "More like watered down? Pipes broke, the heating lamps busted, the generator was a whole thing." I don't mention the sabotage because then I'd get a whole speech about safety, and it would just worry them more. I don't want to stress them out.

"Right," my sister says. "So are you gonna reopen? What's going to happen next?"

I stare down at my oxtails like they are the most interesting thing in the world.

"I'm not sure yet," I say honestly, taking my first bite of oxtail. Long Beach does a lot of things right, but it's a Jamaican food wasteland, so I haven't had really good oxtails in a long time. They're so juicy and saucy with just the right amount of spice, and the piece melts in my mouth. Perfect. I sigh happily. I needed this. I scoop up some gravy and rice to chase the chewy oxtail with, and it's so good it momentarily wipes my brain of the current situation.

"Tessa and I were talking about her coming home. She thinks it's a good idea," my mom says. Except I didn't actually say that, and my sister knows it. Mom does this all the time. Pretends the conversation went the way she'd have wanted.

Cece and I give each other a look to acknowledge that fact, and then she says, "Well, Tessa has a lot to think about. She seems to still be figuring things out."

"Well, she's here now! She needs us. I have a few things I'm throwing away in your bedroom, but we can get that stuff out in no time. It will just take an afternoon. No biggie."

"Mom," Cece warns. She's always been my buffer, and I love her for it.

"What?" Mom says innocently. "I just love you, Tessa, and I want you to be safe and happy, and these last few months you've been so unhappy." They both look at me expectantly.

"These oxtails are so good!" I exclaim, trying to channel my enthusiasm for the piece of meat into my words.

"See! It's a hellhole. No oxtails." My mom rests her fork down like she's made her ultimate point.

"But that's her choice, Mom. She doesn't just want to come home. What would she even do?"

They do this sometimes. Talk as if I'm not actually here. It's an older daughter and mother thing, I think. They also just are around each other more.

"Home Depot!" My mom is excited when she says it. "There's also Pike's Nursery."

As they talk, I realize that it hasn't all been bad, my time without the store. When I let myself relax, let myself forget about all of the chaos, I remember all of the really great moments. I think about watching Bill perform. I think about the aquarium. I think about cleaning out the RV. I think about me and Leo in the bed and how good that felt. It really wasn't all bad, and I experienced all of those things without the store. Then I think about Norma smiling at her phone. Whatever she's been smiling about, it certainly has nothing to do with the store.

"What? Is she going to gallivant around like her father? Is that what you want?" At that, I decide to speak up.

"Mom, why do you think traveling is so evil?" Dead silence. My sister looks shocked. It's something the two of us have talked about in passing—our mom's resentment for travel—but nobody has actually brought it up. "Like really? Is it just because of Dad?"

Mom suddenly looks very young. She keeps eye contact, but her eyes don't have the fire they typically do. Is that some vulnerability? She looks like she's searching for the words.

"It's not safe," she says after another moment. It's something she always says. Her go-to. She reaches for my arm, holds it. "I just don't want something bad to happen to you."

"Lots of bad things have happened to me, Mom. I tried my best to stop them, but they just kept coming, and I couldn't win." I feel like we're on the edge of something. It's right there, like one of those paint-by-numbers kits. You work at it and work at it, and eventually you start to see something.

"Your father—"

"I'm not Dad. I'm not gonna leave you," I cut in. I know her argument. She thinks if she can scare me, she can keep me safe, keep me close, that I won't leave her. Her eyes water a little, and she wipes the tears away. We're silent again, but it feels like something big has shifted, and I feel like there's more coming. "And if I fail, I'll survive. I have survived. I'm surviving right now." I get up from the table and come around to hug her. She puts her hand on my arm, and I kiss her on the forehead. "I am okay," I whisper to her. She pats me again a few times on the arm and leans into my hug.

"Okay," she says quietly, pulling away a little and standing up. "I have some pound cake, let me go get it." She wipes a tear from her eye and makes her way into the kitchen.

When she's gone from the room, I exhale a breath I didn't realize I was holding.

"Oh my god!" my sister says, shoving me in the arm. I shake my head, not sure what happened but feeling like the heavy backpack I've been holding for a while is finally off.

———

My sister and I sit on the back porch together a little later that night. Mom is in bed, and we'd spent the evening cleaning up and washing the dishes before moving out here to relax some. It's a warm but crisp night, and the back porch overlooks one of those retention ponds they've lit up with a water feature to make it more appealing. It's pleasant. The two of us eat our third pieces of pound cake with vanilla bean ice cream. And I tell my sister the whole story. Everything about Plant Daddy, the stores, Leo, the insurance check. Everything. When I'm done she gives a long dramatic sigh.

"I know in front of Mom you said you didn't know what to do, but what are you going to do? Are you going to report that douche bag? You should! He sounds awful."

"I don't know if I can. I wish I didn't care so much, but I do."

"So you're going to give up your store for him? Do you love him?"

I don't know if I'm that brave yet. Especially since there's no chance for a future between us because of our situation.

"It's kind of for him, but it's also for me. I think I'm ready."

"Maybe we can see you more."

I realize I'd like that too, that maybe coming home can be a part of my plan. I nod. "Yeah. Maybe I'll drive the RV here and hang out for a bit in a few weeks."

My sister's face brightens. "I know we'd like that."

I smile back.

chapter thirty-one

Mom: Are you back safe?

Tessa: Mom, you're texting!

Mom: I love you so much, Tessa. I can't wait to see you in a few weeks.

Tessa: I can't wait to see you again too.

Mom: Make sure you make a list of foods you want me to make.

Tessa: I will.

———

It's finally time to tell Norma that I'm not going pursue the store anymore, that I don't have anything left. I still have her steely gaze from our last conversation with the landlord in the back of my mind, how she looked at me like I was failing at everything. I'm hoping some of my momentum with my mom can help me here and can give me the strength I need to somehow deal with Norma without having another breakdown.

When I arrive at the retirement center, they tell me there's a party happening. Someone is turning eighty-nine. The party is in an old gym on the property, one of those places you can tell they haven't put much money into. There's something deeply nostalgic about it—from the bleachers to the spinning lights. It reminds me of an early 2000s formal or nights at the skating rink. Everyone is sitting around in wheelchairs or shuffling about with walkers. Nobody is really dancing. Everyone just sits in little clusters around the dance floor. It feels like the ending scene of a coming-of-age movie.

I scan the gym, looking for Norma. I quickly spot the birthday boy—Benny, according to the posters—holding court among three elderly women, all vying for a shot with him. Then I see Norma. She's sitting in the corner, giggling and whispering to a darkskinned man wearing a party hat. I don't think I've ever seen her giggle before or smile like that. I make my way over to her, weaving through the very slow-moving elderly people along the way.

Norma doesn't notice me at first, so I have time to fully take in the scene. Is she wearing blush? Who is the man she's talking to? I come to a stop nearby, and she finally feels my presence. Much to my shock, she doesn't frown. Her smile stays plastered on her face. I'm so confused. I make a face, but her sunny disposition doesn't shift. She taps on the man's shoulder, and he turns to me.

"Herb, this is Tessa. She's not my daughter, but she might as well be."

I try not to seem too shocked when she says it. Norma has never really talked about me like that. She's never said something so sweet about me. I've always felt more like her mentee than a daughter, but there's real softness in her eyes now.

"Hi, Herb. Nice to meet you."

He gives me a nod. "Nice to finally meet you, too. I've heard a lot about you."

There's a pause, and it's kind of awkward, with both Norma and me struggling to fill the space with something to say. Herb saves us from ourselves.

"Hey, I'm gonna get us something to drink, babe," he tells Norma, kissing her on the cheek.

She preens, still sparkling. "Sounds good, sweetheart." She watches him shuffle away, his pace slow, mesmerizing. I guess I know what those heart emojis were about and why she's been so hard to get ahold of lately. She's been in a love vortex.

"Isn't he sweet?" she asks when I settle down across from her, giving her a look that can only be described as "what the fuck."

I launch into my questions.

"Who is that? Is that your boyfriend? How long has this been going on? How did you meet? I've never seen you smile at a man before!"

"I know, it took me totally by surprise." She glances over to where Herb is shakily pouring drinks. He's moving impossibly slow. "It's been a little over a month. I really feel good about it."

I guess a month in a place like this ends up feeling like a much longer time.

"Norma, I have something to tell you. I don't know how to tell you this but—" She's looking at me now, and her sternness is back. She's scary again. I continue, trying to not be too shaken by her gaze. "The store, I decided I don't want to continue trying to make it work. I know I've been trying so hard on it, and I was going to try to find us a new location and everything else, but I think we should just take the insurance money and let it go."

Norma is quiet for a while, but she doesn't look mad anymore. She goes back to watching Herb, who has managed to pour the drinks and is about to carry them back to our table. It's a long process. She still looks charmed.

"Why?" Norma asks, her gaze staying on Herb.

I have no clue how I'm supposed to begin to tell Norma why. Do I tell her about the sabotage and Leo? I guess it doesn't matter. There's so much that's happened. But I decide to go for the simple answer instead.

"I think I'm ready to do something else, and I'm tired, Norma." It's the clearest I've been thus far, and it feels the most true at this moment. I'm ready to do something else. What is that something else? I don't know. It's silent again beyond the crooning of Frank Sinatra in the background.

I brace myself for the worst, and I start babbling, trying to fill the silence. "You can hire someone else to run the store if you want to keep it open. I have a few locations I looked at, maybe one of them will be good."

She stops me with a look. "I hate that this happened, Tessa. I trusted you with the store."

I nod. She did trust me with the store, and for six years, and I screwed up. I try to think of a good explanation, to talk myself out of what happened, but I decide instead to just let it sit there, to deal with it.

"I know, and I'm sorry," I say. The disco lights dance across her face, and I watch them as they go.

"Okay," she says simply.

"Okay?" My voice comes out much higher than it should. Almost a screech.

"Yeah, I mean, what am I supposed to do from here? This is my life now. It's not my store, it's been yours for a while now, and if you don't want to do it anymore, I can't force you."

Herb is making his way back to us from the punch table—again, very slowly.

"You aren't mad?" I ask.

She throws daggers with her eyes, like the old days. The less lovey version of her floats to the surface.

"I mean, I am a little mad, Tessa. The store I built nearly forty years ago is gone, and you lost a bunch of money. But maybe forty years is enough. Plus, I can't do anything from here. What am I gonna do? Find another you? It's impossible."

Yeah, well, she has a point.

"But I'm glad you're getting away. I'm starting to realize there's more to life than the store," she continues, turning to look at Herb again. He's still on his way back, slowly. "So what happens now?"

"The store gets liquidated, and we get the insurance money and any other assets, which we'll split," I say.

"Eh, it's yours," she says.

"I'm sorry?"

"The money is yours, Tessa. You've done a good job, now you can go do what you want. Maybe use the money to fix that damn RV and do something else."

"What about your house?"

"Maybe we can sell it or rent it or something. Whatever we want to do."

"We?"

"Yeah, you're my heir."

"I am?" The shocks never end.

"Who else? It's always been you, Tessa. You're all I have outside of this place. It was always going to be yours anyways, so you can take it now."

I'm full-on crying now (what else is new?), and Norma pats my shoulder awkwardly and looks a little grossed out, but I don't even linger on it. I'm beside myself.

"Just make sure to call the insurance guy and do all the final meetings so it's all done."

Herb is finally back with the drinks, and he places a kiss on Norma's head and very slowly sits down. She smiles up at him as if he's the most beautiful thing in the world.

"What did you ladies talk about?" he says, looking at me a little concerned. Probably because of all the crying.

Norma gives me a wink. "The future, Herb."

Herb gives a big hearty laugh, like Santa Claus.

"Oh, that's not something I think too much about," he says. "Not sure how much time I have left."

He laughs again, and Norma is laughing. I guess I should start laughing, too. After a few moments, they are fawning over each other, leaving me sitting there to watch them. They're all laughs and smiles, and my brain conjures up Leo, and I wish it wouldn't. Whatever happens next won't include Leo or Plant Daddy.

chapter thirty-two

Norma: Hey, make sure you get all the mail and all my stuff when you go in today.

Tessa: Of course.

Norma: I want our trash cans too. Just store them at the house. The city gets nothing!

Tessa: Yes.

Tessa: I won't leave anything. Are you sure you don't want to stop by and see it? Say goodbye?

Norma: I want to remember it as it was before. That building isn't Plant Therapy anymore.

———

When I arrive at the store for the final inspection and paperwork signing, it's still early. Being in the empty shop doesn't hurt, but it feels sad—like I'm mourning someone who has left. Wildcat is there because I want her to say goodbye, too. The power is off, but it's a bright day, so the sunlight streams in through the windows. Without the plants in here, it's hot, and so I prop the door open. I then walk to the side of the building where the mailbox is, passing Bill's and Allison's old stores. They're both empty and bare, just like mine.

I grab Bill's mail, and when I reach my mailbox, I notice a plant on the ground next to the door. It's the strawberry shake that Paul stole from the store when he sabotaged it. My mailbox is empty except for a single letter with my name written in small, blocky letters on the front of the envelope. I open the door fully and go inside. Then I open up the letter. There's a note inside, along with a $30,000 check signed by the Botanical Brothers.

I read the note silently.

Hope this helps.
   Love,
   Leo

The words repeat in my mind. *Hope this helps. Love, Leo.*

Is he serious? I was kidding when I mentioned a payoff, but I guess this is it. Is this some type of bribe? Some hush money? Am I some mistress he's paying off to keep quiet? Is that all I am to him? Heat rises from my neck, and my hands shake. I'm smart enough to know that taking money from the Botanical Brothers likely comes with strings attached, with stipulations. It's also hush money masquerading as an act of kindness. I guess if this was all some big elaborate plan, they definitely won, and I hate that. I start to tear up the check, but stop as I look at my phone to check the time. I've got plenty of time.

"Wait here, Wildcat," I say, and she sits down quietly in the empty space, watching me as I leave the store. I walk up the street to Botanical Brothers. This time, I know exactly where to direct my rage.

Botanical Brothers is eerily the same. It exists outside of everything that has happened. Leo and Paul cutouts fake-smile at me from outside the door. The doors are open, and there's a crowd, like usual. I try to be as inconspicuous as possible. I see some of my customers, and they try to avoid eye contact with me. I walk around the store, looking at the displays and all the plants. It's been a while since I've been around so many plants. I love the way the air smells like dirt, and I love the steam from the humidifiers on my skin. I walk around the huge space and look at all the smiling faces of the customers. Happy people with their plants.

I spot a hot twenty-something man who looks more like a model than an employee setting up the hoyas.

"Hi, is Leo here?" I ask him.

He looks just past me, and it's clear he doesn't know who I am. Looks like they're always hiring new people. I guess with my store out of the way, it's even easier to get customers. All of my regular customers, even those who remained loyal till the end, are now free to shop here. What a perfect setup for them. My face manages to grow even hotter.

The man nods again, looking behind me and pointing, but I don't need his direction anymore because I can feel it. I know he's there. My Leo spidey-sense hasn't gone away, despite everything. I'm a little afraid to turn around, but I do. His eyes widen as he takes me in, and I wonder what he's seeing, what he's thinking about. His gaze falls to my lips and then lifts to my eyes. He looks tired. He's not wearing his Botanical Brothers T-shirt, opting instead for a plain black shirt. That seems a little odd, but I don't linger there.

"Really, Leo? A check?" I say, shoving the check into his hands. I'm making a bit of a scene, and a few people turn around to see us. But I don't care. I'm not afraid of embarrassing myself anymore.

"Just a problem you can pay to go away? Is that how you see it?" I start to leave, but he follows after me.

"Tessa . . ." I don't fall for the trap of him saying my name.

"Just don't, okay. You won. Paul won. I'm officially out of your hair. It worked. I'm not going to say anything. If this is what you want, this situation is what you want . . ." I lose some of my steam thinking about the twins, about his family. I get why he wants it, why he's done what he has. But that doesn't make it okay. I shake myself and continue. "If that's what you want, then it's yours, but don't throw money at me, not after everything. You didn't have to do this because I wasn't going to say anything anyways."

He reaches out for my arm, but I pull it away.

"No. You don't get me too," I say. There are a few shocked noises from the peanut gallery. I guess the secret is out now. Not that it matters. I care for Leo a lot, but I can't live with what he's doing, what he's choosing, even if I understand it. "And just know this is never going to end. He's going to keep doing this, going to keep putting you in these situations, because he knows that you love him and you love your family and you feel responsible for everyone. But it didn't have to happen like this. You know it didn't. You're just afraid."

I look at him one more time, the sexy merman of my dreams. His lips are puffy, his hair a bit ruffled like he's been messing with it.

"Bye, Leo."

And with that, the battle is over. Botanical Brothers wins.

I take a step back out of his space and make my way towards the door. On my way out, I see Paul, and he stares at me with a gaze I can't identify. I turn away and walk out the door, passing the cutouts. In a cathartic act of pettiness, I knock over both of their cutouts and then start back up the street so I can finally close my store. I hear the echoes of commotion on my way out but I don't turn around.

―――――

"Okay, are you ready?" Frank says, pushing the paperwork over to me. I have my plant from Paul sitting next to me while I look over the papers. This is it. The end. I nod and start signing as Frank directs me. "Okay. So this paperwork is to release your insurance money. Half for you, half for Norma. I already went to see Norma, so these just need your signatures, and we'll be done."

I sign it.

"And these are the reports saying that there was no foul play and it was just an infrastructural accident. The police didn't really find anything, and you won't be pursuing any further investigation."

I sign that one too without hesitation.

"This is the form that officially ends your lease of the building and turns it over and also releases the company from liability moving forward. Basically just means you are no longer connected to this building and you've been compensated for everything."

My hand shakes a little when I sign this one, but I still sign it anyways.

Then I put the pen down, and it's done. It's actually done. I'm no longer running Plant Therapy. This is no longer my store. It's been eight years, and it's finally over. I feel absolutely terrified, but in my heart, I know it's the right thing to do.

"From what I understand, Plant Therapy will not be in operation in any form, so we can also cancel the insurance for the place."

I pick the pen back up, take a deep breath, and sign that form too. I look next to my name and see Norma's signature is already there, giving me strength.

"Okay, that's it." He smiles. "You're done and free. Good luck, Miss Wilder." He puts out his hand for me to shake, and I shake it.

"Thanks."

He gathers his papers up and leaves, and then I'm alone in the silence of the store one more time. It is sadder than I thought it would be. It hurts more than I anticipated. I close my eyes and say goodbye to the space. In my head, I envision all of the plants around. I think about my clients and the events I put on. Garden parties and my prized plant wall. I'm tired of crying. I take another slow walk through the space while Wildcat runs around for the last time, too, saying her goodbyes.

Before I leave, I sit in the chair with my phone in hand. I open Instagram and start writing a message about the official closing of the store. The account has a few thousand followers now, without me even noticing. Likely a combination of the hype around the closing and all of the drama and people trying to catch good deals on my plants.

I pick a photo of me and Wildcat in front of Plant Therapy smiling.

Hi, this is Tessa, the co-owner of Plant Therapy. After 40 years, Plant Therapy will be finally closing its doors. Thank you so much for letting us be a part of the community for the last 40 years. I've really enjoyed serving you for the last 8 years, and I will miss you all so much. Remember to water your plants.

Talk soon,

Tessa.

chapter thirty-three

Bill: Hey, I'm so proud of you. I'll see you on the road.

Tessa: See you on the road.

Bill: Have you talked to Allison yet?

Tessa: Not yet but I will. I will.

Bill: Okay, call me when you head out, okay?

Tessa: Thanks Bill. Thank you for everything.

———

The plan is to take Wildcat on a road trip to Georgia with me and spend some time with my mom and sister. This time, we have a good amount of money to work with, and I plan to keep the whole trip mostly to myself beyond updating a private Instagram account I decided to start. It's small—just my favorite clients and friends—

and low pressure, but it's a nice way to document. One of Bill's bandmates spent a whole day fixing the RV for me before they left for their tour. I haven't turned it on yet, but I heard him start it, so I'm sure it will run fine.

Wildcat and I have been sleeping in the RV to get her used to it. She was fussy at first, but she seems to like it now. We plan to spend the night at the beach one more time before we start driving. I'm packing up some dishes for the road when I hear Allison's voice outside.

"Tessa?"

It's been a while since I heard her voice. I'd planned on texting her today to make sure I would get to see her before I leave Southern California. I step out of the van, and she's standing there in the driveway. It's the first time we've spoken in weeks. We're silent for a bit, and I'm about to speak when she beats me to it.

"I'm pregnant," she says with a shy smile. "Just into the second trimester now . . . . I didn't want to say anything because I was having trouble wrapping my head around it, and I was over-whelmed and stressed and hormonal, but that's what I was hiding."

"Oh! Oh my god!" I give her a tight hug. When I'm up close, I can see it—a tiny bump underneath her tank top. "Wow. That's incredible. A mom. You're going to be a mom." It's hard to believe, but I know she'll be good at it. Party Allison is long gone.

"It's unbelievable, right?" She pulls back a little to look at me again. "Your store is closed. I'm sorry." She hugs me tighter, and I relax into it. I guess I needed this.

"Yeah, I'm sorry too." I exhale into her hair. She pulls away.

"I just thought you should know, but I didn't want to tell you on the phone or talk to you like that . . . so I stopped by." She looks behind me. "You don't have a sexy man back there do you? Can I see?" I try to pull my brain away from the memory of me and Leo in the van.

"I wish. Come on in." I step back into the RV, and she follows me in. Her eyes go wide as she takes in the space, and she's smiling.

"Wow, it looks great."

I've decorated since Leo was there. I also added some plants and some photos of my family and friends. She lingers on a photo of the two of us with Bill at the concert all those months ago. I also have the alocasia black velvet Leo gave me sitting in the kitchen. It's one of the last plants I still have.

"Something else you need to know. Leo is Plant Daddy," I tell her.

"Your internet boyfriend?" She throws it out casually, and it's almost as if nothing has changed, as if the two of us didn't get into that huge fight.

"Yeah, that's him. They're the same person." I grab a bottle of water from the fully stocked fridge and throw it to her.

"Wait, that kind of makes sense. It seemed like you guys were addicted to each other. How do you feel? Does he know?" As she says this, I realize so much has happened.

I settle down and tell her the whole story, everything she's missed. She pulls a snack out of her pocket and eats while I talk about telling Leo that I'm Plant Daddy, the check, Paul, and everything else.

"Oh! That explains the videos!" she says when I'm done.

The existence of videos has traditionally never been the bringer of good news, and I'm afraid to ask, but I do anyways.

"What videos?"

She frowns. "I didn't want to mention it in case you were upset about it? Haven't you gotten a bunch of messages about it?" I shake my head. I haven't logged in to my store account since I did the last post. It was too hard. She whistles and opens her phone. "So there's a video of Paul and Leo fighting after you knock over their cutouts. I figured it was for a good reason, and now I know. He tried to bribe you!"

She pulls up the video, and it's taken from a bit away, by

someone else in the store. There's me leaving the store and pushing over the cutouts as I leave. What I didn't see is that Leo starts to chase after me but is stopped by Paul, who grabs his shoulder. Leo turns, and they start to argue.

"God, are you happy now?" Leo is pacing back and forth, and Paul is trying to settle him down.

"Not here," Paul says between his teeth, grabbing Leo again, this time by the arm. Leo stares at his hand and then pulls away.

"You sent her a check?" Leo booms. "Are you serious? From me? I had to protect you again. I told you to leave it alone, to leave her alone."

"Leo, let's go. Now. Let's go. Not here. Not now."

Leo looks around as if he's just noticing everyone in the room.

"She's right about you," he says, and he then he turns and leaves the store. And it's just Paul standing there while everyone stares. It's so quiet you can hear a pin drop.

Paul puts on his signature smile and holds his arms out in the air. "The Botanical Brothers fight sometimes. It's nothing," he says, still smiling.

The camera goes off.

I'm speechless. She plucks the phone out of my hand and pulls up another video, this one on YouTube. I'm surprised I'd missed so much content. But then, I'd pretty much destroyed my Botanical Brothers habit since seeing them would have been too painful. I've also been really busy and haven't had the time to stalk them.

I press play on the video. In the screenshot, Leo has a bit of a glazed-over expression, his dimple nowhere in sight. His eyes are dark and rimmed red. I know the feeling.

"Hi, this is Leo. I hate that I have to do one of these things, but I feel like it's the best way for me to do it since this is how we met each other and started talking all those years ago. I just wanted to say thank you for everything and all the ways you've supported me. Unfortunately, I will no longer be a part of the Botanical Brothers moving forward. This wasn't an easy decision, and it makes me really sad, but it's for the best. I won't go

into details, but Paul and I have different ideas for what we want to do and how we want to do things, so it's best that we part ways. As for me, I'm not sure what's going to happen next, but I realized that now's the best time for me to figure it out. Thank you again for everything. I hope you keep your love of plants and remember to water. Thank you so much."

I turn off the video and look over at Allison. She's smiling at me.

"It doesn't mean anything," I say.

"Tessa, you won. The Botanical Brothers are gone. He chose you."

"You're on his side now?" I ask, handing her phone back. I get up and pretend to be busy with the pile of dishes I'm putting away, but I just stand there. "It's too late."

I actually feel bad for Leo because I know how hard it must have been for him to make that decision. I think about his niece and nephew and how much he loves them and cares about them. He also loves Paul and the safety and love of his family. I know he doesn't want to sacrifice that.

"You should reach out," she says, and I pause, thinking. I couldn't, right? No, it's too late. But . . . the thing between us is no longer between us. There's no more Plant Therapy. No more Botanical Brothers. "You're thinking about it! What do you have to lose? You've already decided what you're gonna do. You can just let him know that you're open to talking again."

Am I open to talking again? We left things in such a bad place.

Allison continues. "Doesn't have to be anything big. I just remember how he looked at you, how you looked at him."

"You weren't a big fan of it at the time."

"I was jealous. You were having this whirlwind dangerous affair, and I felt like a loser who was in Riverside and who was now pregnant. I'm sorry. I wanted things to change for you too, but I was obsessed with how I wanted it to happen, and I was being controlling about him. I guess I kind of felt like I was being replaced too."

"I'm sorry for not being there and avoiding the reality of you leaving and being too self-centered. All I cared about was keeping things the same, and I just wasn't paying good enough attention. I'm sorry."

She gets up, and we give each other another hug. "You love him don't you?"

I pull away from her. I want to say no, but if I didn't love him, why would I give up my store? Yes, it wasn't just for him. It was for me, too. But he was a big part of it.

"Fine. I'm so bored. Riverside is so boring. Please come visit. What am I gonna do up there? Maybe you were right. It's no Long Beach. I should come down more, and we can do stuff." I'm glad she changes the subject, glad she doesn't push.

"I was thinking I could come up!"

Her eyebrows raise. "What? You're going to come visit me? Leave your beloved Long Beach behind?" She puts a hand across her forehead and pretends to collapse like she's a character in a historical drama. "What has happened to my friend?"

"Okay, don't be dramatic. I'm actually gonna take the RV out of Long Beach for a while. Maybe I can spend a few days in Riverside?"

Allison shrieks and hugs me again. "Yes! That would be great. We can shop for stuff. You can help me set up my nursery! Wait till you see the house! It's so huge and has big windows. Perfect for plants. You can put it together! Wildcat can run around the back-yard! There's this Mexican restaurant near me that's really good. They have $5 margaritas, and I can watch you get drunk!"

―――――

When Allison leaves, I sit down and go online to assess what's going on. It's a mess. There's the clip of me floating around. Everyone has theories about what happened. My inbox is full of angry messages from people saying that I split up the Botanical

Brothers. I've been called a Yoko Ono. There are online rumors about our relationship. Other messages saying that the Botanical Brothers shut me down and I needed to get revenge. When I see the rumblings of people wanting to do a deep dive investigation on what happened, I decide it's time to log off.

I pull up the text message thread between me and Leo and stare at it for a few long moments. A "hi" wouldn't hurt. Especially considering everything that's happened. I don't know if we can go back, but I'll start with a hello.

chapter thirty-four

Tessa: Hey, it's me. I saw your video. I know that must have been really hard and I'm proud of you for doing it.

Leo: Hey, you. I should have done it sooner. I'm sorry.

Tessa: No, I understand. That's your brother. There's a family history there. It's not a contest.

Leo: I don't know about that. I quit. You did win.

Tessa: You didn't quit for me.

Leo: I only quit because of you. If it wasn't for you I'd still be there, I'd still be caught up in that toxic shit with my brother.

Tessa: Are you okay?

Leo: Yeah, I'm in Sacramento right now staying with a few relatives. I can't be in the house with him right now. I hope you know I didn't send that check.

Tessa: I saw the video. How are things with your niece and nephew?

Leo: I can still support them and not be in business with Paul. I'll figure out other ways. I have a bunch of money saved up. I can pay Andrew's medical bills myself if I have to.

Tessa: I just wanted to reach out. I know what it's like to lose your store.

Leo: I just don't know what to do with all my free time. I didn't realize how busy I was.

Tessa: Maybe find a cute guy to spend it with. That's what I did.

Leo: I miss you.

Tessa: Don't do that, I'm leaving soon.

Leo: You are? Where?

Tessa: Just need a fresh start. I'm going to the beach Friday and then I'm heading up to Riverside first to spend some time with Allison and then I'm heading east to spend some time with my family and then I'm not sure what comes next.

Leo: Can we have a fresh start?

Tessa: Maybe this is how we should know each other.

Leo: Chatting like this?

Tessa: Yeah.

Leo: I don't know if I can go back, not after feeling you.

Tessa: Stop saying dreamy stuff.

Leo: Sorry.

Tessa: I can't believe you're Plant Daddy. What are the chances?

Leo: I wanted it to be you so bad. I'd feel so guilty about it, like I was cheating.

Tessa: I was confused too. I was thinking "oh, if I could just combine them they'd be the perfect man for me."

Leo: Are you saying I'm perfect?

Tessa: You know what I mean.

Leo: I don't know. You are pretty perfect to me.

Tessa: Didn't I say to stop being dreamy?

Leo: Sorry again.

Tessa: So . . . friends?

Leo: Friends.

———

"Okay Wildcat, let's go." I load Wildcat into the RV. She jumps up happily into the front, settling in the passenger seat next to me and sitting up at attention, ready for an adventure. I take out my phone and take a photo of her to send to Leo.

> Tessa: And we're off! Hope you are okay today.

I pause for a moment to see if he answers. We've been texting pretty nonstop since I reached out. It is nice to fall back into our familiar old dynamic, even if it hurts a little bit. It doesn't feel like quite enough, but I'm still glad to have him back in my life now that our stores are no longer in competition with each other. He doesn't answer, and I pocket my phone.

"Okay, we're going," I tell Wildcat.

She barks in agreement. I take a deep breath and put my key into the ignition and turn it on. It's a big moment. The engine roars to life, and I can feel it underneath my skin. It feels like my whole body buzzes. I adjust my side mirror and then back out of the driveway really slowly because I seem to have forgotten what it's like to drive such a large vehicle. The rear bumper grazes the mailbox a little, but not enough for me to care, and we head to the beach.

The parking lot at Rosie's Dog Beach is pretty empty because it's the middle of the day. I let Wildcat off the leash, and she runs across the parking lot to the beach. I follow behind her. When I step off the sidewalk, I take off my shoes and bury my feet in the sand. The sand feels almost too hot, but I get used to it. Wildcat circles me a few times before running out into the surf far ahead of me. She grabs a stick and takes off down the beach, as is her way, and I settle into the sand and gaze out at the waves and the huge boats inching across the water. I'll miss this view, and I'll miss this spot.

"Thank you," I say to no one and nothing in particular. I think I'm saying it to Long Beach. Thank you for taking care of me. Thank you for keeping me safe. Thank you for giving me the space to grow up, find my passion for plants, and keep going.

Wildcat is still running in the distance, and as I pull out my phone to take her picture, I notice a little familiar gray blur speeding down the beach. I scramble to stand up, and the blur, seeing me, starts running in my direction. When I see his fluffy ears and wide eyes, I know for sure. It's Alfred.

He arrives at me all tail wags and jumping around. I reach down and pet him, and then he wiggles out of my grasp and takes off running. My gaze follows as Alfred runs down the beach.

And that's when I see him—Leo. Leo, who said he was in Sacramento. He's here. Why is he here? He looks just like the sexy merman he did when we first met on this beach months ago. He's wearing a tank top and shorts and holding his sandals in one hand.

My throat feels like it's closing up, and I try to steady my breathing, but it's not happening. Seeing him brings everything back. The Plant Daddies. Us. He's staring at me as he comes closer, and I can't look away.

Wildcat jumps over to him, demanding attention. He leans down and gives her a quick pet and kisses her on the forehead. Satisfied, she goes running around again with Alfred following her.

"Hi," I say as he comes to a stop in front of me.

"Hi."

"What are you doing here? You were in Sacramento," I whisper, even though the waves are loud. I wonder if he can hear me.

"I know, I drove down. I just needed to see you."

I don't know how to respond.

"You know how you always used to say you're putting me out of business.' " I nod as he steps closer. "You'd say we can't do this because your store and my store, but there's no stores anymore. It's just us."

"It's just us." I nod, and I'm shivering a little bit.

"You were in my head for months before we even met, and since knowing you in real life, you've buried yourself in my heart, and I just can't go back. I can't just talk to you, I can't just be your friend, not when I love you the way I do." I take a shuddering breath, and he reaches for me, his hands on my arms. "Can I just love you as us? No Plant Daddies. No Terri and Josh. Just like Tessa and Leo?"

"There's been so much."

His hands cup my face, and we're there together. I sigh at the contact, at the feeling of being there with him again. His thumbs rub little circles on my cheeks. I wrap my hands around his wrists and hold him close. He smells like salt and sea. It feels so good to be with him now—the first time that there's really nothing in between us.

"I love you, Tessa. So much. And I don't want to be your pen pal anymore, I don't want to pretend to be someone else. I just want to love you. Can I do that? Will you let me do that?" He looks so scared as he says it, and I want to hold him.

"Yeah," I choke out, gripping his wrists a little harder so he knows I'm here, my throat full of emotion. "You can. We can."

"Yeah?" He looks so beautiful, his eyes rimmed with tears.

"Yeah."

He kisses me hard, and I can taste his tears as he wraps himself around me tighter. I slip my arms up around his neck, pulling him even closer, wishing I could consume him. I pull back and give him a few more pecks all over his face.

"I love you, Leo," I whisper into his skin. "I love you, Plant-Daddy54."

"I love you, Tessa. I love you, PlantDaddy13." He chuckles and brings me into a hug, and we're there together, just us with our dogs jumping around and chasing each other in circles.

epilogue

Meet The Plant Daddy, a traveling plant store

Tessa Wilder is a travel writer, and Leo Ahn is a graphic artist. Together, they run The Plant Daddy, a traveling plant store and art shop featuring unique plants and art created by Ahn. For the last two years, the duo have been on the road, hosting plant seminars and bringing plant culture to different communities around the United States. The two met and fell in love in Long Beach, CA as competing plant store owners. Both stores are now defunct, but their passion for plants never wavered.

"We're just plant nerds," Ahn says.

You might remember Paul Ahn, one-half of the Botanical Brothers duo, who rose to prominence a few years ago through their shirtless plant care videos posted on Instagram and YouTube. Since then, Paul Ahn has disappeared from social media completely after a controversy over an internet rumor that he destroyed Wilder's store. When asked about the rumor, Wilder and Leo Ahn both decline to comment.

Wilder was a budding travel blogger more than ten years ago and says she's proof that failures don't have to define you. "I honestly never thought I'd be doing this again. Traveling was always my dream, and once I failed the first time, I didn't think I could ever do it again, so I'm glad this is my life now." Wilder has since restarted her blog as a newsletter and writes about her life on the road, the communities she's encountered, and lessons she's learned along the way.

The name "The Plant Daddy" is apparently a play on an inside joke between the two. When asked about the name, the two looked at each other and laughed.

"It's a long story," says Wilder.

As far as being a couple on the road, they say it works out pretty well.

"Our relationship kind of began in a nontraditional way, so it makes sense we'd have kind of a weird life together, but it works for us," Ahn says.

They say their upcoming wedding is going to be fairly straight-forward. "We both have really big families, so it's going to be pretty traditional, but there will be lots of plants, of course."

If you'd like to shop at The Plant Daddy, they will be posted up at the Myrtle Beach Flea Market and will also have a booth set up outside of the Roxie, where ACAB will be playing hits from the Clash and more.

acknowledgments

This is a super exciting moment for me—it's my FIRST book! I have some folks to thank!

First and foremost, a big, heartfelt thank you goes out to my family, especially my parents. Everything I do, I do with the knowledge that they've got my back. Thank you for making it easy for me to do what I love.

To my AMAZING friends, your support and love have been essential. A special shout-out to Erin Williams, who worked her magic on my development edit, and to Melissa Cassera, my writing buddy and constant cheerleader.

I know it might sound a bit unusual, but I want to express my gratitude to BTS. My obsession with them reignited my passion for writing and set me on this exciting path of crafting books.

A massive thank you also goes to my GAF community, who've had my back for years now. Your support has meant the world to me, and I couldn't have come this far without you.

Lastly, I penned this story with a specific purpose—to resonate with the girls who struggle to find themselves in tales with happy endings because they rarely see or read about them. This one's for YOU, and I hope it touched your heart.

THANK YOU SO MUCH FOR READING!!!!!

about the author

Shenee is a content creator, writer, and director of projects with happy endings for people who don't usually get them. As a fat girl in the suburbs growing up in the 2000's, life was rough and crushes were forbidden for girls like her. Her goal is to create swoon-worthy stories that she never got herself. When she's not writing swoon-worthy men and book besties, she's throwing clay, walking her dog, and thinking about Keanu Reeves. You can follow along her adventures at heyshenee.com.

Get exclusive stories over on heyshenee.substack.com

instagram.com/heyshenee
tiktok.com/@heyshenee